SUICIDE INTENDED

Freddy Gibbon was a blackmailer, drug pedlar, thief and bully. An accomplished juvenile crook, he looked forward to a profitable career in the blacker arts while still an eighteen-year-old schoolboy studying for A levels – albeit without the least desire to gain any: but there was a dark reason for that too.

So when Freddy's body is discovered in Modlen College, a private sixth-form crammer near Cardiff, there are many who have reason to be relieved. But then suicide is revealed to have been a well-organised murder, and Chief Inspector Merlin Parry and Sergeant Gomer Lloyd are called in to investigate...

SUICIDE INTENDED

SUICIDE INTENDED

by

David Williams

Magna Large Print Books
Long Preston, North Yorkshire,
BD23 4ND, England.

British Library Cataloguing in Publication Data.

Williams, David
    Suicide intended.

        A catalogue record of this book is
        available from the British Library

        ISBN   0-7505-1641-0

First published in Great Britain by
HarperCollins*Publishers,* 1998

Published in Large Print 2001 by arrangement with
Harper Collins Publishers Ltd

Magna Large Print is an imprint of Library Magna Books Ltd.

Printed and bound in Great Britain by
T.J. (International) Ltd., Cornwall, PL28 8RW

31569730

This one for
Clifford and Elizabeth Hughes

1

The first thunderclap had been unexpected and uncomfortably close. It had caused one older male juror to stumble while making his way back to his seat. The following jagged fork of lightning was no less awesome for being predictable. It had starkly illuminated everyone in the otherwise badly lit, makeshift and crowded coroner's courtroom, fixing expressions that had been variously grieving, apprehensive, earnestly enquiring or just plain nosy.

'That was like the wrath of God, wasn't it?' Detective Sergeant Gomer Lloyd questioned, in a deep growl, to the uniformed PC Esther Hawkins, after the second round of thunder and lightning. This time the eruption had been directly overhead, and had come, appropriately, the moment after the jury's open verdict had been announced.

'You're right there, Sarge. And if the case ends up as murder, God's wrath will descend on somebody all right. On earth, or in the hereafter,' came the whispered but stern response.

Lloyd's heavy eyebrows lifted. His remark hadn't been intended as comment on the verdict, nor had he expected a pious reflection in return. It set him thinking all the same that at the rate of progress so far, it'd likely be the Almighty that got the case sorted in the end, not the South Wales CID.

Both officers had given evidence earlier: both had been witnesses to the aftermath of the tragedy four weeks before. The death had shocked Aberbach's inhabitants – and was still doing so.

It was Friday, and the delayed funeral had been on the previous Tuesday, with the weather then oppressively dry and sultry. There were almost as many people here today, crowded into the town council's main committee room, as there had been at the service. That had been held in the town's United Reformed Church, with its Doric pillars, and rusticated stone walls that towered over the other buildings in Colliery Road. It had been doing this since it was built in 1862, though then it had been a Congregational Chapel in no need of reform.

The landlord of the Royal Oak, a homespun philosopher, had said that the funeral had been packed as a sign of community guilt. Certainly the inquest, in its turn, had attracted record numbers for this once wholly coal-mining community, set on the eastern side of the valley, twenty miles inland from Cardiff – most of them uphill.

The coroner, Derek Ellis-Preece, nodded gravely at the jury foreman – who, as it happened, was female. 'And you were unanimous in what you've just reported?' he asked.

The woman, a middle-aged housewife, got to her feet again promptly. She was nervous, her upward movement impelled by convention – that her answer might be too important to be given sitting down. 'Yes, sir.' She pushed a wisp of hair back under the narrow brim of the blue canvas hat she had on. This object wasn't exactly suited to the occasion, but it was the only hat she owned, and she and her husband had felt that being on a coroner's jury called for a head covering – in deference.

'Thank you.' Ellis-Preece glanced gravely around the room before his eyes returned to the speaker. There had been murmurs of dissent when the jury's conclusion – or lack of one – had been announced. 'I assumed you were having problems since you were outside so long,' he added, almost conversationally, but with questioning in the tone.

The woman swallowed. 'We were unanimous ... in the end,' she uttered haltingly. This time her words were less audible than before, so that they were missed by a good many present, and not only because the angry beating of the rain at the windows was threatening to obliterate every other sound.

'Unanimous in the end. On an open verdict. I see. Well that's fair enough. Thank you again, and please sit down.'

The coroner was a gaunt, silver-haired solicitor whose legal practice was in the next town. Now he looked down at his notes through gold-framed, half-glasses, but not because his memory needed any prompting. He was aware that he had to choose his next words carefully – to avoid hurt feelings. It was either that or say very little, and Ellis-Preece was never a man of few words.

It was clear that half the witnesses hadn't believed the boy had taken his own life, so to them, at least, the verdict would be more acceptable than suicide. It still wasn't as firm as 'death caused by a person or persons unknown', but it wouldn't be far off, if he called for further police investigations. Except that they'd been investigating since the middle of August without exposing facts that pointed one way or another. For his own part, the coroner was still reasonably sure that it had been a case of suicide.

Mrs Nora Absom, the boy's mother, had been composed enough at the beginning of her evidence, but had become distraught in the middle. It had meant adjourning the court for five minutes until she recovered. Her second husband, Howard, who was not the dead boy's father, had been doing his best to calm her since then.

'Listen to what's coming next, Sarge, for tact and diplomacy. He's a real wordsmith, this one. Goes on a bit, though,' Esther Hawkins confided knowingly to Sergeant Lloyd. She had been stationed for two years in the town where the coroner practised.

'Well, I'm very grateful to all of you who've taken part in our sad deliberations this morning,' Ellis-Preece began, looking up. 'The ending of a young life is always poignant. More grievous than the loss of someone older can ever be. Or that's my experience as a coroner. Peter, at fifteen, had his whole life before him, and, by all indicators, it would have been a successful and rewarding life. As we've heard, he was someone who ... who preferred his own company. And no harm in that. He was a thinker, and a poet. Such folk are often what the world chooses to call loners. Sadly, in this case, his preference reduced the number of people, of friends, who might have been able to help us patch together his movements, and his frame of mind, on the day of his death.' He sighed, while his gaze fixed on Mrs Absom. 'We do know that he was a good son, a loving son, and our sympathies go out in great measure to his devoted mother and er ... stepfather.'

The speaker paused briefly, while continuing to regard the slim and mourning Mrs Absom, a well-preserved woman in her late forties, but whose distraught state was hardly doing justice to her looks today. 'Peter's GCSE levels predicted a brilliant scholastic future,' he continued. 'Who knows, though, whether his failure to achieve his high target of fourteen starred passes was a bit too ambitious–'

'He could have got them,' Mrs Absom broke in, loudly and defensively, but with more pride than rancour.

The coroner nodded sagely at his notes, not at the interrupter. He had no intention

14

of admonishing her. 'In any event, Peter's final results fell short of his target, only just short, mark you,' he said. 'The grades he did achieve would have brought joy to most candidates, but we've heard they were not good enough against the standards he'd set himself. This could have caused him to be depressed, to buy and ingest the tablets, to break into the gymnasium of the empty school, an easy enough thing to do, it seems, and ... and then to the precipitate action of hanging himself, if that's what he did.'

At this point, another mighty explosion of thunder and lightning lent drama, and, somehow, an extra degree of credibility to the last doleful conjecture, before the speaker went on: 'We've been assured that Peter was not a habitual drug taker. Indeed, it may well be that this was the very first time he had ever ... indulged himself in this way. If this was the case, it did more than just enhance the possibility of suicide. The absence of a letter, or a note of any kind, can never, of course, be taken as the sole proof that suicide wasn't intended. As I said to the members of the jury before they retired, young people sometimes take their own lives with little or no premeditation, and without leaving any sign of their ... their sad resolve.'

Ellis-Preece nodded to himself, then leaned forward a little. 'Of course, the jury's unanimous verdict shows that the evidence does nothing specifically to suggest that there couldn't have been some other person or persons present with Peter in the gym. So the possibility that there was a ... an accident of some kind, arising from some horseplay, perhaps, some fooling about, needs examining very carefully. From the start there was nothing that firmly pointed in that direction, but it was why I appealed at the first adjourned inquest, two weeks ago, for anyone who'd been present in the gym with Peter at any point that day, and no matter how innocently, to come forward. No honest person would want to leave such a weighty ... inadmission lying on his or her conscience for the rest of his or her life.'

The lawyer paused again, and stared around the room, allowing time for a belated admission from someone. But there was no taker, only silence, and even stonier stares than before from the mostly adult audience, and particularly from the male members. Every man in the room was self-consciously doing his best not to look like someone given to indulge in horseplay, or any more sinister sort of play, with a

16

sensitive fifteen-year-old boy, in a deserted school gym, in the middle of the summer holidays.

'Finally, there's the third possibility I referred to in my summing up.' Ellis-Preece delivered this last comment more slowly and gravely than the rest. He was alluding to the likelihood of malicious action. 'So, it now remains for me to thank the jury for coming to its inconclusive, but considered and proper verdict. To repeat the court's sympathies to the bereaved family, and to charge the police to reapply themselves diligently to find the true cause in this unhappy matter,' he completed solemnly.

'You could tell the coroner favoured suicide from the start, boss,' Lloyd was recounting to Detective Chief Inspector Merlin Parry, later in the day.

'But you don't agree with him, Gomer?'

The two men were at the Royal Cardiff Infirmary. Parry had been waiting to interview the driver of a security van as a matter of urgency. Along with the guard, the man had been attacked and knocked senseless when the vehicle had been held up at lunchtime by a gang of five men, less than a mile from the city centre. The guard was still unconscious, but the driver was supposed to be recovered enough to talk – except there had been a relapse since Parry had reached the hospital. He had come from the headquarters of the Major Crime Support Unit, at Cowbridge, the pretty market town, eight miles west of Cardiff, the Welsh capital. Lloyd had joined Parry directly from Aberbach.

'I don't think this Peter Absom would have been the sort of lad who'd top himself, no,' said Lloyd, in answer to the question.

'And you've gleaned enough about his character to know that? In depth? There wasn't much to go on though, was there? Secretive type. It sounded like a suicide to me, from what you said at the start.' Officially, Parry hadn't had anything to do with the investigation. Lloyd had been reporting on it to a different senior officer. But for the conscientious sergeant, at least, it had been more than just a commonplace case.

So far as assessing the character and motivations of an unknown dead person from hearsay, Parry reckoned his own view could be seriously off balance. Simply, he was irked beyond measure over what he'd considered to be his recent false evaluation of the intentions of a much known, living person.

'He wouldn't have done it for the reason offered, boss,' the sergeant insisted, surprised at the other's cavalier reaction.

'You mean, because he missed getting top marks in two out of fourteen GCSEs. So what about the ecstasy tablets?'

'He wasn't a regular user, boss.'

'Or so other people tell you. People with an interest in keeping his memory pure and unsullied.' Parry watched a young, white-coated female doctor hurry down the corridor beyond the waiting area where he and Lloyd were seated. She was issuing instructions to the slightly older male nurse striding beside her. The stethoscope protruding from the doctor's pocket, and the nurse's shorter white jacket, acted as their unofficial badges of office.

The thirty-eight-year-old Parry was thinking that the neatly turned out male nurse carried more authority than the scruffy young woman. Then he acknowledged that what was bothering him were the sexes, not the ages or appearances, of the two people. Possibly, and in an outmoded fashion, he still preferred doctors to be men, and nurses to be women – except it was more probable that this was a reflection of his irritation with the prospective woman doctor called Perdita Jones whom he adored, and had confidently been expecting to marry in around eighteen months' time. That had been until four days ago when she had phoned, late in the evening, to say, with apologies, that they shouldn't count on marriage so soon after all. Provided she qualified, and following her junior doctor year at the London hospital where she was training, she'd now been promised two years in the same hospital to begin specializing as a gynaecologist – an opportunity which, she confessed, she'd had reason to expect for some time.

For Perdita to have been planning a further long stay in London had been bad news for Parry – especially since she hadn't mentioned it to him before this. Up to now, he'd assumed she would be joining a general practice in South Wales.

'I don't believe Peter Absom was even an occasional drug taker, boss. I think this may have been the one time he took the stuff. Otherwise, it doesn't fit with what his mother, his stepfather, his friends, his teachers, his–'

'Mothers always think the best of only sons. My mother did. Still does,' Parry put in flatly.

'He wasn't her only son. There's an older one who works abroad. Both were by the mother's previous husband,' Lloyd explained with deliberation.

'All right, but Peter was her favourite, I'll bet. The brainy one who fell into bad company. People who got him into the drug scene. That could have led to abnormal behaviour. Possibly making those exam results look worse to him than they were.'

'I just wish I could get my hands on the pusher, boss.'

'No leads on that?'

'None. A total dead end. Kids at the school are either too scared or possibly too hooked themselves to give us a clue.' He rubbed his chin. 'Those exam results were good really, not bad.'

'But he was a perfectionist, Gomer. So he's found hanging from a skipping rope in the school gym. A case of what the coroner probably believes was suicide, even if the jury veered a bit the other way. So further police investigation is required?'

Lloyd gave a hollow, grumbling noise. 'Still into the possibility of its being suicide,

21

accident, or foul play. Which is how we'd treated it from the start. Except we've got nowhere.' Lloyd took a peppermint from his pocket, examined it suspiciously, blew on it, then put it in his mouth, his expression disconsolate.

'But the Unit's off the case from today, Gomer?'

The older man shrugged, while shifting the peppermint from one side of his mouth to the other. 'That's right. Matter of the most practical way of allocating manpower, I suppose. Local CID have got it now. Should have stayed with them in the first place, probably. The powers-that-be reckoned if the verdict turned out to be an open one, like it has, the case was going to be a no-resulter in the end. It's on the back burner now for good, I'd say. So it doesn't affect me either way. Not that I've minded trying to prove the lad didn't kill himself. For his mother's sake, mostly.' The sergeant shifted his considerable bulk in the quite small chair that was accommodating it. 'So is there anything new on this hold-up, boss? I got the details on the radio coming down. There's a nerve they had staging it where they did. On the Newport Road industrial estate, was it?'

22

'Yes. We expected progress from what the driver had to say. But he may have gone back into a coma. If so, there's no point in us staying. I was at the scene earlier. It was–'

'You can go in now, Chief Inspector. Only for five minutes, I'm afraid. He's very weak.' Parry had been interrupted by the woman doctor who, close to, looked less scruffy than plain tired, while still making an effort to be helpful.

It was from this point that both Parry and Lloyd became immediately immersed in the case of banditry, and lost interest in the demise of Peter Absom and the circumstances surrounding it. In due time – about eight weeks – the robbers were brought to book, or three of the five were. In the nature of things, meaning mostly the availability of police men and women hours set against the determination of criminals not to grass on accomplices, this result was a credit to the detectives involved, notably DCI Merlin Parry and DS Gomer Lloyd.

It was to be some time, too, before the two officers would be indirectly exposed again to anything that might have touched on the Absom affair – and somewhat longer than that before either of them recognized the fact.

2

'I'm very grateful for the sterling work you're doing, Emlyn. Yes, sterling work,' Dr Handel Newsom-Pugh offered with enthusiasm, while towelling his naked nether regions with a matching degree of zeal.

'Thank you, sir. I'm enjoying it. The atmosphere here is–'

'That's good. Settled in nicely too, I gather,' the other man interrupted sharply and breathily. He was briefly balancing on one foot. The opposite knee was bent in the air as he continued to apply a well-programmed drying routine to his astonishingly hairy body. 'Room all right, is it?'

'Well, as a matter of fact, I was hoping–'

'Yes, yes, I remember now, you mentioned that before. Mrs Watkyn is seeing to it. How do you think that boy Gibbon's doing?' The principal of Modlen College moved firmly on to another subject of his own choosing, after remembering, too late, that he should have kept clear of the first one from the start. Both his feet were now grounded, and set well apart, while he worked the towel on his back with the same athletic vigour as before, his ample stomach, and what his effervescent, inventive wife called the dangly bits below – thrust forward in a somewhat unwholesome if not intentionally obscene manner.

'Hardly a natural learner, sir, I'm afraid.' Averting his eyes out of distaste not embarrassment, Emlyn Harries discarded his own towel, and pulled on his jockey shorts.

The two were in the men's changing room of the indoor pool at Modlen Hall. It was seven o'clock on a Monday morning in mid-February. It had stopped snowing an hour before. Harries, in his mid-twenties, was tall, spare but fit, and given to self-effacement. He taught English, and had joined the staff of tutors at the beginning of the current term, at only a few days' notice.

Modlen College was a private crammer, a forcing ground for students of both sexes who had either already failed A levels, or were likely to do so shortly, unless drastic action was taken, and who were anxious to qualify for university places somewhere – anywhere. In truth, the anxiety in the matter usually stemmed from the students' parents who were wealthy enough, or else desperate enough, to indulge this common concern for their offsprings' scholastic futures. The official fees at the establishment compared with those at Eton, although students rarely stayed for more than two years at the most.

The college was housed in Modlen Hall, from which it had taken its name. This was a rambling Victorian mansion set in a high, commanding position, half a mile above the picturesque village of Brynglas – which is Welsh for 'green hill', and, in this case, a designation that had remained appropriate to the present day.

Several miles inland, with views across the Vale of Glamorgan to the Bristol Channel beyond, the hall had originally been built by a mine owner for his own occupation. Since his grandson had disposed of it in 1929, the place had stood empty when not requisitioned by the army in wartime, or rented, as it was for two decades later, by the local authority as offices. Unoccupied again for some years after that, it was next expensively converted into an upmarket, country-house hotel. This worthy enterprise – Wales had too few good hotels at the time – had foundered financially in the fifth year, mostly because it was too many miles west of Cardiff to attract enough of the city's expense-account business, and not far enough west, into real country, to appeal to higher-spending tourists.

It was at this juncture that Newsom-Pugh had taken over the building for his educational enterprise on an annually renewable, nonrepairing lease at a knockdown rate. Four years had passed since then, and he had been expecting to show a profit at the end of each of them, without ever actually doing so. Luckily for him, in the meantime the receivers for the hotel creditors hadn't found a buyer for the place, or a tenant willing to pay a higher rent, so the college had survived, in a sense by default.

Emlyn Harries, now fully dressed, had needed to wait for his employer who, in addition to a suit of substantial Welsh tweed, had come provided with a scarf, hat and heavy topcoat. The heated, though, for economy reasons, not overheated swimming pool, and the adjoining games room, were in an independent, single-storey building, set in a woodland clearing a hundred yards up the hillside, behind the hall.

'Nothing like a swim before breakfast, is there?' Newsom-Pugh remarked, as they moved down the concrete path – he warily, a stout walking stick in his right hand. The way was covered in several layers of ice with a fresh snow topping. Although it was before daybreak still, the clouds having cleared, the moon was providing bold illumination to the starkly white scene. 'Can't understand why others seldom take the opportunity to swim,' the speaker went on. 'Glad you're one of the takers, Emlyn. Not the first time, is it?'

'No, I'm up here a good deal, sir. But in the evening usually.' Harries swallowed guiltily. Needing to corner Newsom-Pugh, he had turned up at the pool today because he knew his quarry was here alone every morning at this time: few members of staff chose to join their principal for the simple pleasure of his company – especially not before breakfast. The problem for Harries was that he still hadn't properly succeeded in airing the subject of his living quarters which, apart from being cold, due to an ill-fitting window, were not in the specific part of the building where he had wanted them to be.

The principal, in his turn, had long since found a defence from being buttonholed in the way the young man had just attempted. He either affected not to hear complaints addressed to him, or fobbed the complainer off on to someone else – as he had done in this instance. Mrs Watkyn was the college housekeeper.

'Hm. So Gibbon is not a natural learner, you say? Cynthia Strange has the same opinion,' Newsom-Pugh reverted to the earlier topic. Miss Strange was the college's forty-year-old history tutor. Single, jolly, overweight, hardly a looker, but memorable, not least because she smoked herb tobacco in a clay-lined pipe, she had been in the job for nearly two years, and had given up a senior post in a top girls' school to work here for less money because she needed free time to write historical novels. 'My wife is inclined to agree with both of you,' the principal observed next, but with a certain reservation in his tone. Mrs Newsom-Pugh, blonde, German, definitely a looker, and half her husband's age, taught modern languages: Harries had learned already that her real opinions, and sometimes her motivations, were not always those her husband credited to her. 'His widowed mother isn't rich,' that worthy continued. 'Far from it. I believe some kind of educational endowment helps pay the fees. Even so, if sacrifices are being made, Gibbon seems hardly to appreciate it,' he ruminated, but not very audibly, while still examining the ground with care before each step – like an obese bloodhound in search of a superior scent.

'Freddy Gibbon isn't a worker, no,' the younger man supplied, while wishing he'd also brought a topcoat. At the rate they were moving, he'd be frozen before they rounded the main building.

'So ... so if we awarded bursaries to less well-off students, you feel he wouldn't be a contender for one of them?'

'I shouldn't think so, sir.' The reply had been as surprised as the question had been unexpected.

Except Newsom-Pugh had no intention of introducing grants or scholarships to help indigent, gifted pupils at his own expense, although it did no harm to imply that he was thinking of something so virtuous – on the contrary, he found it had a satisfyingly inhibiting effect on staff salary expectancies. It so happened that the only time he had relaxed his much flaunted rule of never taking pupils at reduced fees, had been in the very case they were discussing. But this had not been for altruistic reasons. Rather it had been a last-minute effort to improve student numbers at the start of the current academic year, after the candidate's mother had demurred over the size of the fees. Added to which, Freddy Gibbon had been recommended to the college by his former headmaster – a possible source of further such largesse, whose first offering could hardly have been spurned.

Even so, Newsom-Pugh was careful always to protect his establishment's quite high academic success rate and, it followed, that to be nurturing a student who was a certain failure could scarcely do much for the Modlen College image. 'I've already sent a warning note to Gibbon's mother,' he said, a touch of satisfaction, and certainly no regret, in the tone. 'Of course, it's a great pity there isn't a father.' The last comment suggested that the inconvenience invented by this shortfall in the conventional number of parents attaching to each pupil was entirely that of the put-upon speaker's. 'Always difficult, of course, but the lady had to be made aware that keeping the boy here could well mean pouring good money after bad. Yes,' he mused, then looked up suddenly. 'It's a very fine building, you know? Of its type. Even from this side. The snow shows it off well in the moonlight, don't you think?' In changing the subject, the well-insulated Newsom-Pugh had also halted, the better to admire the edifice ahead, and much to his companion's further discomfort.

In truth, the place was considered quite good for its period, if a bit pretentious. A redbrick, Gothic ensemble with castellations, it boasted turrets at every corner, with buttressed, high chimneys, tall slender pairs of windows beneath pointed arches, and a squat tower in the centre of the east front. The north front, which Newsom-Pugh had just seen fit to praise, and which the two men were shortly to pass on their left, had less to commend it than the rest. It was, and had always been, the service side, backing into the hill, with no noteworthy view at any level, except of outhouses and a narrow yard full of mammoth garbage bins.

'That's my room. Second floor, on the right, at the end–' Harries began, seizing what was likely to be the last opportunity to air his grievance.

'Up there, are you? Well, I never. Not in the tower, so that's a blessing, at least. But then climbing stairs is good exercise when you're young,' Newsom-Pugh had cut in volubly, at the start sounding envious, not surprised. The bankrupt hoteliers had never seen fit to install a lift, which, in their case, had been a false economy. 'Not so good at my age, perhaps. Bad for the knees. Like the breast stroke. Or so they say.' The speaker had moved off again at a suddenly accelerated pace with Harries, caught unawares, trailing him at first, past the narrower, west side of the house, and catching up as they turned on to the sixty-foot-wide, and even longer, gravelled terrace. This served the imposing southern front, with its elaborate main entrance. Across from that, on the right, there was stone balustrading, broken in the centre by ornamental steps which led down to garden terraces at three levels. 'Tell me, eh ... Emlyn, in strict confidence, what is your view of Ifor Jenkin?' The principal had stopped again, and drawn much closer to his companion in a definitely conspiratorial style. Since he was four inches shorter than Harries, this involved his looking up at the other's face, which he did with dark, searching eyes, narrowed under flaring brows.

'That's difficult for me to say, sir,' the young man answered with evident hesitation. Jenkin was the tutor in mathematics.

'Quite so. You're showing a proper

reticence over offering an opinion on a colleague.' Newsom-Pugh moved closer still to his intended confidant. 'But I need an objective, fresh opinion on the matter. For the good of all, you understand? Recent maths results have been very disappointing. Jenkin tries hard enough, no doubt of that, but is he up to the standard our students are entitled to expect? And their parents? That's what I keep asking myself. It's partly a question of dedication, of course. I notice he's away on that noisy motorbike of his at midday on the Saturday of every weekend when he's free, and he's never back till start of work Monday.' He looked at his watch, then over his shoulder as if he expected his mounted maths tutor to come roaring over the garden terraces and up the marble steps, scramble style, at any second – and early for once.

'I believe he goes to his mother in mid-Wales, sir. If he's not on duty, he's entitled–'

'Indeed he's *entitled*.' Harries had been forestalled again. 'But he always takes maximum advantage of the time conceded, on every single occasion,' the principal complained, emphasizing the last phrase. Although there were no classes or tutorials after noon on Saturdays, and all students were permitted to go home for Saturday and Sunday nights if they chose, a good many remained on the premises to complete the prodigious amount of preparatory work allotted. For this reason, one senior member of the teaching staff was required to remain at the college too, to give help to any requiring it, on an informal basis, on both Saturdays and Sundays. This was supplemented by the presence of tutors who made the college their homes – like the principal and his wife.

'Most of us get away when we can, sir, I'm afraid,' Harries offered, with what amounted to undue objectivity.

'You don't, Emlyn.' the older man countered accurately. 'I've seen you here over the weekends, when your name's not been on the duty roster. The same goes for Miss Strange.'

'So far, it's often been more er ... convenient to stay, sir. And anyway, as you know, I do a bit of book reviewing. The weekend in college is a good time for that. I think Cynthia Strange finds the same about writing her novels.'

'But you're both here, and make yourselves available if needed by students. That's the spirit I applaud. And Jenkin doesn't have it.'

It was obvious that Newsom-Pugh had it in for the mathematics tutor on all counts, and not all of them either fair or logical. Harries, intimidated and freezing on the edge of the windy terrace, was still trying to find a neutral way of extricating himself from an embarrassing situation, when someone else did so for him.

'Principal, Principal, come quick. Accident,' a powerful contralto voice summoned, clarion like, from the steps of the main door. The gesticulating Mrs Gwen Watkyn, the voice's owner, was already making off, away from the direction of the two men, not towards them.

'Where exactly, Mrs Watkyn?' called Harries, who, glad of the chance, had sprinted across the gravel to catch up with her. A worried Newsom-Pugh followed at an overcautious half-trot.

'At the bottom of the tower. A body,' the housekeeper explained breathlessly as Harries reached her. She was short and stout, her normally imperturbable countenance suffused with concern. The two moved together quickly to the far corner of the building. 'I saw it through the window. We were airing the rooms. Sara's phoning for the ambulance.' Sara Card was the college's sole chambermaid.

'Could you see who it was?'

'I don't want to say till I'm sure. There was only the moon and the car park light, so I couldn't be certain. Not quite,' came the tight-lipped, equivocal reply.

They had rounded the corner now. The tower, a well-contrived architectural extravagance, was the first feature of the hall that most visitors sighted coming up the narrow road from the village which ascended on that side. The tower's leading edge stood out a little in the centre of the east wall, while below both tower and wall was a continuous sunken area, twelve feet deep, which, at a distance, fancifully suggested a narrow moat, protected on its outer bank by low stone battlements. Nearer examination showed that this was simply an area that provided light for the basement right around the house. A bridge of elegant steps spanned the feature when it reached the front door on the southern front – with less fanciful arrangements allowing for egress on the west and north sides of the building.

'About down there,' Mrs Watkyn went on, stopping, and pointing to the basement.

'Oh, I don't think I want to look close to. You'll need to go down, Mr Harries. But don't try jumping, the bottom's treacherous. There's iron steps just round the next corner, through a little gate.'

'OK.' The running Harries didn't stop to peer over the battlements. He found the unlocked gate, clambered down the staircase, then wobbled and crunched his way back over the loose, uneven surface of snow, gravel and accumulated debris, along what was a rarely tended or trodden surface.

'Here, Emlyn. Hurry, man. Who is it?' This came from Newsom-Pugh. He was leaning over the stonework. Despite her previous misgiving, Mrs Watkyn was doing the same, with a gaze wooden and transfixed. 'Is he breathing?' the principal demanded.

Harries was now standing over the splayed and totally naked body of a tall and muscular young man. It was lying, face downwards, at a slight angle to the outer wall, in the shadows at the foot of the tower. The left shoulder was pressed against the rubble surface and the wall, with the upper arm trapped in the same way, but with the forearm and clenched hand free. The other arm was outstretched at right angles to the body, the fingers of the hand open and upturned. The legs were spreadeagled, the left foot pressed harder than the right on the unyielding surface, and flattened out against it.

'I'm afraid it's Freddy Gibbon,' Harries called up, kneeling beside the body. 'He's not breathing, and he's stone cold.'

'He would be cold, wouldn't he? Try the pulse,' the principal instructed from his vantage point, but Harries was doing that already. This was the first dead human he had ever touched in his life, but he'd been sure, without any examination, that it really was dead, and that the ambulance, whose siren was already audible from the valley below, was on a fruitless errand.

While Newsom-Pugh should have been fixated by the tragedy presented, and its possible causes, his first assailing, and unstoppable, thought was a shaming one of relief that Freddy Gibbon had been removed from Modlen College without any apparent intervention in the matter on the part of its principal. 'Better not move him about. And find something to cover him with, poor lad,' he directed. His former low opinion of the deceased was improving by the moment, though he had yet to feel any compunction about failing to surrender his own overcoat.

Harries removed his jacket and draped it over the body as best he could. This provided an outward, visible show of decency and respect at least, despite his view that in life the subject had scarcely earned or even courted such graces.

Mrs Watkyn was doing her best to pray. She had never liked Gibbon – quite the opposite, in fact, because of what she had suspected about his relationship with Sara, and other things. But you had to forgive people: her bible taught her that.

After summoning the ambulance, Sara Card had coolly returned to distributing clean towels. She had been fairly certain from the start that it was Freddy's body they had seen from the window. She had better eyesight than Mrs Watkyn – and a good deal less compassion.

Altogether, the deceased's immediate mourners were hard pressed to find real grief in their hearts, like many others who learned of the loss later.

3

'He was eighteen. Nineteen this May, boss.' Sergeant Lloyd was detailing to Parry as they moved back from the body. It was an hour and a half since Gibbon's remains had been discovered. The police were now present in force, with Scenes-of-Crime Officers examining the open basement area with their search equipment, and working as best they could. The white-hooded overalls pulled on over normal clothing were producing welcome warmth as well as guarding possible evidence from contamination. It was snowing again, and a large section of the space had been tented over, and screened, to shield it both from the elements, and the gaze of inquisitive students who had earlier been enjoying a grandstand view of what was going on from windows overlooking the scene.

'So he was getting on a bit for someone taking A levels in June,' Parry commented. He had arrived only ten minutes before this. 'Isn't the college a forcing house for bright kids?' He was still keeping a watchful eye on the police surgeon who was working methodically on the dead body in very cramped conditions.

'No, boss. The opposite really. It's for the dimmer ones who need extra coaching to get through. Frederic Gibbon had sat for A levels twice already, without doing well enough to qualify for university.' Lloyd had been the first senior officer on the scene, and had already interviewed Dr Newsom-Pugh, Emlyn Harries, Gwen Watkyn, and Sara Card.

'I see. And we don't know what time he came back last night?' asked Parry, who had come at speed from investigating a case of serious domestic violence in Neath, nearly twenty miles west of here, and where he'd been since before dawn.

The student death at the hall was already proving a lot more complicated than the horrendous wife-beating in Neath, where the woman involved had survived against the odds, and was now in intensive care, with her husband safely behind bars. Lloyd had reported to headquarters earlier that Gibbon's demise might not be suicide, and from what he had learned so far, Parry was sharing that opinion.

42

'The lad must have come back after ten last night, boss,' the sergeant replied to Parry's question. 'His car's in the car park. It's a three-year-old, yellow Ford Sierra estate. The car on the left of his belongs to a girl student called Kate Unwin. She says she came back from the weekend with one of her roommates at ten last night, and the space on that side was empty when they arrived.'

'So any time after ten.' Parry frowned. 'Nothing tighter than that, Gomer?'

'Not so far, no. Seems Gibbon left at midday on Saturday. There's no information on his movements since then, but the clothes he was wearing, when last seen, don't seem to be in his room, and they're not in his car either. I've had the car screened off.'

'I noticed that,' said Parry. The car park was a wide piece of open ground at the top of the village lane, between a freestanding, modern, single-storey block of domestic staff bedrooms and the east side of the main building. The newish block was utilitarian but not handsome, and had been built where it was during the hotel period, presumably not to sully the grandiose impression of the hall. 'The Sierra's engine was cold, Gomer?' asked Parry.

'Stone cold when we got to it, yes. That was at seven forty-three. Switched off more than two hours before, I'd say. Difficult to tell with everything freezing up so fast, though. Could be it was there for less than that even. We're finding out now if anyone spotted it being brought back, or even just saw it in the car park. No takers, not so far. As you saw, the car park's like an ice rink. Has been for nearly a fortnight, of course, like everywhere else.'

The chief inspector nodded. 'Dr Maltravers just told me there's no way here he can estimate the time of death with any accuracy. Not with the body as cold as it was when he arrived, but he reckons very roughly three hours or more.' George Maltravers was the police surgeon. A taciturn, weatherbeaten, sixty-year-old GP, he was presently emanating clouds of vapour like an overworked horse. He was clad in an old tweed fishing hat, and an even more ancient sheepskin jacket. He had pulled on the bottom half of the white SOCO overalls over his trousers as token obeisance to forensic-investigator regulations.

'There'll be more chance of getting a time of death at the autopsy, boss. From the stomach contents and that.'

'Assuming we can find out when he last ate.' Parry looked up disconsolately at the covering of orange plastic tenting over their heads. Time of death was often the most critical item in a suspicious-death investigation, but just as often the most impossible to pinpoint. 'And his room's directly above here?'

'Nearly, but not exactly, boss. It's on the top floor of the tower. The centre of three rooms facing this side. The body's three or four feet right of dead centre. That's to our right, looking from the outside of the building. The difference could have been caused by the way he angled himself for the drop.'

'That's if he did the angling. What about the room to the right of his?'

'Belongs to a girl student called Josephine Oswald. She's been home for the weekend. It's possible he could have jumped from there, but the place was locked from noon Saturday, and still is. It's also possible he could have done it from one of the rooms on the floors below his. That's if he jumped at all, of course,' the sergeant cautioned.

Parry nodded. 'So what about those other rooms?'

'There's only two on each of the second and first floors facing this way, all with private bathrooms, by the way.'

'That's pretty grand, even for a private school.'

'A school that used to be a hotel, boss,' the sergeant reminded. 'The most likely rooms would be either of the ones on the second floor. Their bathrooms have a sort of communal double window in the centre. Except the room on the right's been locked and empty the whole term. The other's shared by three girl students. One of them was ill in bed there with a cold most of the weekend. Her roommates were the two I mentioned who came back together in the car at ten last night.'

'And the two rooms on the first floor?'

'Both occupied by senior tutors, boss. The right-hand one was empty and locked all weekend. The other was in use by the occupier, the history tutor, most of the time, and certainly all last night.'

'And you said the lad couldn't have got out on to the tower?'

'That's right. Access blocked by a padlocked door, boss.' Lloyd glanced at his watch. 'Want to go up and see his room? SOCO team's been sweeping it since eight.

Should be through by now. Different team from the one down here. DS Wilcox split up the people he brought when I said there could be two independent sites.'

'Who's he put in charge up there?'

'DC Vaughan, boss.'

Parry nodded his approval with a smile, bringing into relief the good-humoured wrinkles at the outward corners of both eyes. Detective Sergeant Glen Wilcox was a young but highly experienced chief Scenes-of-Crime Officer. The older Detective Constable Vaughan wasn't as versed in supervising SOCO work, but was still a meticulous detective. 'We'll go up as soon as we've talked to the doctor,' said the chief inspector. 'Anyone been on to the boy's parents yet?'

'His mother, boss. There's no father. Dr Newsom-Pugh's been trying to reach her on the phone since eight, but there's been no answer yet. She lives in Hereford. Moved there recently. He's asked that we don't try getting her through the local police. Not yet. He'd rather give her the news himself. Thinks she may have been away for the weekend.' Hereford was approximately sixty miles from Modlen Hall. 'If Dr Newsom-Pugh doesn't–'

'Hang on, Gomer. Are you all through, Doctor?' Parry had interrupted, and switched his attention to Dr Maltravers, who had stood up creakily after his long crouch beside the body, the white overalls slipping down further than they had been before.

'I'm all through, yes, in more ways than one,' the doctor replied, arching his back slowly, while removing his spectacles. 'Bloody overalls,' he added, giving a half-hearted upward tug at the offending garment. 'There'll be no shifting the body yet, Merlin,' he continued. 'Home Office pathologist will want to look at this one *in situ*.' He breathed hard on his fingers after peeling off the surgical gloves he'd been wearing. Then he pushed one hand into a fur-lined, leather glove, and sent the other searching for something in the confines under the sheepskin and the overalls.

'Anything we should note about the body, Doctor?' the chief inspector pressed encouragingly.

'One thing, certainly.' Maltravers blew his nose loudly into the capacious white handkerchief just removed with some difficulty from a trouser pocket. He considered the handkerchief for a moment,

48

then looked up at the speaker before he added: 'Seems not to be damaged enough after dropping, what is it, forty feet at least.' He glanced skywards as if to check his estimate of the distance, only to find himself staring at an opaque ceiling of orange sheeting which was already beginning to sag with the weight of snow gathering on it.

'He dived, you say, Doctor?'

'Well, sort of skydived, I'd say. That is, it certainly doesn't seem he just tipped himself out head first, or feet first either. Not judging by the way he landed. Certain amount of histrionics involved, I'd say. As if he was playing to an audience. Like the fairground performers who used to dive off towers into ... into wet flannels.' He sniffed at his own limp witticism, then rubbed the sides of his face with both now warmly gloved hands. 'You see, a naked body dropping that distance, at that angle, on to this sort of surface, ought to be more bashed about generally than this one is. And bloodier, probably. Which reminds me, there are two small incisions just below the ribcage. Probably dried-up cuts from the fall, but it's hard to tell with a frozen corpse. Worth noting, anyway.' He looked again at the sheet he'd just put over the body, before

49

adding: 'I could be wrong about the lack of general damage. If it was suicide, and if he was drunk or drugged, well, that might have made him relaxed on impact, and less knocked about, that's if he just hit the bottom of this basement area squarely – and nothing else en route, like the fake battlements, for instance.' He slapped the wall with the back of a well-protected hand. 'You could say he was lucky or unlucky over that, of course, depending on his real intention. With such a comparatively soft landing he might not have killed himself, just been crippled for life. Such things do happen.'

'The place where he ended up is still pretty ragged all the same, Doctor,' Parry put in. The implication in part of what Maltravers had said fitted with Gomer Lloyd's first reported impression that the body seemed not to have travelled anything like the distance from the top floor.

'Er ... yes,' the other replied grudgingly, 'and with protrusions that might have dented him much more seriously than they have. It's a difficult one, Merlin, and certainly not one I'm equipped to pronounce on.'

'Will the pathologist be long, do you think, Doctor?' Lloyd enquired.

'I'd guess he'll be here within the hour. I put in a call to the hospital soon after I got here.' He glanced again in the direction of the body. 'Right, I'll be off. Surgery full of flu patients waiting to give it to me, I shouldn't wonder. Happy prospect. I'll do the paperwork in the car with the heating on. Don't let anyone go near the body. Your SOCO team was being extra careful when I arrived, Merlin. They're learning, aren't they, Detective Sergeant Wilcox?' Maltravers completed, smiling broadly at the youthful, white-clad sergeant who had just appeared at Parry's side.

'That's right, Doctor. And no chance this time you've contaminated the evidence rearranging his clothes,' Wilcox responded with matching good humour.

The doctor gave a grim chuckle. 'That's true enough. Naked as the day he was born, poor lad. If he was pushed out, or died some other way, let's hope his skin, hair and orifices will tell us something pertinent eventually. Cheerio then, everyone.' Balancing his steps carefully, and still clutching the sagging overalls with one hand, he moved off towards the iron staircase.

'Hell of a drop, even on to our tenting,' said

51

Lloyd pointedly.

'Yes, and with the tenting in place, it's hard to judge how he came to miss landing on the battlements. Hmm, good view on a fine day from here, I should think,' Parry mused. Both men were leaning from the open set of double casement windows to Freddy Gibbon's close-carpeted room. DC Alf Vaughan was standing behind them expecting questions: his team had finished going over the place some minutes before. The chief inspector returned to calculating the angle of the drop for the body to have landed where it had in the basement area.

The squat, castellated tower had four storeys above the basement – only one more than the rest of the building. The three sets of paired windows on the east side of this uppermost floor were different from the ones below – half the height, and not arched, but flat-topped under shouldered architraves. The same applied to the other two rooms there which faced south. All five rooms let out on to an L-shaped corridor with stairs at the north end coming up from the third storey, and carrying on to the roof of the tower, though this part of the stairs was barred by the heavy door and im-pregnable-looking steel padlock Lloyd had described. The arrangement on the opposite side of the corridor to the hapless Gibbon's room was similar, but not identical, to that on his side. The three doors here led to a complex of shower rooms, bathrooms and lavatories, their windows looking out on to Welsh slate roofing.

Lloyd turned away from the window and scanned the room again. 'Originally servants' quarters. With a lot more than one to a room,' he said with grudging assurance. His grandmother had been a parlourmaid in a similar house in a dissimilar age.

'Yes, but somehow you'd still expect a tower room to be grander, wouldn't you?' said Parry reflectively.

'When the place was a hotel, Mrs Watkyn told me the rooms up here were guest doubles, big, but without private bathrooms, boss. Cheaper accommodation, with no lift, of course.'

Parry nodded. 'Anyway, the furniture's better than you'd expect for a school.' He sat on an adjustable metal office chair and opened two drawers. These were fitted under a built-in desktop with a lap computer and a small printer on it. The upper drawer yielded half a dozen slim cardboard files containing both typed and written notes on A4 paper. Each file had a subject label such as History or English. Unexpectedly, the lower drawer was filled with a jumble of socks and sweaters.

The desktop was part of a unit that included a wardrobe-cum-chest of drawers and which occupied the whole of one wall. Opposite was a single divan bed, and shelving that housed a selection of standard school textbooks, a pile of car magazines, and a CD player with around a hundred discs stacked haphazardly beside it. The top of a low cupboard on the window wall was supporting a TV receiver and video tape deck. There were two small easy chairs and a narrow coffee table in the centre of the room. Heat was emanating from a long slim radiator, painted white like the walls, and set under the window. Lighting was indirect from two wall brackets, a desk lamp and a standard lamp, all of which were switched on.

'Only two of the rooms on this floor are being used this term, sir. This one, and the one you passed as you came in,' DC Vaughan volunteered. He was a few years younger than Lloyd, and a good deal lighter, but balding, with an intrusive smoker's cough. The SOCO gear he had on, hood now removed, made him look weightier than he was.

'And the other room belongs to Miss Oswald, and was locked all weekend?'

'That's it, sir. Seems she should have been back by now but isn't.'

'And one of the two rooms below this is also empty, so the place is a long way off being full,' said Parry absently. He and Lloyd were now moving around the room, examining with their eyes before touching anything. 'And who are the teachers who use the two tower rooms on the first floor?' he went on, sliding open the wardrobe door for the second time.

Lloyd pulled out his notebook. 'One is Mr Ifor Jenkin, who teaches maths and has only just got back. The other is Miss Cynthia Strange, the history tutor.' He narrowed his eyes as he deciphered more of his own notes. 'The large single ground-floor room under that is one of the two language laboratories. Access to it at weekends is by key, kept by the duty tutor. It's not been used since four on Sunday, or that's what the principal told me. Incidentally, the room next to that on the south side of the tower is the principal's study. He was in it most of yesterday evening, and it was locked when he wasn't.'

'He doesn't sleep there?' Parry was examining a Japanese camera he'd found on the top shelf of the wardrobe. It was a model he'd toyed with buying before being put off by the price.

'No, boss. He and his wife have a self-contained apartment on the south side of the building. First floor. Lovely outlook, the housekeeper says.'

'And nobody in these tower rooms has reported anything unusual at any time during yesterday or in the night?' He looked at Lloyd, but not overexpectantly.

'Not so far, boss. But we haven't talked to all of them yet.'

'And what about your lot, Alf? Anything useful found in here? No suicide note, I know.'

'Nothing like that, sir, no,' Vaughan replied. 'And nothing on the computer so far as we can see. DC Price was here with us. He did, a quick check on the index of all the headings on the computer main menu.' Mike Price was the Unit's computer expert. 'The latest jobs listed have nothing personal in them, and, anyway, Mr Gibbon doesn't seem to have put anything on the machine since last Wednesday.'

Parry sniffed. 'If the stuff in those

56

coloured files is all the work he's done this term, there's not much of it,' he remarked, while scanning the room once more. There had been no evidence of other original material, except for the answers to some history questions lying on the desktop itself, with a reprinted examination paper. Parry had noticed that the pages of answers were photoprints, and in a different typeface used on the notes in Gibbon's flies.

'Perhaps Mr Gibbon didn't like working on a screen,' said Lloyd. 'Some people don't.'

'Or perhaps he just didn't like work,' Parry responded caustically. 'For a chap who's supposed to be cramming for A levels, there's precious little in this room to prove it.'

'And if he took stuff away with him to work on over the weekend, it wasn't in his car,' said Lloyd. 'Of course, according to Dr Newsom-Pugh, Frederic Gibbon wasn't very scholastic by nature.'

Parry pulled a face. 'But he must have been doing some kind of work, otherwise why was he here?'

The sergeant shrugged. 'To please his mother, perhaps,' he offered, as a young uniformed constable entered through the open door.

'Mrs Watkyn, the college housekeeper, asking to speak to DS Lloyd, sir,' the newcomer announced. 'She's outside in the corridor.'

'Come in, Mrs Watkyn,' called Lloyd loudly. When the lady appeared, he introduced her to Parry and Vaughan, then asked: 'So what can we do for you?'

Mrs Watkyn, in her mid-fifties, moved with a slight lift at the end of each step. Her jet-black hair was cut short and waved. She wore no make-up save for a fiery-red lipstick, liberally applied, and some dark pencilling over plucked eyebrows. She had discarded the wraparound cotton overall she had been wearing earlier, to reveal a long-sleeved, tailored navy-blue dress. This emphasized her classically curved silhouette which, in one given to a degree of plumpness, suggested assistance from a competent corsetier. 'It's to do with something you asked me about earlier,' she said. 'About a window latch in this room.'

'I remember, Mrs Watkyn, yes. You mentioned the latch on the left-side window was open.'

'Yes, well, thinking it over, I'm not quite sure now that it was.' The housekeeper pursed her lips. 'I know you said it was

58

important, and I've been going over it in my head ever since. I'm not certain even now, but what with the shock of finding the body, I ... I may have made a mistake.' The hesitation over the last phrase indicated that the speaker was rarely mistaken and was diffident, if not actually resentful, at having to admit the lapse.

'It's very responsible of you to come and tell us, Mrs Watkyn. I wish everyone was so public-spirited,' said Parry, with deep conviction in his tone. 'Why don't you sit down, and run over the point again with us.' He nodded at Vaughan, who left the room as the lady went to a seat, with a look of growing self-satisfaction. 'Now, I gather you and Sara Card were airing the rooms? The ones that hadn't been used over the week-end?'

The housekeeper beamed at her questioner. 'Well, it was more than that really. Every Monday we put clean towels in the students' rooms, but Dr Newsom-Pugh's very keen on rooms getting an airing, like you say. His wife's the same. She's German, you see?' she continued earnestly, as though that wholly explained the lady's matching whim. 'They both like windows to be opened for five minutes, even during cold weather. Well, I'd opened one window next door, in Josephine Oswald's room, then I came in here–'

'Sorry to interrupt, but what was Miss Card doing at that point?' asked Parry.

'Sara? She was following me round with the clean towels, and collecting the dirty ones. When I came in here, I went straight to the window. I'll never know what made me look down after I opened it, but when I did, and saw the body, I called for Sara straight off. She was on the stairs and–'

'Hang on, can we go back to your opening the window in here, Mrs Watkyn?' asked the sergeant.

'Well, I was going to, but I wanted to say first why I may have got mixed up. You see, I remember the latch I used in one of the two rooms was open, but the more I think about it, the more I think now it was the one next door. Only it was more likely I'd *imagined* it was the one in here.'

'Why is that?' Parry's knitted brow indicated solid interest.

'Freddy Gibbon was always opening his windows and leaving the latch off.'

'Fresh-air fiend, was he?'

'No. It was to get rid of the sickly smells of his smoking.'

Lloyd glanced at Parry. 'Do you know what he smoked?'

Mrs Watkyn shook her head. 'I've no idea, but sometimes the smell in here was ... fetid,' she announced, with strong emphasis on the first letter of the last word. 'But I realize now it's not likely he could have left a window latch open over the weekend.' She stopped speaking while she touched the end of her nose with a blue-bordered handkerchief.

'Why is that, Mrs Watkyn?' the sergeant coaxed.

The housekeeper frowned as if she might have forgotten, but it was only because of the difficulty she was having in pushing the handkerchief back up her sleeve. 'Sara and I were dusting, and changing the sheet and duvet cover in here on Saturday morning,' she answered, looking up. 'We always make sure the window latches are closed in the rooms after we've done that. Later I was told Freddy Gibbon had left the college straight after lessons ended. If that's true, I shouldn't think he'd have come up here, and if he did, he'd only have been picking up his things for the weekend. He wouldn't have opened a window.' She paused, looking from Parry to Lloyd, then back again. 'Of course, I do understand why it's important to know whether that latch was open or not this morning. That's why I'm here. It stands to reason, doesn't it, that if he threw himself from one of those windows, he couldn't very well have closed the latch after him, could he?'

4

'Is it usual, Dr Newsom-Pugh, that students can come and go here without needing to report to anyone?' Parry questioned.

'Certainly not.' The studiedly downcast principal shook his head vigorously from where he was sitting behind a capacious desk in an even more capacious, though quite sparsely furnished, study. The desktop itself was arranged with a blotter and the other normal accoutrements, though these were overshadowed by a much larger than normal framed photograph of a strikingly attractive young blonde woman who both the visitors rightly took to be Mrs Newsom-Pugh. 'As I've already told Sergeant Lloyd,' the speaker continued, 'on Saturday,

Frederic Gibbon reported to my wife, his course tutor, that he'd be going home for the weekend. It's the rule. When he returned, he should have reported at once to the duty tutor, who happened also to be my wife.'

'But he didn't do that, sir?'

'He hadn't done it up to the point where he appears to have taken his life, no. There could have been any number of innocent reasons for that. For there being a ... a delay.'

Parry looked at Lloyd, who was taking notes in the chair beside his. The two detectives were seated across the desk from Newsom-Pugh. It was now ten to nine. 'But mostly when Gibbon went home for the weekend, he came back on the Monday morning, sir, not Sunday night?' the chief inspector pressed.

'That's right.'

'And often he made it only just before the start of the first class, at, nine o'clock on Monday, and sometimes after the class had started?'

'I'm afraid so, yes. I know he'd been cautioned on that. I fear that when it came to timekeeping, he wasn't the most conscientious of students.'

'Was he any more conscientious in other ways, sir?'

'He was not ... not academically inclined, which meant he needed to try harder.'

'And did he try harder, sir? At his studies?'

'I hardly see what that has to do with his losing his life, Chief Inspector.'

'Perhaps not, sir, but we have to be the judges of that.'

With a pout and a lift of his wild and bushy eyebrows, Newsom-Pugh replied: 'He wasn't progressing perhaps as well as he should have been, no.' He sighed heavily.

'At least it seems the caution about time-keeping may have done some good, sir,' Lloyd put in cheerfully, shifting in his chair. 'He must have been here well before nine this morning. We think he could have been dead for some hours before he was found.'

Newsom-Pugh, who was now wearing a black academic gown over his tweeds, leaned back magisterially, both podgy hands rubbing the rounded ends of the leather chair arms. 'If he came back in the middle of the night...' The eyebrows demonstrably lowered again before he went on. 'And, by the way, that's something else we don't encourage, but if he did come back in the small hours, he wouldn't have disturbed my wife then, of course. He'd have waited to report to her after breakfast.'

'Thank you, sir.' The sergeant glanced at his notebook. 'The engine of his car was stone cold when we examined it. That means he could have parked it where it is now any time after ten o'clock last night, the time when the space he used was last seen empty. If he got back very late at night, would someone have had to let him in, and if so, who?'

'He might easily have been noticed by someone, a member of staff, or another student. Your people are presumably asking everyone about that now.' The principal cleared his throat. 'But no, he'd have let himself in. He had a key. All students have keys to the main door, and to their own rooms.'

Parry looked surprised. 'And you have thirty-seven students currently on the books, sir. That's a lot of main-door keys to have lying around.'

'I'm aware of that, Chief Inspector, but the keys are hardly left lying around, as you suggest. We've tried other systems for allowing students access, and they don't work. Besides, all our students are sixteen years of age or more. They're old enough and responsible enough to have keys to their own homes, which is why we consider them responsible enough to have keys to this college. It's normal practice at the universities they'll be attending after leaving here. For instance, many Oxford and Cambridge colleges give their undergraduates keys. They have to. Otherwise it means having a porter on duty around the clock, as it would do here.'

Parry nodded, while wondering how many students of Modlen College ever qualified to go on to Oxford or Cambridge. 'You say Gibbon told your wife he was going home on Saturday. That would be to Hereford. As we explained to you earlier, since you hadn't been able to reach his mother by phone, I'm afraid we had to ask the local police to send officers to her home. They got no answer there either. A neighbour says she doesn't believe there's been anyone at the house for more than a week, but the Hereford police say there are fresh tyre marks in the drive, so the lady may have returned from wherever she's been, and then gone out again. The house is being checked at regular intervals.'

Newsom-Pugh exercised his lips, in concert with the end of his substantial nose, like a rabbit tentatively checking on the edibility of a dandelion leaf. 'Yes, I was most anxious to speak to her before anyone else. To tell her the sad news. She hasn't lived in the area long, of course,' he volunteered, as if conceivably that could be a reason why someone wouldn't answer the telephone or the doorbell. 'But I should explain that when a student says he or she is "going home", it's not assumed to mean just that in every case. It only applies to younger students, who are certainly required to go to their homes, or other specified destinations, if they leave here at the weekends. It's so we know they've returned to the ... the custody, as it were, of their parents or other approved guardians.'

'And so that you won't be responsible for them once they're off the premises, sir,' Lloyd put in cheerfully. 'That's to cover your back, is it?'

Newsom-Pugh's cheeks stiffened, as if he didn't care for the last expression, before he replied: 'You could say that, yes, Sergeant. Certainly it's meant to provide legal protection for the college.'

'But Gibbon was eighteen, wasn't he?'

'Indeed, and for him, "going home" for the weekend would be a loose term indicating he ... he simply wouldn't be here.'

'Because he could go where he liked, and no problem to the college, sir?'

There were more rabbity movements in the centre of Newsom-Pugh's face before he pronounced: 'That's about it, yes.'

'We gather six of the students live fairly locally and don't board in the college, sir. They go home each day,' said Parry.

'That's right, Chief Inspector. Some of those have their own cars or are transported daily by their parents.'

'Do many of the boarders have their own transport? Like Gibbon?'

'About half of them do. They tend to be the older ones. Of course, there's a perfectly good bus service to the village.'

'Could Gibbon have gone to the home of one of the other students this weekend?'

'I don't know where he went. I'd have thought if that was the case we'd have known by now.'

'Quite so, sir. Otherwise, you've really no idea where he could have gone?'

'None. I'd hoped one of his tutors might know. Or one of the students, but that hasn't proved to be the case so far. We may learn more shortly, now everyone's here to be questioned.' He looked at the time.

'You mentioned his course tutor was your

wife. I gather Mrs Newsom-Pugh teaches French and German. Were those Gibbon's main subjects?'

'No. I should explain the full-time tutors are responsible as, what we term, course tutors for counselling half a dozen or so students over their general and ... and moral wellbeing.'

'But Gibbon did do French and German, sir?'

'French, not German. French was one of the subjects he failed an A level in last summer. That was at his previous school.'

'Could you tell us what else he was studying?'

'Mathematics, history, and English.'

'And had he failed in all of them?'

'I fear so, Mr Parry, yes. Oh, I recall now he got a D grade in English, and was hoping to improve on that by sitting the subject again.'

'But he would only have needed three reasonable A levels for university entrance, wouldn't he, sir?' put in Lloyd, whose five children had each achieved that or better.

'That's so. But we normally have a fourth subject in reserve. As a makeweight. Even so, in Gibbon's particular case, I fear the possibility of three good grades was fairly remote. Now, of course, the matter is ... hmm, academic.' A brief, rueful smile crossed the principal's face.

'If that was as apparent to him as it was to his tutors, sir, would he have been depressed about it?' asked Parry.

'I don't believe so.' The speaker began tapping the fingers of one hand lightly on the desk. 'He seemed to have a very fatalistic attitude to life.'

'You mean exam failure wasn't something that fazed him?'

'Not especially. He was scarcely a scholarly boy. I did tactfully point that out to his mother at the end of last term.' He ran his tongue around his lips, before adding ruminatively: 'There was a time when a commission in the army suited that sort of individual. Strong athletic type, aggressive to a degree, with latent leadership qualities, but not er ... not overly endowed academically, if you follow me? However, the educational requirements covering officer recruitment in the services have been set a good deal higher in recent years.' Newsom-Pugh made a pained face, but offered no compensating assurance that Her Britannic Majesty's armed forces, and the protection of Realm and citizens, had benefited all

70

round as a consequence – assuming his whole assertion bore any resemblance to fact.

'So why was Gibbon kept at an expensive school like this, sir?' asked Lloyd.

'Some parents are optimists. Also, we do have a reputation for getting results against the odds.' The last claim brought a passing expression of prim satisfaction to the speaker's well-nourished countenance.

'And his mother's well off, is she, sir?'

'No, not at all. As a matter of fact, there was a ... a small problem over the fees here, but we overcame it. I believe there was a modest insurance settlement of some kind, which was supposed to provide for the boy's education. Miss Thomas, our bursar, can give you what details we have on that.'

'But it was too modest for a school of this calibre, sir?' Parry questioned.

Newsom-Pugh seemed to be testing the point before he answered carefully. 'You could say that, yes.'

'But Mrs Gibbon was ambitious for her son? Ready to make sacrifices?'

'I'm sure that's true.' This response had also been a cautious one, signalling his diffidence about being drawn further in the matter.

71

'He certainly doesn't appear to have had personal money problems,' the chief inspector continued, aware of the stiffening attitude on the other side of the desk. 'We've checked through his room. His possessions border on the lavish. On top of a pretty good car he owned a lot of expensive clothes, a Contax camera, a CD player, a TV set, a computer–'

'You surprise me,' Newsom-Pugh interrupted. 'I should point out, however, that students are ... are encouraged to bring a personal computer to keep in their rooms. Even so, the college provides all the equipment they need for their studies, including computers in the classrooms. We aim to be a centre of excellence. Yes, a centre of excellence,' he completed.

'And would you know if Gibbon used illegal drugs, sir?'

The principal sat back sharply – as though physically as well as mentally assaulted by the question. 'Good heavens no. Whoever put that idea in your head, Chief Inspector? If I learned that any student here took drugs, he'd be out on his ear in an instant. Thankfully, we've never encountered the problem.'

'No one's directly suggested the opposite

to us, sir.' Parry had no wish to stir things up for Mrs Watkyn. 'But I'm afraid it's a question we need to put in cases of this kind,' he added, far from reassured by the previous overly confident reply.

'You have no other address for Frederic Gibbon's mother, Miss Thomas?' Lloyd was asking a few minutes later in the connecting room to the principal's. It was half the size of the one they had just left, but with walls, carpets and curtains in the same well-coordinated shades or patterns. The two rooms had probably been an entertainment suite of medium size when the place had been a hotel.

'No, I don't. It's very worrying not to be able to reach her. Dr Newsom-Pugh is deeply concerned about it. Please sit down, won't you?' Debby Thomas was an attractive and buxom brunette in her late-twenties, who wore well-applied make-up and noisy jewellery. When the two police-men had re-emerged through the double doors, she had greeted them with a grave smile that Parry sensed would have been a good deal more engaging on a less melancholy occasion. Her gaze had lingered on his face before assessing the rest of him, returning to his eyes after she had answered the sergeant's question. Dressed in a chunky wool sweater, a knee-length tweed skirt and high leather boots, she was seated at an open-fronted, white metal desk which matched the filing cabinets behind her.

'As bursar, I gather you're responsible for all the college's paperwork. That's a big job,' Parry went on, as he and Lloyd moved to the chairs she had indicated.

'Fairish,' she commented with a modest smile, removing her rimless, oversized spectacles. 'The principal and I share the work between us. I do all his typing as well as my own. That keeps me in touch with everything that's going on. It works out very well. We've never employed secretaries.'

'Saves on overheads,' said Lloyd encouragingly.

'Yes, it does, but that's not the only reason.' The reply had been clipped. Evidently, the speaker was happy to indulge the speculations of youthful chief inspectors, but not those of aging sergeants. 'College bills are pretty straightforward and computerized,' she added, nodding at the computer to her right. 'Salaries are handled by outside accountants, and paid direct into people's banks. We have a very good housekeeper and an excellent cook, both highly motivated. I only need to approve their accounts for payment once a month.'

'And do you live in the college?' Parry asked.

'No.' She had elongated the single word, and accompanied it with an inquisitive arching of one eyebrow, which might have been a signal that she thought the question had been more personal than official. 'My partner and I have a house on the far side of Llanishen. It doesn't take me long to get here. My partner needs to be close to Cardiff for his job. He's in the security business. As a matter of fact, he's an ex-policeman.' Llanishen was an outer suburb on the north-east side of the city.

'Go on. What's his name? Perhaps I know him?' said Lloyd.

'It's possible, Sergeant,' she responded. with a glance at the questioner which expressed the opposite, before she returned her attention to Parry. 'His name's Colvin Russell. He's Welsh, but not from round here. Used to be in London, with the Met. He's a supervisor with Home and Corporate Security now, in Cardiff.'

'No, I don't think I know him,' said the sergeant, shaking his head, while Parry didn't volunteer anything. 'So, could you tell us, were you here on Saturday morning?' Lloyd went on.

'Not last Saturday, no.'

'So there was no chance you heard Mr Gibbon say where he was going for the weekend?'

'Afraid not.'

'Did you have much to do with him, Miss Thomas?' Parry put in.

She hesitated. 'No more than with any of the other students, I suppose.' She blinked several times before adding: 'Well, a bit more, come to think of it. Col and I ran in to him one Saturday afternoon in Cardiff last term. In October, it was. He came back for tea. He was meeting a girl later, I remember.'

'Bit of a one for the girls, was he, miss?' asked Lloyd.

'I suppose he was, yes. He could be quite amusing, and he was very good-looking, of course.'

'We noticed that from photos in his room. He was older than most of the students.'

'Not that much. He looked older, though.'

'Did he visit you at home often?' Lloyd enquired.

'Why, has someone told you he did?' she came back sharply.

'No, no, miss. I was just wondering.'

'Yes, he did come to see us again. But not often. Once, or maybe twice. I think he enjoyed our company. I got the impression he preferred being with older people. I mean, as opposed to students.'

'But you didn't see him at all over this weekend?'

'No, I've already told one of the other officers that.'

'Would you say Frederic Gibbon was capable of suicide?' Parry enquired.

She fingered one of the gold pendant earrings she had on, in the process making the bracelets at her wrist jangle. 'Always difficult to say, isn't it, Mr Parry? He wasn't doing at all well with his work here.'

'But according to Dr Newsom-Pugh, that didn't seem to worry him,' offered Lloyd.

'That's probably right. He could have been worried about other things, of course.'

'A girl, perhaps?' pressed the sergeant.

Miss Thomas shrugged. 'Who knows. Except...' She hesitated again before going on. 'Except he was pretty sure of himself. I mean, I imagine he was probably the kind of boy who broke hearts fairly often.'

'Not the kind who'd worry if he made a girl pregnant, for instance?'

'Who is, these days, Sergeant? In any case, isn't it the girl who used to commit suicide in those cases, not the boy?' The reply had come with some acerbity. 'No, I think he'd have coped well enough with something of that kind.'

Parry frowned. 'He seems to have lived pretty well, but the principal doesn't think his mother's at all wealthy.'

'I know. That's a bit of a mystery. When they came here for the interview last August, she was very upset because she felt she couldn't really afford the fees. She asked to speak to Dr Newsom-Pugh alone about it, just before they left. Since she was a widow, he broke the rule and brought the fees down a bit. She was terribly grateful to him. At Christmas, though, Freddy told me he paid the fees himself out of a family endowment of some kind. He said his mother worried about money unnecessarily. He didn't even know she'd pleaded for a reduction here. I've not mentioned this to the principal. No, Freddy never seemed to have trouble getting money for whatever he wanted.'

'You mean for clothes and girlfriends ... or drugs, perhaps?'

'I wouldn't think drugs.'

'You sound very sure of that.'

She crossed her legs under the desk. 'Only as sure as it's possible to be, just from observation,' she answered, it seemed more undecided than evasive.

'I see. And his funds were always from his own resources, were they?'

'How do you mean?' Her answers seemed now to be more carefully considered than before.

'Well, could he have had other sources? His student friends, perhaps? Richer ones?'

Miss Thomas shook her head slowly, making the earrings flash. 'I'd say he didn't have many friends amongst the students, though, in general, I got the impression he was rather looked up to by them. And I don't believe anyone here was staking him. As I said, he didn't seem to need it.'

5

'Well, it's been a pretty unprofitable exercise so far,' Parry complained, staring through the window at a blank wall. 'Thirty-five students, plus virtually the whole staff, and nobody with the first idea where Gibbon went, or when he came back. It's hard to credit.'

'Unless some of the people are lying, sir,' offered sharp, twenty-four-year-old Detective Sergeant Mary Norris. 'A few of them have been incredibly tight-lipped as well.'

Parry swung round to face her. 'In which case we need to know what they have to hide. It's a small community. People living on top of each other, taking classes, tutorials, and meals together all week. You'd think weekend plans would be a ... a major topic of conversation. And a harmless one as well.'

'But Gibbon didn't mix much, sir. Not a friendly type. The opposite, I should think,' blurted out lanky Detective Constable Alison Pope, then wished she hadn't. She was standing behind Mary Norris. As a consequence of offering unsupported opinion, not fact, to a senior policeman, she shifted nervously from one foot to the other, disturbed at the prospect of having that opinion challenged. She was an earnest officer who made up in dedication and intelligence what she lacked yet in confidence – and also in gainliness.

'That's the impression I've been given

too,' Parry replied, with an encouraging nod. 'Except by Debby Thomas, the bursar.'

'She did say he got on better with older people, boss,' said Lloyd.

'That didn't apply to Miss Strange, the history tutor, or Mr Jenkin, the maths tutor. I interviewed both, sir,' Sergeant Norris put in. She and Lloyd were at a small rectangular table checking their notes. 'They didn't have much of an opinion of Gibbon as a pupil, or as an individual. Miss Strange was hostile about him under the surface. When I suggested she was, she kind of dodged the issue. Said he wasn't up to the mark scholastically, or keen to improve, which meant he was wasting everyone's time being here at all.'

'And Jenkin?' Parry pressed, now joining them at the table.

'He was different, sir. Very nervous with his answers. He asked me twice when Gibbon had died. The second time was after I'd told him we didn't know. He thought Gibbon got other people to do his schoolwork. I suppose that was the worst thing he actually said about him. But it was obvious he didn't like him.'

There was silence for a moment, until Alison Pope, still standing, was encouraged

81

enough to offer: 'There's still the two students who haven't turned up yet, sir. From what we've been told already about the boy, Alwyn Bowen, he should have some input on Gibbon. And Josephine Oswald is the same. She's the one who has the room next to his.'

'Who hasn't come back from Brecon, where her father can't get his car out of a one-inch snowdrift,' the chief inspector responded disparagingly. 'Surprising he managed to collect her on Saturday. She's the one who's been described as unsociable by at least three people.' He sniffed. 'She must have known Gibbon quite well, but somehow, I don't think she had anything to do with his weekend.'

'Well, you never know,' said Lloyd, with what was meant to be a show of optimism.

'You can have premonitions though, Gomer,' Parry muttered testily, while riffling through a sheaf of other people's notes.

It was 10.25. The four officers had been involved in interviewing since nine. Some of the questioning had taken place in the basement lecture room they were in now.

'So this'll be all right if we need an incident room, will it, boss? Plenty of electric

82

points, and we can use the small inter-connecting room for interviews,' said Lloyd, temporarily changing the subject to get a decision he needed in any case.

The chief inspector looked about him. 'Sure. It's big enough. And from the way the pathologist was talking, I'd say we're definitely going to need an incident room.'

The body had already been taken to the hospital mortuary. Dr Ironmonger, the young Home Office pathologist, had left shortly before that, after bounding up the stairs to check the windows in Gibbon's room. Normally even more diffident than DC Pope over offering conjectures not founded in provable data, he had still expressed doubts over the suicide theory. His immediate view had been that there should have been more blood from the wounds if the deceased had still been alive at the time of the impact. He had also been interested in the two incisions in Gibbon's stomach noted by Dr Maltravers, both of which seemed to be more than just surface wounds, though he couldn't investigate them properly on the spot. His parting words had been an invitation to Parry to call him at the hospital much later in the day, when he should have completed the preliminary parts of the autopsy.

The close-carpeted lecture room was on a corner, and was the largest of four similar basement rooms in Modlen Hall. Like the others, it had earlier been fitted out as a hotel conference room, only this one also had a small anteroom. At present the main room contained only twenty or so stackable chairs, a few tables in assorted sizes, and a movable blackboard. Its three windows faced east, and although they had only the castellated wall for an outlook, the single window to the anteroom was at the base of the tower, only a few feet from where the body had been found. The space had been offered to the police because it was too big for even the largest college classes – and in the bleak midwinter, like today, it was also the darkest of the basement lecture areas, and the hardest to keep warm.

As Parry had remarked, the time spent interviewing had been largely unproductive in terms of moving the enquiry along. Newsom-Pugh's opinion of Gibbon had been a more diplomatic version of what other members of the teaching staff had thought about him. As for the students, apart from the two still unavailable, only three had admitted having anything to do with the dead youth on a regular basis. These had been the girls occupying room twenty-eight – one of the two student bedrooms on the second floor lying directly below his. Two of the girls, Abby Kennedy and Kate Unwin, had been the ones who had returned together by car the evening before. Their other roommate, Mair Daltry, was still suffering from the cold that had kept her indoors over the weekend, but she had appeared for lessons and thus for questioning by the police.

The three girls were all well-developed seventeen-year-olds, and physically the most attractive of the female pupils at the college, with Mair Daltry judged to be the more intelligent of the trio. This last had been the joint opinion of DS Mary Norris and DC Alison Pope, who had interviewed the available eleven girls enrolled.

'So they're a sexy trio, but only one's at all bright, Mary,' said Parry a minute later. when they were discussing the occupants of room twenty-eight. He looked across the table at the woman sergeant, and then Alison Pope who had seated herself there as well. 'The dimness of the other two could have been a ploy, of course. To make you think they weren't bright enough to have

85

had anything to do with Gibbon's death,' he speculated.

'But if they were bright kids, they wouldn't be here anyway, would they?' put in Lloyd. 'And hadn't they already volunteered knowing Gibbon better than other students?'

'Not really, Sergeant,' answered DC Pope, sure of her ground here. 'It was people we'd interviewed before them who said they were special friends of his.'

'So they couldn't get out of it.' This was Parry. 'Except, you say they denied being that close to him. Or was that just to stop you thinking they should have known where he was yesterday? Where were they, by the way? The two who weren't here for the weekend?'

'Abby Kennedy went home with Kate Unwin, sir.'

The chief inspector folded his arms tightly across his chest. 'Well, it's still odd that hardly any of the kids in the college seem even to have spoken to Gibbon,' he remarked. 'He was in his second term, after all.'

'Conspiracy of silence, could it be, boss?' said Lloyd.

'Possibly. Even these three girls only finally admit to what? A sort of group acquaintance, because they kept bumping into him on the stairs.'

'They did admit they went up to listen to his CDs sometimes,' put in Alison Pope. 'Always at least two of them together though.'

'Hmm.' Parry pulled a face. 'Safety in numbers, or a way of showing none of them was his special girlfriend.'

'If one of them was, sir, it wouldn't have been Mair Daltry,' put in DC Pope.

'That's right,' added the woman sergeant beside her. 'She had almost nothing to say about him.'

'Was what the others said complimentary?'

'Their opinions were ... bland, sir. We got the feeling they were holding plenty back, for their sakes', not Gibbon's.'

'I see. So were the two telling the truth when they said Gibbon's car wasn't in the park when they got back?'

'I'd say there's a fifty-fifty chance they weren't, sir.'

'But if they're lying, why?' asked Lloyd, while offering his peppermints to everyone, and finding an enthusiastic taker in DC Pope.

Parry considered for a moment, then

shrugged. 'No reason I can think of yet, Gomer. So who's seeing this Bowen boy, and when?'

Alwyn Bowen, day boy, and the only male student alleged by others to have been a friend of Gibbon, hadn't been available yet for interview because of a dental appointment.

DC Pope glanced at the time. 'Ah, I was just going to say, by now he should be at a lesson in the lecture room across the hall, sir,' she offered, and sounding as if her mouth was chock full of peppermints. 'Shall I see him, sir?'

'No, DS Lloyd and I will. Wheel him in, could you? Oh, and can we find some coffee?'

'Yes, sir.' The detective constable jumped up and made for the door with long, purposeful strides.

On first appearance, the seventeen-year-old Bowen, who entered a few minutes later, seemed to Parry as physically unattractive as Gibbon's female friends were alleged to be the opposite. His shortness accentuated the fact that he was seriously overweight, and his slovenliness compounded it. The dark-green tracksuit he had on was in need of a wash. His uncombed hair hung over his forehead in a long fringe above a pair of slightly crooked, John Lennon glasses. His pasty face was scored by acne, and the dark hairs at the sides of his upper lip were too few to rate as a burgeoning moustache but too long not to warrant taming. His sullen contemplation of the two policemen – DS Norris and DC Pope had left the room – hovered somewhere between suspicion and downright hostility.

'Please sit down, er ... Alwyn, isn't it? The lady officer offered you a coffee, did she?' Lloyd enquired warmly, indicating a chair on the other side of the small table from himself and Parry, while he stirred the brown liquid in one of the two polystyrene mugs Alison Pope had brought in.

'Didn't want any coffee. Not from the machine she got it from,' the boy responded darkly.

'Know what you mean,' said the sergeant with a grin. 'We've got machines at our office too, but interviewing's thirsty work. Anyway, I'm Detective Sergeant Lloyd, and this is my boss Detective Chief Inspector Parry. We're enquiring into the sad death of Freddy Gibbon. We understand he was a friend of yours.'

At the mention of the word friend, Bowen's sullen look altered to register a puzzled but not actually hostile reaction. His expression remained in that fresh mode, suggesting that his face was to be a faithful mirror of his thinking, without any outward attempt at guile on the part of its owner – or perhaps any capacity for it. 'Oh, yes,' he uttered, but without voicing the challenge most of his fellow students had made in response to the same or a similar question. Both detectives wondered whether the young man couldn't be bothered with a denial. He seemed preoccupied with twisting both feet around one front leg of his chair. The feet were encased in a pair of badly scored white trainers.

'Yes. Well now, we gather you don't board in the college, Alwyn. That's right, isn't it?' The sergeant took the responding nod as confirmation before he went on. 'But you were on the premises here for some of the time yesterday, and for part of Saturday afternoon?'

'Yes. Saturday I was using the language lab.'

'Was that the one next door here, or the one upstairs?'

'Upstairs. They don't use the one down

here weekends.'

'I see, so you were here to study? That's very conscientious.'

Bowen's face now showed a measure of incredulity – or possibly pity. 'My dad made me come,' he said flatly. 'And I had an extra session booked Sunday afternoon. With Mrs Wattis-Milne.'

'That's Mrs Wattis-Milne who teaches physics and chemistry?'

'Yes.'

'And I believe she came in specially for you.' Sheila Wattis-Milne, whom Lloyd himself had questioned earlier, was middle aged, married and lived in Cardiff with her university-lecturer husband. She had never taught Gibbon, nor, as she recalled, even spoken to him. Hers had been a particularly fruitless interview, excepting only that it had covered Bowen's whereabouts between three and five the day before.

'And your home's in Pontyglas, isn't it?' the sergeant continued, sipping the coffee.

'Near there. My dad's a farmer. Dairy farmer.'

'I see. So you don't have too far to come. And you've got a car.'

'Yeah. Only a banger. That's all my dad'll pay for. Still, it goes.' He smiled for the first time – a somewhat bitter and fleeting smile.

Parry drew his chair closer to the table, and pushed the only once sampled coffee to one side. 'Did you talk to Freddy Gibbon on Saturday morning, about his plans for the weekend?'

'Hardly talked to him at all Saturday, except for a minute before lessons started.'

'Was that in the classroom?'

'No, upstairs in his room. I ... I was giving back a CD he lent me.'

'I see. Did he mention to you where he'd be going for the weekend at any other time last week?'

'No.'

'And you didn't see him on Sunday? Him or his car?'

Bowen shook his head.

'Can you even guess where he might have gone?'

The boy shrugged. 'Home?'

'No. We don't believe he went home.' Parry smiled. 'As Sergeant Lloyd said, we'd gathered he was a special friend of yours? Do you want to tell us about that? Did you have any big interests that brought you together?'

The boy searched in his pocket before producing a grubby, screwed-up tissue with which he rubbed the end of his nose. 'Not a special friend.' He paused. 'I don't have friends here. I did have in my last school. in Pontyglas.' The tone, like the grieved look that went with it, made it crystal clear that the change of school had been resented.

'But surely you and Freddy were pretty close, all the same?'

'I used to help him. With his work.' There was a pause. 'He wasn't so bright with school stuff. That goes for me too, but I'm brighter than Freddy was.' The statements had been solidly matter-of-fact, not boastful.

It was Lloyd who then put in: 'So far as you know, Alwyn, did he have any close friends at all amongst the male students?'

Bowen pulled a face. 'Don't know.'

'What about girlfriends?'

'Depends what you mean by girlfriends.' The speaker's upper lip had curled slightly at the end of the sentence.

'Well, the usual, I suppose. Girls he sat next to in class. Girls he took out,' the sergeant offered. 'Kate Unwin, Abby Kennedy, and Mair Daltry, for instance.'

'Wouldn't call them his girlfriends, exactly.'

'What would you call them, then?'

93

The eyes narrowed, indicating either calculation or caution. 'Just girls he talked to a bit more than the others, probably. I don't know.'

'What about Josephine Oswald, who has the room next to his?'

'She's weird. Doesn't talk to anyone.' Which at least seemed to corroborate the views of others.

Parry cleared his throat. 'You're a bit more than a year younger than Freddy was, of course,' he said. 'So if you weren't especially friendly with him, and you helped him with his work, was that because he did something for you in return?'

This time, Bowen's small dark eyes widened unblinkingly. 'What do you mean?'

'What I say. Did he return the favour you did him in some way?'

The boy scratched the nails of five podgy fingers against the back of his other hand, but made no immediate reply.

'Did he pay you, perhaps, Alwyn?' the sergeant took up the questioning.

The long-delayed response, when it came, was too mumbled for the words to be distinguishable.

'Sorry, could you repeat that?'

Bowen raised his chin and his voice a

fraction. 'I said, sort of. He sort of paid me. Not in money... He ... he gave me things. Or lent them. Like CDs. He ... he had a fantastic CD collection.' It was as though he was making up the explanation as he went along.

'Did he ever offer you drugs of any kind, Alwyn?'

'Freddy? No. Freddy wasn't into drugs.' The answer had been so prompt, and firm, and the expression that went with it so ingenuous, that both policemen debated whether it had been totally honest or possibly just the result of long anticipation.

Lloyd produced his mints again and offered them to Bowen, who took one. 'This help you gave Freddy, what sort of help was it? I mean, were you teaching him things, or ... or just giving him answers so he'd get better marks?'

In contrast to DC Pope, the boy was a sweet cruncher, not a sucker. 'Both, I suppose,' he replied between bites. 'I just helped him with his prep. In the evenings, or the mornings sometimes. I'd get here early, specially for that. They give you a lot of prep. Mostly old exam questions.'

'I see. So what it amounted to was you did his prep for him? Or let him copy your answers?'

'Yes, he copied my answers sometimes. We mostly did the same subjects. Except he didn't do physics. But usually he couldn't copy the answers straight, could he? If he had they'd have known. Except for maths questions sometimes.'

'So did you sometimes leave him what you'd done, so he could ... rearrange the wording for his own answers?'

'I left it sometimes, yes.'

Parry leaned forward across the table. 'Did you give him some of your answers you'd photocopied recently? Very recently?'

The boy gave a long sniff, then reached again for his tissue. 'I took some stuff up to his room Saturday morning, when I gave back the CD. That was answers I'd done Friday night. I'd made copies when I came in. There's a copier in the hall.'

Since the broaching and denying of any drug offer, his answers had been somewhat more relaxed and lengthier.

'That wasn't much help to him long term, though, was it?' questioned the chief inspector. 'You're all supposed to be here cramming yourselves with knowledge that'll get you through A levels next time. If Freddy was just cribbing your work–'

'Freddy didn't care about A levels,' Bowen

broke in, very confidently this time. 'Just so he got good enough class marks here ... so the teachers didn't get on at him.'

Parry grimaced. 'You make it sound as if he was just killing time, here, Alwyn.'

'That's what he said he was doing.'

'Said to whom?'

'Everyone, I should think.' He frowned. 'Not the teachers.'

'You're the only one who's mentioned that to us, Alwyn.'

'Ask the ones you call his girlfriends, then. He told everyone he was coming into money when he was older. When he was twenty-one. It was a family will, or something. He never gave details. Anyway, he said he could do what he wanted after that. He wasn't bothered about going to any university, either.'

'And you think he was telling you the truth about that?' asked the sergeant.

'How would I know? I'm just saying what he told me.'

'Alwyn, are you quite sure you didn't take those copies up to his room yesterday, after your special physics lesson?' Parry asked suddenly.

'No ... no, like I told you, that was Saturday morning.' The vehemence in the denial,

97

reflected in the eyes, seemed genuine.

'And you didn't go up to his room at all yesterday?'

'No. Wouldn't have been any point, would there? Not if he wasn't in college. His door would have been locked.'

'So you knew he wouldn't be here, although he'd never told you that?'

'Freddy was never here at weekends.'

The chief inspector continued to watch the boy's eyes carefully as he put the next question. 'So – what time did you leave the college last night, Alwyn?'

'About half-six.'

'Not straight after your lesson?'

'No. I had a game of table tennis after that.'

'Who with?'

'Phil Evans. He's another boy here. He asked me.'

'And you didn't go up to Freddy's room before you left, to see if he was back?'

'No, I told you, I–'

'And you didn't see his car in the car park as you went to leave, and *then* go back to have a word with him?'

'I never saw Freddy's car.'

'All right. Tell me, Alwyn, would you think Freddy was the sort to commit suicide?'

The boy hesitated. 'Yeah, he could have, I suppose. He was a nutter in some ways.'

'You say he didn't have many friends. Did he have enemies, perhaps?'

'Might have had. I don't know.'

'Just now you said he was coming into money. Did you think he had plenty already?'

'Always seemed to.' The caution was back in his voice as he went on. 'It's why the girls...' Then he stopped in mid-sentence, and changed the way he was sitting in the chair.

'Why the girls what, Alwyn?'

'Nothing. I didn't mean anything.'

'Why the girls were ... were especially nice to him, perhaps? Did him favours?'

Bowen offered the beginnings of a leer. 'Ask them.'

'What sort of favours would you think, Alwyn? Don't leave us in the air,' said Gomer Lloyd in a man-to-man voice. The three girls from room twenty-eight had been asked in their separate interviews about whether any of them had been sexually involved with Gibbon. Each had firmly told the women detectives they hadn't been – only the answers had sounded orchestrated and rehearsed.

99

Before Bowen could reply to the last question, Parry's cellphone began bleeping. Within seconds of his answering it, his face clouded. 'Hold on, will you?' he said into the mouthpiece, then turned to the interviewee. 'That's all for the moment, Alwyn. You can go back to your class. Thanks very much for your help.' The boy needed no second bidding, and left the room in the first show of alacrity he had demonstrated since he had entered it.

'No question about it?' said Parry, speaking into the phone again, then listening while making notes. 'I see... Yes, I'll speak to him later... I'm glad you rang. And thank him for giving us the headlines, will you?' He put down the instrument. 'Well, we can start fitting this place out as an incident room, Gomer. That was Dr Ironmonger's secretary. He's been called out urgently to view another body. Car accident. But from the examinations he's made on Gibbon so far, it's fairly certain he'd been dead for at least four hours before he was found this morning. Actual cause of death still isn't clear, but it wasn't the fall. He was dead before that happened. But those stomach wounds were made before he died. He doesn't think they were deep enough to be important. Caused by a round metal rod with a pointed end, maybe a plumber's probe, or a small butcher's steel. Something like that.'

'Anything on when he last ate, boss?'

'Not yet, no. Organs taken from the body are still being tested,' Parry completed without enthusiasm.

'So all a bit negative, isn't it, from our viewpoint?' The sergeant grinned before adding, 'Unless they've had a plumber up here who went beserk and stopped him breathing with one of those rubber bungs.'

6

'Hi, Josephine. You got back in the end, then?' the plump history tutor offered brightly, while shifting a load of books from one short, stout arm to the other. She smiled benevolently at the stooped waif of a girl who, eyes lowered, had done her best to sidle past on the stairs without being noticed.

'Yes, Miss Strange. Half an hour ago.' It was one thirty. 'My dad brought me in

Mum's car in the end. He couldn't get his to start.'

'Terrible snow they've had in Brecon, I gather. Worse than here. Get something to eat, did you?'

'Yes, miss. A snack before we started.' The girl pushed a long wisp of mouse-brown hair away from the pale and winsome face.

'Well, that must have been a long time ago. Come for a coffee in my room. I've got some mince pies, too. My mother sent them, to stop me wasting away.' She gave a deep chuckle. 'You can give me your prep at the same time. In your bag, is it?'

'Yes, miss.' Josephine Oswald followed her tutor who was already thumping determinedly along the first-floor corridor, brogue-clad feet splayed well outwards, her top enveloped in several layers of woollens, the lower part of her sturdy body encased in an immense pair of corduroy trousers. Shortly, she unlocked a door on the left, thrust it open, stood back as if in the expectation that she might have surprised a belligerent burglar, then marched through into a large bed-sitting room.

When Josephine was seated, she undid the zip of the soft canvas bag she had been clasping to her bosom. Thrusting aside some clothes, she pulled out a sheaf of typed papers. 'In the end, I did the question on Robert Walpole as well as the one on Pitt the Younger, miss.'

'Bully for you. I'll read them later. I don't have a two o'clock class. When's our tutorial – five, is it?' Her hands were full, but she stopped to look through an oversized pair of spectacles at the open desk diary on her work table in the window. 'Yes, five o'clock. Shared with Abby Kennedy and Alwyn Bowen again.' Then she moved towards Josephine. 'You don't take sugar in coffee, do you?'

'That's right, miss. Oh, thank you.'

Miss Strange put a green earthenware beaker of coffee and a sugared mince pie on the little table beside the girl's armchair. 'You've heard what's happened to Freddy Gibbon, have you?'

'Yes, miss. Terrible, isn't it? Two police-women have been asking me about him.'

'I thought they would.' She had hoped to have spoken to Josephine in advance of this happening. 'So what did they want to know?'

'About when I'd last seen him. And ... and if I knew where he'd gone for the weekend. I didn't.' The voice had been hesitant, and the disclaimer close to apologetic.

'So what did you tell them?' Miss Strange's question was casual enough, but she was all attention for an answer.

'Only that I saw him Saturday morning. Upstairs. After the end of lessons.'

'In your room or his?'

'In my room. But he never said where he was going after.'

'Did they tell you whether it was suicide or murder?'

Josephine seemed genuinely shocked. 'It wasn't murder, was it? I thought it was suicide.'

'Everyone did at the start. Now there's a strong rumour he may have been killed by someone.'

'They don't know for certain, miss?'

'There's been no official announcement, no. Not so far as I know. There will be soon, I expect.'

The girl shook her head, while staring at her untouched coffee. 'But when I got back, everyone was saying he'd committed suicide.' She bit her lip. 'I'm so ... so sorry for Freddy.'

'Are you really? You were fond of him, I suppose?' The tone was a touch dis-approving.

'Well ... sort of, I was, yes.' She began to blush, while still staring hard at the beaker of coffee, and feeling like St Peter after he'd denounced Jesus: Josephine Oswald was deeply religious both by upbringing and persuasion. 'I'm ... I'm sorry for his mother, too,' she completed.

'We're all sorry for her, of course. Did they tell you, nobody knows where she is?'

'Yes, they said.' She picked up the beaker, using both hands to steady it before she drank some of its contents.

'The terrible trio in room twenty-eight were friends of Freddy's, too, of course,' said the tutor pointedly.

'Have the police talked to them as well, miss?'

'Yes. But then, they've questioned everybody, including me. I was never overfond of Freddy, I'm afraid. Tell me, did the police ask if he'd ever been ... ever been unkind to you?'

The girl breathed in sharply through her mouth in overreaction to the unexpected question, and just as she was taking her first bite of mince pie. The castor sugar, sucked to the back of her throat, produced a violent fit of coughing. When she had recovered, she swallowed hard twice, then answered in

105

almost a whisper: 'They asked me whether
... whether he'd ever made me do things I ...
I didn't want to do. I told them he'd never
done anything like that.' The narrow lips of
her tiny slit of a mouth were now pressed
tightly together, as she appeared to be
making a spirited attempt to have her head
sink into her body.

'And had he? You can tell me the truth,
Josephine. I shan't tell anyone else.'

The student took a long breath, this time
through her nose. 'He was never unkind to
me.'

'I'm glad to hear it. I er ... I managed to
give the others a word of warning before
they were interviewed. I said to tell the
truth, but to be careful not to overstate
things. Understatement is better on these
occasions, I always think. That's also
between you and me, of course.' Except in
the case of the others, Miss Strange had the
feeling that they hadn't been in need of
cautioning, whereas Josephine could certainly have used some.

Cynthia Strange was course tutor to the
demure, timid creature with her now, as well
as to the three other girls. She took this
responsibility very seriously. In her view, it
could be vital to the future reputation of

these four young moral charges of hers that they weren't tarnished by Gibbon's death. She had always considered him to be potentially, if not already, a bad lot – with the capacity to corrupt the lives of others. For instance, she'd suspected for some time that he'd been seducing the maid Sara Card. Probably the flighty puss wouldn't have needed much pushing into bed, which was partly why the tutor had never done anything about the matter. Even so, it was typical of the boy that he'd take advantage of a menial, which was wrong in principle. On the other hand, Miss Strange now took to wondering if, in the light of recent, very recent, events in her own life, whether she had been overprotective, too censorious even, about the moral actions of other people? On mature reflection she persuaded herself she hadn't. Her concern had always been for the young people in her care: adult activities fell into a quite different category.

'So did he die here, Miss Strange?'

'I'm sorry, Josephine?' Her thoughts had been elsewhere. 'Oh ... oh, no one seems to know. As they say in the detective stories, the police are baffled.' She offered a broad, conspiratorial grin, adjusting the heavy spectacles on her rosy, button nose. She was seated now, facing her visitor, her swivel chair turned so that she had her back to both the table and the window. 'The important thing is that none of us gets more involved than we have to be,' she said, holding her coffee beaker in one hand, and stirring the contents vigorously with the other – too vigorously, because some of the liquid slopped over the top. 'Damn.' She opened her knees to avoid the drips, then put the beaker down on the table before she reached for one of the pipes in the rack behind her. 'I'm sure they'll find Freddy Gibbon's death had nothing to do with any-one at the college,' she said with conviction, then blew hard through the pipe, producing a hail of burnt-out bits of herb tobacco.

'Yes, miss.' Josephine took a surreptitious look at the time. She was desperate to know what to do with the stuff Freddy kept in her room. She'd been on her way there, for the first time since her return, when she'd been accosted by her tutor. She'd accepted the invitation to coffee because, on the spur of the moment, she'd hoped she might be able to confide in Miss Strange, to ask her what she should do. But that was before she had learned that Freddy might not have killed himself.

The possibility of murder changed things: the girl could see that well enough without Miss Strange's caution. If she became in any way tangled up in a murder, her parents would never forgive her. At least she hadn't told the police anything that mattered – not yet.

Freddy had made her swear she'd never let on to anyone what she did for him – and once he had actually threatened awful things if she did. Afterwards, he'd said he'd been joking, that he'd never hurt her. But you never knew with Freddy – not that she'd cared. He'd sworn his relationship with her was different too, not in the least like it was with other girls, and she'd believed him totally. Now that he was dead, she felt she still owed him the same loyalty – unless, perhaps, if telling would help find whoever killed him. But she couldn't believe it would, not even if she told everything: she cringed at the very thought.

Josephine needed more time to think. She'd loved Freddy so much, despite the way he'd used her sometimes. Losing him was the end of her world, especially in the new circumstances. She didn't know yet whether she could go on without him – or even if she wanted to.

'Murder's a lot different from suicide. It sheds a frightening light on ... on everything and everybody involved. The college, the staff, the pupils,' Newsom-Pugh lamented, metaphorically wringing his hands, and he would probably have been doing so physically if he too hadn't been holding a cup of coffee. The cup in question was china – Royal Doulton china. Neither polystyrene mugs nor earthenware beakers were admitted to the Newsom-Pughs' milieu.

The principal of Modlen College had escaped briefly to the privacy of his own apartments. He had been too busy for lunch, and, in any case, he'd had no appetite. Parry had told him an hour before this that Gibbon had been murdered.

'Suicide wasn't exactly going to cast a warm glow on things either,' his wife Inga responded tartly, while examining a broken nail at the end of a long and exquisitely tapering finger. Born and nurtured in Hamburg, she was a Nordic blonde, with high cheekbones, light-blue eyes, a well-chiselled nose, and an angular body given naturally to the sensuous kind of movements that, at thirty-two, continued to enthral a good many males of most ages. The residual accent in the husky, Garbo voice she was aware added to her allure, and she maintained it for that reason. If she chose, she could pronounce her nearly impeccable, idiomatic English like a home-counties native – and her French was close to perfect too. She had joined the college staff three years before this, and had married the widower principal a year later. But anyone unacquainted with her who theorized that the notedly tight-fisted Newsom-Pugh might have taken her for his wife to save a salary was quickly disabused of the notion on first sight of the lady.

On the other hand, the motives that had prompted Frau Inga Braun to take Handel Newsom-Pugh for her husband had been diverse, complex, and had, it must be admitted, involved monetary considerations. Her first husband, a German corporate lawyer with an international practice in London, had himself taken his own life a day or so ahead of being arraigned for fraud on a gigantic scale. She had stayed in Britain, a penniless, childless, desperate widow, with her languages her sole likely means of future support. At the time, only Newsom-Pugh and some shamefully underpaying language schools had been ready to compete for her services. Newsom-Pugh had won the day because, for once, he had forced an unnatural generosity into matching his almost boundless capacity for guile – later harnessing both again in the achieving of his earliest resolve to marry the lady.

'Suicide in the young is usually the resort of a tormented, often temporarily crazed mind,' he philosophized, a touch wistfully, with a continuing, and what might reasonably have been considered a careless, disregard for the chosen fate of the not-so-very-late Herr Herman Braun.

'Oh, yes,' said his wife, seated, like him, in an overlarge armchair in front of a rough stone, open fireplace, with flames dancing in the hearth. This was in the sitting room of what the previous proprietors of Modlen Hall had hopefully described as the hotel's royal suite, with its impressive, first-floor, southerly outlook. 'So it could be,' she continued, carefully filing the broken nail, and applying no conscious, enduring sensitivities to the method of death under discussion – she had come to loathe Herman in any case. 'So it could be,' she repeated, looking up briefly, 'if it had been suicide, according to you, the deranged Gibbon might have mown down half our student body in advance with an automatic rifle. So in a way we should be thankful.'

He accepted this bizarre speculation without savouring it. 'And where would he have got an automatic rifle?' he asked flatly.

'The way he got a lot of other unusual things. He was a very resourceful young man.'

'How do you know that, my love?'

'Because it was my business to know, my sweet. You made me his course tutor, remember? Responsible, amongst other things, for his moral wellbeing.' She gave a little snort.

'But he never showed this ... this resourcefulness in any positive, intellectual way? Any way that helped his academic advancement? You didn't describe him as resourceful in his report last term.' He was eyeing her carefully.

'Because I didn't know him so well then. I'd have said it in this term's report, probably.'

'When you'd got to know him better. I see.' His eyebrows had lifted a fraction towards the crinkled grey hair above the creased forehead. 'And is this something else you told the police, but didn't mention to me? That he was resourceful?'

113

She had thought he was about to follow up on her knowing the boy better. 'I told you exactly what I said to the police,' she replied lightly, examining her open palm. 'And I'm sure I said that was part of it. He had charm and good manners, that's when he chose to exercise them. I expect he could be cruel too,' she continued, her eyes, if he could have seen them, reflecting something quite close to nostalgia. 'And yes, I said he was resourceful. I also said his schoolwork left a lot to be desired.'

'So what about those three girls the police are so interested in. He was ... playing about with them, was he?'

'You mean sleeping with them?'

'I didn't say that.' He had lurched forward suddenly at her words, swinging his free arm once in a curiously nervous, reflex way, as if he was throwing wood on the gas-fuelled, simulated log fire. 'I didn't say that,' he repeated heavily, but almost to himself.

'It's what you meant, though?'

'It's the extreme of what might have happened, perhaps, but we've no reason to suppose it did. It's just that he was obviously a ... flirtatious kind of boy.'

'He was hardly a boy. He was a very well-developed, attractive young man.'

114

Newsom-Pugh breathed in and out deeply. 'Did he ever make advances towards you?'

'My dear, he never stopped,' she announced triumphantly, crossing her long legs. 'Always chatting me up, from the day he got here. And I rather enjoyed it. It made a change at my age to be lusted after by someone as young, handsome and virile.'

'Good God, you didn't tell the police that?'

'Of course not,' she chuckled, leaning back in the chair.

'But you admit you ... you–'

'Fancied him? Sure, but naturally I never let him know I did.' Her lips made a kissing motion at him. 'Darling, don't be jealous, there's no cause.' She continued to stare straight at him, unblinkingly: bold denial was her standard method of defence.

'Well, all I hope is parents don't take pupils away because of what's happened,' he said, partly changing the subject.

She looked down at her hand again. 'There's no reason for parents to get upset. It must be obvious that someone had it in for Gibbon specifically, not the college.'

'But how could people know that?'

'They would if they'd known young Freddy.'

It was the first thing she had said that seemed to have given her husband prospect of mental solace. 'How do you mean?' he asked anxiously.

'Well, he had our sexiest-looking girls falling all over him. Not that that's saying much. He seemed to have more money than anyone else. He was a maverick with his own rules, and he didn't bother with friends of his own sex, not here, anyway. Plenty of cause for envy, hatred and malice in that little lot. Murder too, given the right provocation.'

'He did have some male friends. The police have been told the Bowen boy was one of them.'

'The only one, I should think. And that wasn't a real friendship. Bowen's quite bright, relatively speaking. He did Gibbon's prep for him, that's all. Probably got paid for it.'

'If you knew that—'

'Knowing wasn't the same as proving. It was Cynthia Strange who told me. She was pretty sure, but couldn't prove it.'

'As his course tutor, you should have asked Gibbon.'

'I did. He denied it, and probably made poor Bowen do the same.'

'Bullied him into silence? Was that it, do you think?'

She hesitated for a moment. 'Yes. I think he probably was a bully,' she answered reflectively, and not in a critical tone. 'Anyway, there wasn't a lot of harm in his getting his prep done.'

'There was harm to the college's reputation if he failed all his examinations.' His response had been both pompous and aggrieved.

'Nonsense. You said last week you were going to ask his mother to take him away because we weren't teaching him anything. Which, by the way, I thought at the time wasn't much of a compliment to me.' She smoothed her hand along the length of nylon-stockinged thigh exposed beyond the hem of her skirt. Mrs Newsom-Pugh didn't favour heavy, figure-cloaking garments indoors, even in midwinter.

'You weren't his only tutor.' He frowned, thinking of Ifor Jenkin before he went on: 'In any case, I only said I was thinking of doing that. And I wish you'd told me all this before. I mean, what about the Oswald girl? She got back as I was coming up. The police will probably want to see her. You said she–'

'She was crazy about Freddy, poor mite,'

his wife interrupted. 'I'd say he was definitely bedding her, when he remembered. She was in the next room, after all.'

'You're serious?'

'Fairly. He probably livened up her sheltered existence no end, and that of quite a few other girl pupils.' She had reasons of her own for not believing this, but it would keep his mind off other possibilities: perhaps she had been too rash in what she'd told him about her own relations with Freddy.

'But are all the students here fixated by sex?'

'Probably not quite all of them. But we do make them work practically around the clock. There's no organized sport–'

'There's swimming,' he broke in, defensively.

'Yes, and can you think of anything more erotic than shoving a bunch of nearly naked, frustrated teenagers of both genders into a small heated swimming pool? It's about the only unsupervised activity they're allowed.'

He shook his head rapidly several times, as if he was trying to shake off something perched on it. 'Well, not many of them go in for it.'

'Not at the crack of dawn when you're

there, no. And not when it's snowing outside, either.'

'So you're saying the motive for the murder has to do with ... with sex?'

'His sex life could have had a lot to do with it, but the chances are it wasn't the sex life he was into at the college. Remember he was never here at weekends, and he didn't go to his mother's then either. Not ever, it seems. So who knows what other kind of life he was leading two days a week? If he was killed hours before he was found, the chances are it didn't happen here at all. His killer could have brought the body back to make it look like a suicide jump from his room.'

'They don't really know how long he'd been dead,' her husband objected. 'Not with any accuracy.'

'That's because the body was frozen stiff. What are the chances he was killed somewhere else in the late evening, his body brought here in the small hours? If he'd come back earlier on his own, surely someone must have seen him? His car wasn't noticed in the car park, even. And another thing, the clothes he was wearing on Saturday aren't in his room, or anywhere else in the college. I had to describe them to the police because I was one of the last people to see him before he left. He couldn't have walked back into college naked. That woman sergeant told me before lunch they're still searching for his things.'

'And they've no idea why he was naked?'

'No, except it fits with his being killed somewhere else, and then stripped because ... because his clothes could have given away where he'd been. Then he could have been brought here in his car, in the middle of the night, the body just tipped over the wall into the basement, while whoever did it left in another car.'

'But why?' Newsom-Pugh looked at the time. He should have been back downstairs again before this.

'I've told you why. To give the impression his death was to do with Modlen College, when really it wasn't.'

'I hope you're right.' Her account seemed so assured.

It would have been hard for an impartial observer to decide whether the theory just expounded brought more satisfaction to the person who recounted it than it did to her single listener: certainly both Newsom-Pughs had seemed temporarily buoyed up by the proposition.

7

'I've just seen the low loader collecting the Ford Sierra, boss,' Lloyd reported on his return to the basement, to what had now been formally designated the Frederic Gibbon incident room. Parry nodded an acknowledgement as he put down the phone. He had earlier ordered a more extensive examination of the car than could be carried out in a snowbound car park.

The now busy room had already been fitted up in a rough, practical way with necessary gear. A bank of telephones, a fax machine, computers, printers, photo-printers, pinboards and filing equipment had been brought over at noon from Cowbridge. The men and women police officers and civilian employees assigned to the case had been at work since then, most of them still logging and cross-referencing the data so far collected.

Lloyd had staked out a working area in a corner for Parry and himself, next to a window, and close to the door of the small

121

interview room.

The chief inspector nodded at the phone. 'That was the Hereford police. Freddy's mother has turned up at the house. She got back there first thing this morning, apparently, but had gone out again. She'd been to Tenerife with a friend. On a week's package holiday which should have ended last night. The return flight was delayed.'

'Charter flights always are, aren't they? That's when they take off at all,' commented Lloyd, whose only family holiday ever planned to take place outside Wales (a fortnight in Minorca) had been cancelled on the day of departure when the tour company had gone into liquidation. This inexcusable event had been years before, but not forgotten – or forgiven. 'Is Mrs Gibbon coming here, boss?'

'Not today, no.'

'Too shocked, I expect. Funny though. Most mothers would want to see the body straightaway. To be sure, like.'

'I thought that too. She told the local police she'll come tomorrow. We need her, of course, to identify him.'

'Is her friend er ... living in, do we know?' asked Lloyd, diplomatically.

'No. And it's a woman friend, another

widow I think, from where she used to live. Not a relative, either.'

'Pity. A relative could have done the identifying.'

'Yes. But in view of what's happened, the friend's staying with Mrs Gibbon, which is helpful all round. I'm going up there now. Mrs Gibbon may have an idea why her son was killed, and we can't afford to wait two days to hear it. It shouldn't take me long to get there.' It had stopped snowing, which was making driving conditions easier, although there was no sign yet of the predicted thaw.

'Want me with you, boss?'

'No. Too much to do here.'

'Right.' Lloyd was turning to pick up some new typed reports from one of the two tables they were using, when the college housekeeper appeared in the doorway across the room. 'Over here, Mrs Watkyn,' he called when he saw her. 'Something else you've remembered, is it?'

The newcomer moved briskly, weaving her way through the people and impedimenta. 'No, this is something new, Mr Lloyd. These girls would like to talk to you and Mr Parry, please. About Freddy Gibbon,' she asserted, although neither of the two young women trailing in behind her looked in the very least determined, or as if they wanted to talk to anyone – and certainly not to a policeman.

Parry had stood up. 'Then let's all go to the next room where it's less noisy,' he said.

'Don't you have to be away, boss?' Lloyd asked tactfully, after ushering the others through, and organizing the necessary chairs.

Parry shook his head. 'That can wait a minute.' He was impressed by Mrs Watkyn's look of dedication.

The lady sat as invited, and pointedly watched her two companions until they did the same. It was as though she expected they might suddenly change their minds and leave. 'You both know my ... my assistant, Sara Card, of course,' she offered, hesitating over the job title, deservedly so, it seemed to Parry, because it suggested someone older than Miss Card, and someone with more authority. Perhaps the term chambermaid – even head chamber-maid, since he knew there was only one – was now unacceptable. 'And this is Bronwyn Tate. She's Mrs Edward's living-in kitchen maid.' Mrs Edwards was cook at the college. 'Sara and Bronwyn have rooms next

124

to each other in the staff extension,' Mrs Watkyn completed. She hadn't troubled to find a more euphemistic title for the job of her second somewhat woebegone cohort.

Sara Card, who Parry knew was eighteen, was a tall, skinny blonde with a dark parting. She was wearing a sulky look, a lot of make-up, and a tight, short, blue button-through overall. The lower two buttons of the garment were undone, revealing generous expanses of thigh – before an urgent and penetrating glare from her employer prompted the girl petulantly to do some buttoning up and tugging down.

In contrast, Bronwyn Tate was a round pudding of a girl, with naturally rosy cheeks and a pitifully nervous demeanour. While it was later revealed that she was younger than Sara by a few months, immediately she seemed a lot more so in her personality and comportment. She had on a wraparound white overall that was much too big for her, and which, while extending from her well-covered larynx to six inches below her knees, was still shorter than the black skirt protruding from under it. Her eyes were presently redder than her cheeks, and puffed, almost certainly indicating recent tears.

'I think Miss Tate was interviewed by one of our women detective constables this morning, weren't you, miss?' asked Lloyd in the avuncular manner he usually reserved for over-anxious witnesses or lost Labradors, and while he searched for the relevant bit of paper.

'That's right, isn't it, Bronwyn?' The girl was still hesitating when Mrs Watkyn, sitting stiffly upright, answered for her. 'And Sara's been seen before, too, because she was second to see the body, after me, of course,' the housekeeper completed, as though her own act of good citizenship warranted reminder.

'Indeed, Mrs Watkyn. And you've all been very helpful, as well. So do you have fresh information for us now?' encouraged Parry, keen to be away.

'I haven't, because I've told you all I know already. But these two have.' Her lips pursed before she continued. 'He'd been putting upon them. Freddy Gibbon, I mean. Bronwyn came to tell me about it after lunch. She's a good girl, and she hadn't meant to hold back anything that might be important. Neither did Sara, not really. They've been a bit remiss, that's all it is. Only Sara should have spoken up earlier, being the oldest. But she's forgetful by nature, as I well know.' The lips closed even more tightly.

Sara Card's response to the criticism of her conduct, and to the other last comment, which had to relate to the way she did her work, was to exhale breath noisily and impatiently, while uncrossing then recrossing her bony legs. She didn't speak, but continued to exhibit pointed indifference towards the whole procedure.

'So, would you like to tell us what you told Mrs Watkyn, Bronwyn?' Lloyd prompted the other girl.

Bronwyn Tate pulled her folded arms more tightly across her bosom, and rocked her trunk several times. She gave a furtive glance at Sara, before mumbling some words that proved to be totally inaudible to everyone present.

'Speak up, love,' encouraged Mrs Watkyn, with a touch more understanding in her tone than before.

The girl lifted her chin slightly. 'He got us to take an envelope for him. To Cardiff. Every week. And bring back stuff in a shopping bag,' she uttered brokenly.

'What was in the envelope, Bronwyn?' asked Lloyd.

'Money.'

'And in the shopping bag?'

'He never told us. He said we didn't need to know.'

Sara sighed loudly. 'So we did deliveries for him? Where's the harm in that? What was in the bags was his business, wasn't it? He paid for it, whatever it was. So why all the fuss?'

'Because, like I said, one of you should have told someone about this before, Sara,' Mrs Watkyn broke in. 'The police asked you all to report everything you knew about Freddy.'

'Yes, we'd like to have known this straight-away, when we first talked to you,' Lloyd put in, but in an amiable enough tone, not wanting to upset the girls any more than was necessary before they'd unburdened more. 'Anyway, no lasting harm done because you forgot the first time round. So let's go back a bit. Freddy asked you both to—'

'He asked me first. Last term. In October,' Sara interrupted, again impatiently. 'He bought us drinks. At the Prince of Wales, the pub in the village.'

'In Brynglas?' Lloyd was making notes.

'Yeah. He was chatting us up there one

night. It's a dump, but there's nowhere else round here of an evening. I mean, you can't afford to go to Cardiff every night. Not on our wages.'

'You've got telly and table tennis in the staff room,' Mrs Watkyn put in sharply. 'And you're allowed swimming at weekends.'

The girl ignored the comment as she went on. 'Bronwyn left early by herself. She walked back. It's not far. Freddy gave me a lift up later in his car. It was a Monday. He asked if we'd do him a favour the following Wednesday.'

The housekeeper tutted her disapproval. 'Of course, he should never have been out of college on a weekday in the first place,' she said. 'Dr Newsom-Pugh's very against that.'

'Which is why Freddy couldn't go to Cardiff himself on the Wednesday,' said Sara in a half-triumphant, half-justifying voice.

'And this delivery run became a regular thing, did it?' asked Lloyd who, like Parry, wished Mrs Watkyn would leave the girls to speak for themselves.

'Pretty well every week after that, yes.'

'And you did it together?'

'Freddy liked there to be two of us,' said Sara. 'And we both get Wednesday after-noons off, don't we, Bron?'

'That's right,' the other girl confirmed.

'What sort of shopping bags were they? Big or small?'

'Small. Ordinary white plastic, with the opening stuck down. Not so anyone would notice, but they always were. Stuck so you couldn't get at what was in them.'

'Were they heavy?'

'No, light.'

'And you're positive Freddy never said what was in them?'

'Positive.' The single-word response had been instant and firm, as though Sara had been as well prepared for the question as she had been with her answer.

Lloyd leaned forward in her direction. 'But you had a good guess all the same, didn't you?'

'If we did, it was guessing not knowing, wasn't it?' The response had been almost comical in its prissiness. 'Anyway, we didn't bother guessing. Like I said, it was none of our business.'

'And the envelopes, what size were they?' asked Parry.

Sara shrugged. 'Long and narrow. Like for business letters.'

'And you knew they contained money?'

'Yeah. Freddy told us. And how much was

in them. In case the person we gave them to said there wasn't enough. If he did, we had to tell him to recount it. But that never happened.'

'And was it always the same person at the same place?'

'Yeah. One o'clock outside the snack bar at the Central.'

'You mean the Central railway station?'

'That's right.'

The sergeant smoothed down his moustache with thumb and forefinger. 'Let's see now, as I remember, that snack bar has two entrances. One to the street, the other to the booking hall.'

'It was the booking hall entrance.'

'And who was this person you gave the envelopes to?'

'Dunno. He had ginger hair.'

'Don't you know his name?' Lloyd asked, but not hopefully.

'No.'

'What sort of age was he?'

'Old. Over thirty. Thin, with freckles. Always had a bomber jacket on, and a black crash helmet. You could hardly see his face when the visor was down.'

'So how do you know he had freckles and red hair?'

'Once we were early and saw him coming out of the cigarette shop by the bus station. He was carrying the helmet. He didn't see us.'

'And he came on a motorbike?'

'He did that day, but he parked it behind the bus station and walked over to the snack bar.'

'You didn't notice the number of the motorbike?'

Both girls shook their heads.

'And is there anything else you remember about him?'

Bronwyn drew breath sharply before she put in: 'He had a limp, didn't he, Sara?'

'Yeah, he had a limp,' the other girl agreed.

'Which leg?'

'Right,' said Bronwyn.

'Left,' said Sara firmly.

'So which was it? Think now,' the sergeant cautioned.

'Like Sara said, it was his left leg,' Bronwyn responded quickly, and evidently because she trusted her companion's judgement more than she did her own.

'And what about his speaking voice? What kind of accent did he have?'

Both girls hesitated before Bronwyn

offered: 'Was it like Irish, Sara?'

The other girl shrugged. 'We didn't talk much. I think he was Irish, except sometimes he sounded a bit American.'

'Irish people often do,' said Lloyd. 'So did you just give him the envelope, in exchange for the bag each time?'

'He needed to count the money before he'd give us the bag,' said Sara.

'But he was ever so quick doing it,' Bronwyn added.

'Where did he count it?'

'On the shelf by the booking office.' This was Bronwyn again, with confidence. 'Where people wouldn't notice. That's where Freddy told us the man would go. We were to stand behind him like we were all getting ready to buy tickets.' It was her longest and most useful contribution yet.

'How much money was there?' asked Parry.

'It was different each time. Last week it was eight hundred pounds, all in ten and twenty-pound notes, as usual,' said Sara.

'The time before it was twelve hundred and fifty, and the time before that a thousand,' Bronwyn volunteered, with another rush of new-found courage, further emboldened by what she had clearly taken to be her friend's more open response. 'The last delivery before the Christmas holidays was fifteen hundred, wasn't it, Sara?'

Sara glared back at her stonily before commenting: 'Was it? I don't remember. It wasn't usually as much as that.'

Parry smiled and kept his gaze on Sara. 'Always totalling up to a round fifty or a hundred pounds, was it?'

'That's right.'

'So it was serious money. Very serious money. And are you still going to insist you didn't know, or didn't guess, what was in the bags?'

'Like I said, it wasn't our business.'

Lloyd gave a dismissive grunt. 'Well, if it had been illegal drugs you were paying for and collecting, and if you'd been caught, it would have been your business all right, wouldn't it? Because you'd have been in deep trouble. Did you ever think about that?'

'We never knew it was–'

'All right, we're not saying you knew, not for certain,' the sergeant had interrupted the shrill protest. 'But we're asking you now if it had ever occurred to you there might have been drugs in the bags. That Freddy was using you to trade drugs for him?'

'No. We never thought that, not ... not really.' But Sara's denial had been as shaky as her tone.

Parry spread both his hands flat on the table in front of him. 'Look, the two of you, Sergeant Lloyd, and I, and all those police officers out there are working to find out who murdered Freddy Gibbon. Murder's a deeply serious crime. The most serious there is, and we're going to catch who did this one. That's not only for Freddy's sake, but so we can lock up whoever did it before he murders anyone else. Meantime, we're not concerned with things you two may have done wrong without knowing it. But we do want to know all about the envelopes, the bags, the bloke you did the trades with, and anything else you know about Freddy you haven't told us yet. But we're not after you. We're after a dangerous killer. So you don't have to be afraid. Is that clear?'

'Yes, sir,' said Bronwyn, while Sara nodded with more willing assent in her expression than she had shown before.

'I should think so too,' contributed Mrs Watkyn. 'Bronwyn, you haven't said yet about the other thing you forgot before. What you heard Freddy say to Mr Jenkin on Saturday morning. About the weekend.'

Bronwyn cleared her throat. 'That's only because no one's asked me about Saturday yet, Mrs Watkyn.'

'Well, let's say someone's asking you now, love,' said Lloyd, smiling broadly.

'It was something I heard through my window. It's next to the car park. Freddy was there with Mr Jenkin alone, just after school was over. They were both leaving college. Freddy asked Mr Jenkin if he'd be going to Oscar's again at the weekend. Only it was in a joking sort of voice.'

'And what did Mr Jenkin say?' the sergeant asked.

The girl gave Mrs Watkyn a quizzical look.

'Well, don't be afraid, girl, tell them,' the housekeeper insisted.

'He said' – Bronwyn took a deep breath – 'he said, "Get stuffed, Gibbon, you slimy bastard." After that, Mr Jenkin rode off on his motorbike.' As soon as she finished speaking, the girl began to blush furiously.

'So was that all either of them said?' asked Parry. He and Lloyd exchanged glances.

'I think so. It was all I heard.'

'And you swear that's exactly what was said?'

'Yes, sir.'

'I heard the last bit, as well. What Mr

136

Jenkin said,' offered Sara in a grudging tone. 'I walked into Bron's room when he was saying it.'

'Well, that's clear enough,' said the sergeant cheerfully, scribbling in his book. 'And thank you for telling us, both of you. Right, girls,' he continued. 'Next, we'd like to know what Freddy gave you for these delivery jobs you did for him.'

Bronwyn looked at Sara who fingered the small silver crucifix hanging round her neck before she said: 'He gave us some money.'

'Just money? Nothing else?'

'What else would he have given us?'

Lloyd disregarded Sara's question, but asked, 'How much money did he give you?'

'I can't remember exactly.'

'I can. It was fifty pounds between us, every time, and he paid our bus fares to Cardiff on top,' offered Bronwyn, pleased to be supplying a correct answer again.

'Thank you. And did Freddy tell you what to do if anyone asked what was in the bags? For instance, did he warn you what to say if you were stopped by a policeman?'

Bronwyn wiped her nose with her handkerchief, then replied without looking at Sara. 'He told us to say we were doing a favour for an old lady, a Mrs Evans who we'd met at Cardiff bus station, where we got on. We were supposed to be taking a present to Mrs Price, her sick friend in Brynglas, to save Mrs Evans the journey. Mrs Price was supposed to be meeting us at the bus stop in Brynglas. Only she wouldn't, not really. Freddy said to stick to that and nobody could prove different. Oh, and we were never to say we were doing it for Freddy. Not ever.'

'Well, I'm blessed,' commented the sergeant, with another glance at Parry. 'And after all that, you really thought what you were doing for Freddy was honest and above board?'

'We thought he had his reasons for not saying what was in the bags, that's all,' said Sara defiantly.

'We thought it might have been duty-free cigarettes and scent,' said Bronwyn. 'He always had plenty of those. More than he should have had, we thought, didn't we, Sara?'

'Yeah.' The other girl gave a dismissive shrug.

'And apart from the deliveries,' put in the chief inspector 'did Freddy ask you to do him any other favours?'

'He sometimes asked me to make him a

sandwich. From the kitchen, out of hours. That's all,' Bronwyn offered ingenuously.

'I see. And you, Sara?'

The older girl ran a hand down over her knee, then up again, while staring wide-eyed at her questioner. 'I don't think he fancied me, if that's what you mean. Not that I cared.'

Ignoring the censorious huffing noise emanating from between Mrs Watkyn's teeth, Parry went on: 'And you didn't fancy him?'

'Not when I began to get to know him, I didn't, no. There was something about him ... I dunno. You had the feeling he wouldn't treat you right. Know what I mean? We had a ... a bit of a cuddle in his car that first time. On the Monday. That was all.'

'That was enough for you, was it?'

'Suppose so, yeah.'

'I see. So where did you collect the envelopes from? Was it from Freddy's room?'

'Yeah. After lessons on Wednesday mornings. I took him the bags there too, after we got back in the evening. I never went to his room for anything else, except to clean it,' she completed with emphasis.

'You always did the visits to his room

alone, though? Bronwyn wasn't with you?'
Parry looked at the other girl.

'Bron doesn't have a reason to go to
anyone's room. She works in the kitchens,'
Sara replied quickly.

The chief inspector waited for Bronwyn to
respond as well. When she didn't, he asked
Sara: 'Do you know of anyone else who
went to his room? Students, perhaps?'

'No. I wasn't up there that much.'

'What about when you came back on
Wednesday evenings. Was there ever anyone
with him then?'

She shrugged. 'Could have been, I
suppose. I always knocked on the door.
Sometimes he came and opened it, and I
didn't go in.'

'So if he'd had someone with him, you
wouldn't have seen?'

'That's right. Oh, a student called Alwyn
Bowen was with him last Saturday morning,
early. He passed me when I was getting out
the clean sheets from the cupboard on the
first-floor landing.'

'So how did you know Alwyn Bowen was
going to Freddy's room?'

'Because he told me. Alwyn's always
starting conversations with me. He's a day
boy at the college. He's wanting me to go

140

out with him.'

'I see. But you never saw any girls go to Freddy's room?'

'No. Oh, I saw Miss Strange coming up the stairs to his floor once when I'd left his room. That was two Wednesday nights back. She may have been going to see him.'

Or to see Josephine Oswald in the room next door, both policemen were thinking. There was a brief silence, except for the background noises of activity next door – the murmur of a high-pitched voice on the telephone, the chatter of a fax machine as it spewed out a message.

Then Bronwyn Tate gave a little cough. 'I don't think Freddy fancied me, either,' she offered earnestly, while closing the V of her overall even more tightly under her throat.

8

Parry had driven across the border into England by the fast road that reached up through the valleys, skirting Merthyr Tydfil and Abergavenny. Traffic had been lighter there than on the lower motorway route because of the weather conditions, and he had enjoyed the way his aging Porsche responded on the tricky iced surfaces. He found the house easily enough, in a tree-lined cul-de-sac off Barton Road, on the west side of the city. It was detached, with an integral brick garage, a small garden at the front, and a larger one at the back, both fairly unkempt, with overgrown, evergreen bushes effectively screening the lower floor of the building from the road. The house was partly within sight of Hereford's busy single-span, modern Greyfriars Bridge – though not of the picturesque and still functioning fifteenth-century multiarched bridge, now dwarfed beyond it.

The policeman had crossed the new bridge on the way in, slowing briefly to savour the majestic cathedral on the far bank of the freezing River Wye. It had been placed there, high above the water, by the Saxons, eight centuries ago – though not before they had erected ramparts to keep out the marauding, despoiling Welsh. Today it was a Welsh lawkeeper not lawbreaker who was infiltrating the city bastions.

'Come in then, out of the cold. I'm just making a cup of tea,' said the woman with the South Wales Valley accent to whom

Parry had introduced himself when she opened the door. He had been surprised to learn from her that she was Mrs Glenda Gibbon, and not, as he had assumed, the friend who was staying to comfort her.

Mrs Gibbon didn't seem to be in any particular need of comfort, but Parry was content, even relieved, to believe that she probably chose to keep her sorrow to herself. She was a big, even muscular, woman, clearly of energetic disposition and, in some ways, memorable appearance. Aged about fifty, she had tightly waved brown hair, and a long, freckled, horsey kind of face. Her unusually pale-blue eyes stared with earnest friendliness from behind thick lenses whose composition seemed designed more to occlude vision than to assist it – so the apparent earnestness might have been due to the need for concentration. The widely flared nostrils of a considerable nose, while contrasting with a quite small mouth, balanced with the protruding two top teeth which were angled a degree or so away from each other. The chin, a long way below all this, receded dramatically, but was still more bone than flesh, punctuating the top of a permanently outstretched neck.

The lady's substantial upperworks were

canopied in a heavy, shapeless, off-white, fisherman's-knit sweater worn over a skirt in pinkish tweed. Her legs were encased in the sort of impermeable wool socks that sailors wear inside seaboots, but this pair were at least knee length, and possibly longer: nor was there much tapering or changed contour along their presently visible parts to identify the sequence of calf and ankle. The stockings were black, but, in view of the other clothing, it seemed unlikely that this was intended as Mrs Gibbon's single outward concession to mourning, particularly as her feet were sunk into red carpet slippers.

'I'm dressed for the Arctic, and no mistake, aren't I?' she exclaimed, after leading Parry into the kitchen. 'But it was over seventy degrees in Tenerife, and you feel the cold after that when you come back to snow, don't you?' She poured boiling water into the teapot. 'So let's go into the lounge, shall we? More comfy.' She looked down at the tray she was carrying. 'There's biscuits but no cake, I'm afraid. Haven't had time to bake since we got back. I could make you a ham and cheese sandwich?'

'Thank you. Tea and biscuits will be fine. And I'm ... I'm deeply sorry about your

144

loss, Mrs Gibbon.' The policeman had at last managed to work in what he had intended to say at the start, though there had been no appropriate opportunity till this moment. He still felt a certain degree of embarrassment that their exchanges had so far centred on near trivia, even though his own contribution had perforce been limited, due to Mrs Gibbon's garrulous disposition.

'Well, there's good of you, I'm sure. The Hereford police were very kind, as well. It was a shock, of course.'

Except, even now, the lady wasn't making what had happened to her son sound like too much of a shock, something which Parry was finding increasingly curious. He had followed his hostess back to the hall, and through to a room whose adequate proportions were still not up to containing the amount of furniture that had been squeezed into it. Instead of the almost regulation three-piece suite, there were two sofas and five armchairs which, though only a little over double a normal complement, seemed grossly greater when first en-countered – the more so because they were all covered in the same material, a design depicting large yellow roses in full bloom, with a profusion of deep-green leaves on a shiny black background. The wallpaper also had a heavy floral pattern, the large flowers this time being mauve rhododendrons and the background pink.

'Sit by there, won't you, Mr ... Mr Parry, it is, isn't it? Yes, thought I'd memorized it right. I'm usually good on names. I've worked in shops and hotels all my life. Customers like to be called by their own names, don't they? Well, that's natural, I suppose. This room looks like a warehouse, I'm afraid. I still haven't decided what I'm going to keep since I rented the house, or what I might need again in the future. I'm a hoarder, you see and this is all very serviceable stuff.' She considered one of the chairs, then one of several occasional tables, in a way that was both ruminative and proprietorial. 'I had a much bigger place before this. Just outside Aberbach. A private hotel. Unlicensed, but very nice. Lovely lounge, it had, with a view of the hills behind. That's where this furniture came from. I've got a lot of dining room chairs and tables too, and beds, but I've stored most of them.'

Parry assumed the wallpaper must have been here when Mrs Gibbon moved in, and that she wasn't responsible for the fake and overpowering botanical symposium it was forming with the chair coverings. She had motioned him towards a very deep chair on one side of the fireplace, where a small coal fire was burning, but not very brightly, in a wrought-iron basket grate on bowed legs. She sat herself on an equally deep, three-seat sofa next to him, balancing the tray on a footstool that was also covered in the all-pervading floral chintz.

'I've got a real fire in here,' she said, 'because of the friend who's staying. Mrs Beth Hooson, her name is. I'm sorry you won't see her. Lovely person. She notices the cold more than me, even. We've been to Tenerife together. She and I'll have our supper here, in front of the telly, in time for the nine o'clock news when she gets back. You miss the news when you're away, don't you? Nothing much else, though. You take milk and sugar, do you?'

'Just milk, thank you. We gathered you didn't feel up to coming to Cardiff straight-away, Mrs Gibbon. Very understandable, of course, but–'

'Oh, it wasn't that, Mr Parry. There was so much to do here,' she interrupted. 'The shop's been closed for a week, so I had to be there today, to deal with all the mail first thing, and then to open at the usual time. Otherwise people might think I'd gone out of business already. And in the middle of the season too. Though I had my winter sale in January. Anyway, that's where we'd both gone when the police came first time.'

'Dr Newsom-Pugh did try to reach you by phone earlier,' said Parry, by way of promoting that worthy's responsible attitude.

'Ah, if it was before eight, we'd pulled out the phone plug. Didn't remember to put it in again till just before we were leaving for the shop. It was so we could get a bit of sleep after that terrible journey. I gather the neighbour the police talked to thought I was away, and I don't think she knew I had a shop. I've never met her. I haven't been here long, you see.'

'What sort of shop is it, Mrs Gibbon?'

'It's called Glenda's Skirts and Sweaters. Small business, but growing. I specialize in national tweeds, knitwear and woollen travel accessories. Welsh mostly, of course, but some Scottish and Irish, too. The knitwear is nearly all from Wales or the Welsh borders. Original designs, of course. There's a thriving knitting industry in the area, and weaving. Cottage industry, I suppose you'd say. Lovely stuff, like this.' She plucked at the front of her sweater. 'I get all my wools direct from the producers. A lot of it's undyed, and soft as cashmere. In most cases I supply my knitters with all materials, patterns, implements, everything. Anyway, Beth's solved a problem by staying on to help me again tomorrow so I can come to Cardiff. She's a widow, too, but in her case quite recent. She and her husband used to have a little shop of their own. Knick-knacks, and second-hand jewellery. It was her husband's whole life, really, but she was the jewellery expert. She sold the business after his death last autumn, so she's a free agent. We've talked about her coming to join me here with a share in the shop. She'd meant to stay last night, but only for the one night. Except the plane was delayed, like I said.'

'It would help us if you would identify the body tomorrow, Mrs Gibbon. That's if you feel up to it.' Parry had taken advantage of the pause in her soliloquy when she sipped her tea for the first time.

'Oh, yes. That was mentioned to me this morning, as well. Of course I'll do it to-morrow. I'll get an early train. I don't fancy driving in this weather. My little car's not here at the moment. I took it in for service before the holiday, and haven't collected it yet.'

'And if there's anything you can tell me, now or tomorrow, to help us catch your son's murderer.'

'Problem there's to know where to start, isn't it?' Mrs Gibbon interrupted earnestly and, from Parry's viewpoint, enigmatically. Then she stretched her neck to its maximum length. 'And you have got it straight, haven't you? Freddy wasn't my son. He was adopted. No blood relation.' The nose wrinkled, bringing the front teeth into even greater display. 'Oh yes, I have to be thankful for small mercies.' She drank some more of the tea.

'Good afternoon, Mr Jenkin. I'm Detective Sergeant Lloyd. If you remember, you and I had a chat this morning. I don't think you've met Detective Constable Alison Pope. We were wondering, could you spare us a few more minutes now? I know you're a very busy member of staff. Busier still after this tragedy, I expect.' Lloyd was advancing further into the room as he spoke, which suggested that he wasn't wondering about the interview so much as already conducting it. The detective constable closed the door behind them.

The short, full-bearded and prematurely bald twenty-seven-year-old mathematics tutor looked seriously perplexed at the sergeant's last comment. When the two officers entered, he had risen uncertainly from where he had been seated behind the desk, his back to the window. 'To be accurate, I'm less busy now than I should have been. Frederic Gibbon was one of my pupils, and I was to have given him a tutorial at four,' he offered pedantically, kneading his palms together with effort, as if he were applying a dryish balm to them. He next made a performance of looking at his watch which had been covered by the sleeve of his sweater. It was ten past the hour.

'Well, well. Is that so, sir?' The sergeant looked suitably solemn over what the tutor might have been doing, waited another moment, then added: 'D'you mind if we sit down?'

'Oh, of course not. We'll ... we'll need another chair. It's cleaning day, and the maid's messed everything around in here. So irritating.' The speaker sighed loudly, made as if to move to the right, then hesitated, blinked and turned the other way:

it was as though the sudden appearance of police officers was overtaxing his nervous system – even more than the machinations of the maid had done.

'I'll get it, sir.' With long steps across the carpet, the lanky Alison Pope brought back a light plastic chair with a padded seat which matched the one Lloyd was pulling up to the desk across from Jenkin. The internal arrangements here were similar to those in Cynthia Strange's bedsitter-study next door. The carefully made-up bed was in one corner, with the work area under the window. There were three inviting easy chairs grouped around the fireplace, probably used for tutorials, and certainly for social occasions, although Jenkin had evidently considered a police interview didn't qualify under the last heading.

'Anyway, we won't keep you long, sir,' said the sergeant, seating himself after making a last covetous glance at the armchairs. 'I notice you've got a good view of the car park from here,' he said, gazing beyond Jenkin through the window behind him.

'I told you before, I wasn't here last night, so I didn't see Gibbon's car come back,' the tutor responded promptly, and a touch defensively.

'So you did, sir. No, I only meant you can probably keep a general eye on comings and goings from here.'

'Not if I can help it, I don't, and certainly not consciously. It's why I work with my back to the window.' Jenkin produced a handkerchief and blew his nose hard into it before adding: 'I couldn't help noticing them take away Gibbon's car earlier, of course. They were so noisy about it.' He folded the handkerchief carefully before returning it to his pocket.

'Sorry about that, sir,' DC Pope apologized, pencil poised over notebook. 'Awkward things, low loaders, especially on ice. The car had to go for forensic tests.'

'That's right,' Lloyd affirmed. 'Now, let's see, you told us earlier you were away from the college for the whole weekend.'

'Yes. I left on Saturday before lunch.'

'And returned this morning at eight fifty, sir. Well, that's clear enough. Could you tell us where you spent the time in between? We're having to ask everyone that question, you understand?'

'No. Why? I don't understand.' The speaker's whole upper body gave a pronounced upward twitch. 'You didn't ask me that this morning.'

'Ah, that's because we didn't know then we were investigating a suspected murder, sir, not an accident or a suicide.'

'I still fail to see what my movements had to do with a murder that happened at the college.'

'I can see your point, sir. But you have to let us be the judge of that, I'm afraid. You see, we aren't sure yet the murder *did* take place at the college.'

'But the boy's body was found here, under his window.'

'And under this window, too, sir, as it happens. And all the other windows on the east side of the tower. But, as you say, that can't be any concern of yours, since you weren't here. And please accept, these are only routine questions. A matter of being sure where people were, mostly so they can be eliminated from further enquiries.' The sergeant followed this with what was meant to be a look of benign reassurance, although it seemed to have a further unsettling effect on Jenkin.

The tutor produced the handkerchief again, and wiped the sides of his face above the beard with it. 'I spent some of the time at my mother's house in Builth Wells.'

'In Powys? It's lovely there,' Lloyd

commented with genuine enthusiasm. As the crow flies, Builth Wells and Hereford were roughly the same distance from the college, but Builth Wells lay almost directly to the north, in hilly mid-Wales. The roads to it, though good, were more tortuous than those to the east. 'That's a tidy distance on a motorbike, of course, in present weather conditions,' the policeman continued. 'Did you go there straight from here on Saturday, sir?'

This time the twitch registered only in the other man's left cheek, as he hesitated before answering: 'No, I ... I went there on Sunday. In time for lunch.'

'And before that, sir?'

'I was with a friend. A friend with a flat in Cardiff.'

Alison Pope looked up to ask: 'Could you tell us what part of Cardiff, sir?'

'Rumney. Look, does it matter? Surely the point is I wasn't here, or ... or anywhere near here. I was either with my friend or my mother for the whole weekend.' Rumney was an inner Cardiff suburb lying on the eastern side of the city on the way to Newport.

Lloyd smiled. 'Except when you were braving the elements on the road to Builth

Wells yesterday, and back from there ... this morning, was it, sir?'

The tutor cleared his throat and leaned forward, his hands holding the edge of the desk. 'Yes ... well, no ... not exactly. I came down lateish last night, in case the weather got worse. I didn't want to risk being late back here this morning.'

'Very commendable, sir. All the same, you didn't actually come back to the college last night, did you?'

'No. I broke the journey in Cardiff. Stayed with my friend.'

'Your friend in Rumney, sir?' DC Pope questioned earnestly.

'Yes. It's only twenty minutes from there to here.'

'Quite so, sir,' said Lloyd, it seemed pointedly. 'So had your friend been up to Builth Wells with you, sir? On the pillion?'

'No. I was by myself.' He looked up. 'My mother will confirm that.'

'Oh, I shouldn't think it'll be necessary to bother your mother, sir.' The sergeant sounded affronted at the very idea. 'If you could give DC Pope the address later, though, for the record? And the same with your friend. If we could just have her name and address, as well.'

156

Jenkin swallowed again. 'It's ... it's a man, not a woman. A male friend.' He seemed to choke on the statement, then his face reddened, while his expression turned to one of not very convincing defiance – as if this were an attempt to cancel out his evident discomfort.

'Ah, right, sir. Sorry about that.' Lloyd smiled directly at the tutor, keeping his eyes on the face for a second more before looking down at his notebook again. 'Anyway, DC Pope can get the details after.' He sniffed. 'So, on mature reflection since this morning, have you any better idea than you had then as to whether Freddy Gibbon had enemies in the college?'

'No, I haven't. And I didn't need to reflect on it.'

'You haven't thought of anyone who might have had it in for him? Enough to attack him? Like it was someone he provoked? I mean, it wouldn't have needed to be a premeditated attempt on his life. Just a punch-up, perhaps, that went wrong. These things happen.'

Jenkin took a deep breath. 'I'm sorry, I really can't tell you any more than I did before. Gibbon was simply a pupil. I knew nothing about his private life.'

'You didn't see him out of school time, then?'

'No. Why should I?'

'No reason, sir. Except this is a tight little community, with a very small ratio of pupils to teachers, very enviable ratio, really. Anyway, I thought it was worth asking.' He paused for a moment. 'And we gather Gibbon wasn't a very studious pupil.'

'That was the general impression amongst the teaching staff, yes.' Jenkin seemed to relax a little as he went on. 'But his maths weren't ... weren't irrecoverable. I thought there was an outside chance he'd get a C grade this summer. That's if he did some work.'

'So he was lazy, not stupid?'

'He certainly wasn't stupid.' The answer came quickly, and with some acerbity attached to it.

'I see, sir. But you still don't think he could have done better than a C in maths?'

The tutor frowned. 'He might have squeezed a B grade, perhaps, if he'd worked very hard indeed.'

'Which he certainly never seemed to do at weekends, did he, sir? Always away as soon as classes finished on Saturday mornings, and not usually back before they began

158

again on Mondays.' Rather like his maths tutor, the sergeant thought to himself, but then, Ifor Jenkin must have passed all the exams he needed to long since.

'Well, again that has to be an assumption,' Jenkin replied. 'He could have been studying somewhere else at the weekends. I only know he wasn't ever in the college when I've been duty tutor.'

'So that would have been the only times you could have seen him at weekends, sir. When you were on duty?'

'That's right.'

'Which we understand is about one weekend in four?'

'One in every four or five, yes. But as I said, he was never here. So I really only ever saw him in the week.'

And even then, it seemed, only for formal lessons, Lloyd was thinking, still surprised at the lack of extramural contacting that seemed to be practised – at least between this tutor and his pupils. 'And you didn't ever run into him anywhere else at weekends, sir?' he asked

'Where would I have done?'

'At Oscar's, for instance? The club at the top of Bute Street, Cardiff.'

The blushing this time began ahead of any

audible response. 'No ... I couldn't have. I never ... I don't go to drinking clubs.' The speaker shook his head violently, as the tic in his cheek went into overdrive, and the handkerchief reappeared. 'Who said I met Gibbon at Oscar's?'

'It's alleged someone overheard him ask you whether he'd be seeing you in Oscar's again at the weekend, sir. That was on Saturday morning, after lessons were over. Did he ask you that, sir?'

'I ... I don't remember.'

'I see, sir.'

He nodded at Alison Pope, who wet her lips and read from her notebook: 'It's also alleged, sir, you answered him with the words: "Get stuffed, Gibbon, you slimy bastard."'

'Do you remember the episode now, sir?' Lloyd waited for the answer with his mouth remaining open in rapt anticipation.

'Certainly not. I'd never address a pupil in those terms, and I demand to know who said I did. That's slander. I could sue.'

'I wouldn't know about that, sir. You see, there's a second person who's alleged to have heard your reply to Gibbon. Are you saying you'd never seen Gibbon in Oscar's?'

Blinking furiously, Jenkin looked from

160

Lloyd to Alison Pope, then back again. 'I don't believe so. I ... I don't remember. I've hardly ever been inside the place.'

'But you're a member, sir?'

'No... Yes. I think I was made a temporary member once, when I went there one night for a drink, after the pubs were closed. You have to sign on as a temporary member to get in. I haven't ... I mean, it's not the sort of club where...'

'You might want to become a permanent member. Quite so, sir,' Lloyd completed gravely, when the confused tutor failed to finish. 'You know, of course, it's a popular venue with the gay community?'

'I may have. But you meet all kinds there.'

'No doubt, sir. I've been there myself,' the sergeant beamed, without adding that he had been very much on duty at the time. But it wasn't the sexual orientation of the members that had prompted his and Parry's interest in Oscar's. It was the fact that the place was currently under surveillance as a suspected centre for illegal drug trafficking.

9

'I never believed those bits in the Bible about casting out devils, Mr Parry. Not till I was sure Freddy had the devil in him. And not just in the way people say some kids are full of devilment – boisterous, or really naughty, even. Oh, no, Freddy was truly possessed by demons. Truly. He was evil, I'm certain of it. And, you know, I've never admitted it as plain as that to anyone before. Not even to Beth, who says there's good in everyone. A real Christian, she is.' Mrs Gibbon sighed, it seemed in relief, not sorrow. She eased the weight of her heavy spectacles with the thumb and first finger of one hand. 'It's getting dark, isn't it? I'd better pull the curtains.' She got up and went to the window.

'How did Freddy get on with girls, Mrs Gibbon?'

'He treated them badly,' she answered without hesitation. 'He admitted to me he'd been the cause of two abortions. Bragged about them, really. And he was so rough with his girlfriends. Always putting them down, and hurting them. Physically, I mean. In front of me sometimes, when he was only fifteen or sixteen. I never knew why the girls put up with it. But they did.' She pulled the curtain cord which revealed yet another material decorated with floral patterns, but this time depicting daffodils and tulips. 'But it wasn't only girls he hurt,' she continued, patting a fold in a printed spray of yellow springtime blooms. The bunched curtains were too wide for the window, which suggested more fugitive stock from Mrs Gibbon's private hotel. 'The number of times I'd be called to his school because there'd been complaints of his bullying. And that started when he was five. Later it was sometimes masters or mistresses he'd be hitting.'

'And you adopted Freddy at what age?' Parry asked.

'Six months. He was such a lovely baby.' She had returned to the sofa. 'It was my idea to adopt. Edwin wasn't keen.'

'Edwin being your late husband?'

'That's right. But I wanted a child so much, and Edwin couldn't give me one. We knew that, and in those days there wasn't much could be done about it. Different if it'd been now, I expect.' She stared reflectively for a moment at the burning coals. 'Anyway, my parents supported me. Edwin was worried about what a baby would cost, an extra mouth to feed, and so on, though I felt he was only like that because it wouldn't be his baby we'd be getting. Mind you, the cost of things did matter. He was only a low-paid clerk in local government. He hated the work. His ambition was to be a professional magician and escapologist, would you believe? He never made it, of course, even though he was good – a good amateur, at least. He was such a quiet man, too, not an exhibitionist by nature. I've still got his tricks and equipment, somewhere. Don't know why. Hoarding again, I expect.' She smiled. 'So, money wise, I married badly. Married for love. Then my parents promised that if we adopted, they'd settle an income on the child, a growing income, from the time he was five till he was twenty-one, so long as he stayed in full-time education. My father believed strongly in education, like a lot of people who didn't get much of it themselves. Have another biscuit, Mr Parry.' She held out the plate.

'Thank you. So your parents did what they'd promised?'

'Yes. It was arranged through insurance policies and a trust managed by the insurance company. It cost a lot, but my parents put down the money in what was a good year for my father. A very good year. He was a bookmaker, and like most bookmakers, he was filthy rich some of the time, while not knowing how to make ends meet for the rest of it. He put up with Edwin, but he never really understood him, or ... or accepted his judgement. Especially over anything to do with money. That was why he arranged for insurance company trustees to keep control of what he gave to our baby.'

'Was that for all time?'

'Yes, but once Freddy was eighteen, the money was paid direct to him every month, not to me.'

'I see. And it was this allowance that originally swayed your husband into agreeing to the adoption?'

'The prospect of it, yes. He thought there'd be something in it for him, you see. And there was, of course, in what we would have saved through it. Except he didn't live long enough to benefit. Edwin and both my parents were killed in a car accident when Freddy was four.' One hand went to smooth the heavy skirt as she went on: 'They were on their way back from Chepstow races. Edwin didn't like racing, but he'd gone along as paid help, because my father's clerk was sick. I've been on my own ever since, and the extra income used to be a godsend. It was two thousand pounds in the first year, and got bigger as time went on. A lot bigger.'

'And that's why Freddy was still taking A levels?'

'After his fashion, yes. The trustees would have paid him ten thousand a year for another three years yet. Or nearly three. It suited him well enough, to go with the money he was making out of what he called his sidelines. He didn't do much school-work. Just enough to get by. Otherwise, it was no hardship for him to stay in school. He enjoyed being a big fish in a small pond. Gave him a sense of power, with plenty of girls to choose from, and boys to terrorize, I expect. And he was being paid for it by the trustees, of course. That's how he saw it.'

'He wasn't coming into more money when he was twenty-one?'

'Oh, no. That's when the trust money stopped. Had he told someone he was getting more then?'

'Something of the sort, I believe.'

'Typical. He was showing off, that's all.'

'Do you know how much he made out of these sidelines?'

'No. But he always had plenty of money in his pocket, and hardly any for me,' she completed bitterly.

'You mean he didn't provide for you in any way? Not for room and board when he lived at home, for instance?'

'He gave me fifty pounds a week the last two holidays, when he was at home, which wasn't often, and when he remembered, which was even less often. And he thought that was generous. But it was only half what I'd allowed *him* in the days when the trust money came direct to me. A hundred a week I used to give him. That was on top of his board, his clothes, any schooling costs, holidays and so on. I paid all of it out of the insurance money. And what wasn't used up that way, I saved for Freddy over the years. Gave it to him on his eighteenth birthday. More fool me. He never said thank you for it, or for anything else.'

'Later, you couldn't have got a fairer deal for yourself than that fifty pounds a week? Through the trustees?'

'No. As I said, once he was of age, all the trust payments had to go direct to him. The trustees couldn't transfer any to me. I often imagined my father turning in his grave over that. He left me very little, you see. I'm afraid he died in one of his bad years, relying on what my mother made running a small hotel, like the ones I've run later.' She smiled philosophically.

'And this extra income of Freddy's, did he tell you how he got it?'

'No. Oh, by trading things, he said to me once.'

'He didn't say what things?'

She bent her head to one side and then the other, as if she was engaged in a spine-stretching exercise. 'He told me he bought and sold used cars. He started that while he was at Modlen College. Used to keep his stock in that big car park they have there. He said no one ever noticed. It may only have been one car he ever sold, of course. He loved to exaggerate.'

'Did he mention anything else?'

'He gave me a bottle of scent last Christmas. Said he was getting it wholesale and duty free from the Continent. Quite expensive stuff, it was. I gave it to Beth's married daughter. Oh, and early last summer, I know he took a hired van to Calais and brought it back full of wine, beer

168

and smokes to sell in Cardiff. He did that at least twice. Had to get an older boy to help the first time, when he was too young to hire the van himself, or to bring liquor and tobacco into the country, I suppose.'

'It sounds as though he trusted you.'

Mrs Gibbon shook her head slowly. 'He did tell me things sometimes that ... that could have got him into trouble, that's if they were true. You never knew with Freddy, of course. I suppose he was certain I'd never do anything worse than argue with him. Try to make him behave better. He never did behave better, though.'

'So he was just bragging to you? I mean if some of the exploits weren't true?'

'Not always. I think some of them were true, or half true. Only there probably wasn't anyone else he could brag to who he was sure would never tell on him. To the authorities, I mean.'

'Why didn't you? If you felt as strongly as you say you did?'

She looked across at the speaker with understanding and tolerance in her eyes. 'Are you married, with children, Mr Parry?'

'Neither. I'm a widower. No children, and my wife died two years ago.'

'Oh, I'm so sorry.' She leaned forward,

and now bent her head towards him. 'But what I was getting at was, with children there's a limit to what you'll put up with, before you give them a good clout, or whatever. But there's a limit to how far you'll go the other way as well. And that's what stops you turning them in. I could never have brought myself to do that. In Freddy's case, if I'd got close to reporting him even, there'd have been something else stopping me.' She paused, took a deep breath and then exhaled it. 'You see, he wasn't my child. I was responsible for him, but I didn't give birth to him. I chose him, but he never had the chance not to choose me, after he'd been ... well, turned down by his real parents. So I was ... I was responsible for his safety. For protecting him from others, but more than that, for protecting him from himself. And you could say I was responsible in another way, too. Edwin was supposed to be his adopted father, who should have been there to give him a father's guidance. Only Edwin never lived to do that. It all fell on me. And in the depths of my soul, for most of the time I've felt guilty for doing such a bad job. Do you understand?'

'I think so.'

'Well, it's true, isn't it? Or that's how it seemed to me all those years. And I hope it answers your question about why I stood by him?'

'Yes, it does. So tell me this.' Parry was reverting to something less emotive. 'Freddy must have had funds for all his enterprises, but how did he manage with school fees boring such a hole in the money he was getting from the trustees?'

'Ah, he was always at state schools till last summer. He'd been at three in the last five years. Seven altogether in his life.' She shook her head.

'And been ... expelled from all of them?'

'Never actually expelled. Not formally. Instead, I'd be asked politely but firmly if I'd remove him. Headmasters are usually very considerate to lone widows. If Freddy left voluntarily, it meant I could get him into another school, without questions being asked. Well, not too many questions.'

'Although you had to move to a fresh school catchment area?'

'Not always, no. Before I came here, we lived in the hotel for three years.'

'And Freddy went to the comprehensive school in Aberbach?'

'That's right.'

Parry had been searching his mind. 'So he was there last summer when a tragedy–'

'When a boy called Peter Absom hanged himself?' Mrs Gibbon interposed. 'No, that happened in the holidays. A month after Freddy had left.' She seemed to be relieved by the admission. 'Only there was an open verdict at the inquest, meaning it might not have been suicide,' she continued. 'I hope that was wrong. It was rumoured, too, the headmaster didn't agree with the verdict. Privately he didn't. Except no headmaster wants to advertise there could have been ... goings-on at his school, does he?'

'What kind of goings-on, Mrs Gibbon?'

She shrugged. 'Foul play, I suppose. In the case of Aberbach Comprehensive, a lot of unpleasantness going back two years at least.'

'And what sort of foul play was it, do you know?'

'Bullying of boys, and girls. And teachers sometimes.'

'Did you ever hear of drugs being involved?'

'Oh, yes. That too. The headmaster is supposed to have known about it all, but he couldn't prove it. Not without risking someone suing him. Nobody was ready to admit anything. Not the children, the teachers or the parents. Well, I don't think the parents knew, or the teachers probably, but a lot of the children did. It was a very unhappy school, and it was easiest for the parents to blame the headmaster and the staff. Well, it always is, isn't it?'

'And where did Freddy figure in all this?'

'At one time, the headmaster, his name's Clarke, he as good as told me Freddy was the centre of the problem. Freddy and two other boys, but mostly Freddy. Mr Clarke asked to see me about it twice last year. The first time was in March. He said he was sure Freddy was at the root of disgraceful conduct in the senior classes. I told him he'd have to prove it before I'd take Freddy away. I could have bitten my tongue for saying it, because I knew all the time it was probably true.'

'But the headmaster must have had some proof of what he said to you, or he wouldn't have dared say it, surely?'

'Not really. There was just the two of us in his study. I think he'd made sure there were no witnesses. It finished up with his agreeing to give Freddy a last chance, after I said I'd read the riot act to him. Of course, it didn't work.' She straightened her jumper as she continued. 'It was in the middle of the last summer term that the headmaster sent for me again. And I could tell this time he was desperate, angry but desperate too. He said that if I didn't take Freddy from the school he'd expel him, and if I objected he'd report him to the police for causing bodily harm to one of the women teachers. The woman was ready to testify that Freddy had tried to rape her in a classroom after school hours, and hurt her when she was resisting.'

'But if that was true, why hadn't it been reported to the police already?'

'Because the teacher was middle aged, unmarried, and shattered and ashamed at what had happened. And since there'd been no witnesses, she was scared people would think she'd made up the whole thing. On top of that, it had taken her three months even to tell her best friend about it. It was the friend who'd insisted they go to the headmaster.'

'So did you confront Freddy with it all?'

'Yes. He denied everything, of course. He said exactly what the mistress said he'd say. That she was a frustrated bitch who was always touching him. Egging him on. I didn't believe him, of course. Indeed, Mr Parry, I felt like braining him myself for what I knew was lies, and for what he'd done. I told him he'd have to leave the school. That he had to avoid a scandal at all costs. I mean, if there'd been legal action, he'd have risked other women and girls coming forward to witness against him about other incidents. I said there'd be too many accusers for the police not to think he was guilty of something. That he'd end up in prison. I had no proof, of course. I was working on instinct. But I was right. He gave in.'

'You mean he agreed to leave the school?'

'Yes, after he'd seen the headmaster himself, alone. That was at Freddy's own request. I don't know what was said, but afterwards Freddy told me he'd weighed up the consequences of staying and decided to leave. He said he was fed up with the place anyway. That was to save face, probably. The other two boys were allowed to stay in the end.'

Parry considered for a moment. 'And all of this was before the Absom boy's death in the holidays. It happened on the school premises, didn't it? In the gym?'

'I think so, yes.'

'And was Freddy living at home at the time?'

'On the face of it, yes, but he was only home there for the odd night, about once a week. Although he was pretty thick-skinned, he wasn't comfortable in Aberbach any more. I think he felt local opinion was too much against him.'

'But did he ever ... ever hint to you that he knew anything at all about the Absom death?'

Mrs Gibbon hesitated. 'After it happened, he swore to me he didn't.'

'And did you believe him?'

Once again she was slow to answer. 'Despite everything, yes, I did believe him over that.'

For the first time during the interview, the chief inspector was aware of the evasion in her answer. But after all, it was one thing to think badly of a dead son, but quite another to face the possibility of having that son posthumously accused of some crime – possibly even murder – with all the muck-raking that would follow. 'Would you think the headmaster suspected Freddy had been involved with young Absom?' he asked.

'I haven't talked to the headmaster since long before that happened. As I said, Freddy had already left the school, and I was busy trying to find another state school to take him. At his urgent insistence, I may say. As usual, he was using me. He even said he'd only left Aberbach Comprehensive because I'd made him. The trouble was there was no other school in the area willing to have him.'

'Is that why you moved here to Hereford, Mrs Gibbon?'

'Well, I have to admit, not really. The lease of the hotel only had six months to go, and I didn't want to renew it. I'm afraid the place had started to lose money, and it needed a lot spending on it. I'd always wanted to open the sort of shop I've got here now, only it wouldn't have paid in Aberbach. Freddy leaving the school just gave me the opportunity I wanted. Or brought it forward, like.'

'But did you try to get him into a school here?'

'Yes. But none of them would accept him either. They had the excuse that he was eighteen already, and had really poor A level results last year. But I think the real reason was they were suspicious about the number of schools he'd been to already, so they made enquiries about him. In depth, as they say.'

'And did he get himself into Modlen College?'

'No. It was Mr Clarke, the Aberbach headmaster who did that. He got in touch with Dr Newsom-Pugh. It was very good of Mr Clarke in the circumstances. I'm afraid, again, it was because he'd taken pity on a widow. Modlen College is feeling the pinch, of course. Not surprising, in view of what they charge. Really they need many more pupils.' She paused ruminatively. 'Freddy found out about that and made me press for a reduction in the fees. We got them too. Except that at the end of his first term, at Christmas, Dr Newsom-Pugh wrote to say Freddy wasn't reacting well to the teaching and needed to try harder. I got the feeling Freddy was up to his old tricks, causing more trouble than he was worth. The college suited him, though. It was near Cardiff where he wanted to be, and he was treating it more as a hotel than a school.'

'Though presumably he couldn't expect to stay there till he was twenty-one in any case?' Parry asked.

'Probably not, but he'd have found somewhere else, I expect. Or got me to do it for him, more like.'

'Did he ever come here at the weekends?'

'Once or twice, yes. But never for more than a night.'

'But he had his own room here?'

'Oh ... oh, yes.'

'Would you mind if I look round it before I leave?' He checked the time.

'Not at all. It's the first room on the right at the top of the stairs. But there's not much belonging to him there. Tell you the truth, I've been using his room for extra shop storage.'

'Well, I only need to take a quick glance.' Parry leaned forward, putting away his notebook. 'And you've no idea where he did go at weekends?'

'None at all, I'm afraid.'

'And is there anything else you want to tell me about Freddy, Mrs Gibbon? Anything at all that could possibly help us find his murderer?'

She looked up at the ceiling, then down again. 'I've told you he was an evil boy, who caused any amount of harm to others. Perhaps one of those others decided to take his revenge. The awful thing is, it may have been justified.'

'That's a difficult thing for you to admit to a policeman, Mrs Gibbon.'

She remained still and silent for several seconds. 'Yes, it is,' she said eventually. 'But it's something I've lived with for years. God knows, I didn't want him dead. But since it's happened ... it's like ... it's like a great weight's been lifted from me. There, I've said it now, haven't I? But I can't help it. I loved him so much at the start, but gradually, very gradually, against my instincts, the love turned to ... not hate, but a kind of permanent ache of despair. It was the feeling that he didn't belong to me any more. Or that he'd never belonged to me at all. That in going his own way he'd rejected everything I'd ever done for him. It was a dreadful feeling, and it made me so lonely. I'd only had Freddy left, and he'd cast me aside.'

Mrs Gibbon was staring hard at the burning coals, and for the past minute it seemed as if she had been talking more to herself than to Parry. Then suddenly she sat up straighter, and turned her head towards him again. 'But now I don't have to worry any more about what he's done, do I? That he'd be arrested some day for something, and sent to prison? I couldn't have borne that. It's over. All of it. Only I do so hope it wasn't a painful death. But you're right, it's an awful thing to say about my own son. My own adopted son.' For the first time tears had begun to form in her eyes, but she was fighting them back. 'I did my very best for him, you see? I brought him up to be truthful and honest. I defended him to others, even when I knew he was in the wrong. And I always hoped it'd come right. That ... oh, I don't know, that again as it says in the Bible, he'd see the error of his ways. But he never did.' She was sobbing now through the words. 'Talking like this is such a relief. Now I know I'll never have to lie awake again wondering if some day Freddy was going to do something, something horrible. Something unspeakable.'

Parry nodded his understanding, while debating if her nearly unnatural but heartfelt relief was based in the knowledge that Freddy had done the unspeakable already, but had been put beyond facing any earthly reckoning for it.

10

'Message from public relations, boss, confirming the news conference is ten thirty in the morning. At the college,' Lloyd reported, before taking a first swallow from a pint of Brain's Best Bitter.

'Did you ask Dr Newsom-Pugh if he wants to be in on it?' questioned Parry.

'Yes. And like you expected, he wasn't keen at first. Didn't see the need for a news conference at all, until I told him it could help us find the killer. He came round a bit after that. I said it'd help keep reporters and photographers at bay for the rest of the time, as well. He's had enough of them already, specially since we announced it was a suspicious death.'

'And you explained the conference would be in the car park?'

'Unless it's snowing, yes. That cheered him up as well. He hadn't liked the idea of strangers having free access to the building. His wife was pleased too, when I said the TV news people are coming, BBC and ITN.'

'His wife was there when you spoke to him?'

The sergeant nodded. 'It was in their private apartment. Very grand, that is. She told him to be positive. Said they should be glad to give interviews. To say encouraging things about the college, balancing against the tragedy. When I left, she was telling him it'd all be good advertising for them in the end.'

182

'Was she? Well, I suppose she could be right, in a way,' Parry commented uncertainly, and wondering if the stunning, extrovert Mrs Newsom-Pugh was simply relishing the prospect of appearing on television, and having her picture in the paper. 'Anyway, we'll put up the photo of Freddy Gibbon on TV,' he added, 'and ask anyone who saw him at the weekend to phone in. Worth a try. Have you talked to the landlord here about him?'

'Yes, boss, just before you arrived. That's Mr Mills and his wife. He's had to go out since, but Mrs Mills is here. She's the one who took your order. They both recognized Gibbon from the photo. They say he's only ever been in three or four times to their knowledge. Mrs Mills remembers the night he was here with the two girls last term. She couldn't remember the date, or even the month, but thinks it was probably in October. Another time, nearer Christmas, Mr Mills definitely remembers Gibbon asking if he'd be interested in buying fifty cartons of duty-free Gold Leaf cigarettes. Gibbon said he'd bought them in Calais. Legit. But the price he was asking was still phoney. Too low. Mr Mills told him he only got his supplies through the brewer.'

183

'Figuring they were nicked?'

'That they might have been. Yes.'

'Fits what I've been learning about our Freddy. Good-looking, personable, veneer of intelligence, a loner who controlled things through bribery or bullying, and fancied himself with women.' Parry had been contemplating his own beer as he spoke. He now picked up the glass and took a long draught from it before he went on. 'Seems he was into a variety of scams. A natural crook with no moral scruples, but a master at making sure he was never shopped by anyone. I'd have guessed drugs would have been his main stock in trade, except we haven't found any.'

'Which could mean we haven't been looking in the right places yet, boss.'

'Sure. But his rooms here and at his mother's should have turned up something.' The chief inspector looked about him. 'Let's sit over there. And are you sure you don't want something to eat as well, Gomer?'

'Nothing for me, boss. I had supper in the college refectory earlier on, with Miss Strange.'

Parry grinned. 'Brushing up your history, or detecting by stealth?'

The two officers had been standing at the

bar of the Prince of Wales in Brynglas. It was just after eight thirty. They had arranged by telephone to meet here when Parry had been driving back from Hereford – or more precisely from Aberbach, which he had taken in on the way.

Far from being the dump described by Sara Card, the venerable, thatched-roof pub was an attractive whitewashed building with a cosy, low-ceilinged interior, beamed, with blazing coal fires at both ends of the room. There was a caged Mynah bird near one of the fires, and, a massive black cat curled up asleep by the other. The establishment served hot food up to an hour before closing time every evening except Sundays. This had been handy intelligence that DC Alison Pope, a logistics fiend, had gleaned and logged for everyone's future benefit early in the day.

'Miss Strange is a gen lady, boss, and jolly with it. I think Gracie's read one of her books.' Gracie, Lloyd's wife, an avid knitter, also read a lot. She and Cynthia Strange had plumpness in common, something they shared with the sergeant, who was pre-disposed towards well-nourished women. 'Historical romances, she writes,' he continued. 'I can tell you she's dead bothered about those four girls she's responsible for. She's their sort of moral tutor, as well as the other kind.'

'Course tutor, they call it, Gomer. You mean the three in the room below Gibbon's, and Josephine Oswald?'

'Right,' the sergeant replied. 'She's concerned about Josephine Oswald in particular. She's the one Mary Norris interviewed at lunchtime, after the father brought her back. She was very nervous. Miss Strange says she's lived a very protected existence. That when she was interviewed, she may have exaggerated the extent of her relationship with Freddy Gibbon.'

'And did she?'

'Doesn't seem so from Mary's written report. I mean, the girl didn't say they were that close. She lived in the next room to his, so of course she ran into him more than most people.'

'Was the father present at the interview?'

'No, boss, he'd left before either he or Josephine knew about the death.'

'Perhaps Miss Strange was fishing to find out what the girl did say.'

'Well, if she was, she didn't get anything from me, boss. But it didn't seem like she was fishing.' And Gomer Lloyd considered he was a fair judge of when he was being suborned.

The two men had moved to a corner table away from the bar, also from the three other customers present, and close enough to one of the fires to enjoy the heat without being roasted. Another feature that commended the Prince of Wales was the lack of custom on a snowbound Monday evening – though the same sentiment probably wasn't shared by the brewers, S. A. Brain & Co, who owned the place. Parry had ordered home-made steak-and-kidney pie from the surprisingly extensive bar menu. 'So did Miss Strange volunteer anything else?' he asked.

'She didn't trust Gibbon, boss. Well, she as good as said that to Mary earlier on. Only she was more forthcoming with me.'

'It's those peppermints you ply them with, Gomer.'

'No, she doesn't eat sweets. She smokes a pipe,' Lloyd responded almost wistfully. He had become addicted to peppermints five years before this when he'd taken them up to stop himself smoking. 'She didn't know why Gibbon was attending the college in the first place, nor why he was accepted on reduced fees when no one else is. Or not that she knows of.'

'Is it likely she'd be given that kind of information?'

'I wondered that, too, boss. But Debby Thomas, the bursar, happened to tell her about Gibbon's fees.'

'His mother told me he got in on the cheap because the college is hard up. Found itself very low on numbers at the start of last term.'

'Ah, Miss Strange sort of guessed that too, boss. And it bothers her. She likes it here. Wouldn't want the place to close. Suits her lifestyle to have a regular salary coming in as well as what she earns from her books. I mean, she's not a world bestseller. Not yet, anyway.' Which implied Gracie Lloyd had talent-spotted a future literary star ahead of the field.

'Why didn't she trust Gibbon?' asked the chief inspector.

'Amongst other things, she thinks he was playing fast and loose with the domestic staff. When I asked if she had evidence, she said she'd seen Sara Card coming out of his room one night. I didn't say we knew about that. And why Sara was there.'

'Or why Sara told us she was there,' Parry

corrected with a frown. 'Assuming it was the same night the girl mentioned. Oh, thanks very much, Mrs ... Mills.' He looked up at the bearer of a heaped plate of steaming comestibles now being put in front of him, together with a knife and fork wrapped in a paper napkin.

'Pleasure, I'm sure, sir. Hope you enjoy it. Would you like mustard or anything?' asked the landlord's comely wife, a cheerful, middle-aged woman with cheeks as rosy as Canadian apples, and almost as shiny.

'No, thanks. Oh, and we're grateful for the help you and your husband are giving with our enquiry.'

Mrs Mills shook her head. 'Nasty old business, isn't it? While I was waiting for your food to heat, I rang Doreen. She's our regular barmaid, works from eleven till three every day except Sundays. She knew Freddy Gibbon by name. Said he'd twice met a man here, by prior arrangement, at around twelve thirty, on a Thursday, both times. Once was in November, the other in early December. The man was in his late-thirties, good-looking, heavy build, fair hair and moustache. Oh, and he wore a dark blazer and flannels. She says he wasn't local, and not from the college either. I never saw him myself. I'm in the kitchen at lunchtime, and my husband always has the day off Thursdays. Anyway, I gather Doreen rather fancied him.'

'Hence the accurate description?' offered Parry with a grin.

'That's right. She said she got the feeling they were talking serious business. Anyway, I thought I ought to mention it.'

'Glad you did, Mrs Mills. Doreen didn't get the man's name?'

'Afraid not, though I think she meant to, for reasons of her own, like.'

'Pity. Perhaps she noticed what sort of car he was driving?'

'No, and I don't think she would have. There's no view of the car park from in here. I probably saw him and his car through the kitchen window, but they wouldn't have meant anything to me, and we get so many customers at lunchtime, you wouldn't believe.'

'I would if all the food's as good as this pie looks,' Parry responded affably. 'Well, I'm sure you'll let us know if anything else about Freddy Gibbon occurs to you, or Doreen.'

'Of course. Mr Lloyd gave my husband your phone number. Enjoy your meal.' Mrs Mills left them to return to the bar.

'Seems he was using this place as one of his trading posts,' said Parry. 'Let's try the regular midday customers with Gibbon's picture, and a description of the man he met. Get this Doreen to do an Identikit picture of him.'

'Right, boss,' said Lloyd, scribbling in his notebook. He looked up, just as the freshly awakened black cat sprang on to his lap, and from where it could get a better view of what Parry was eating. Pet animals liked the sergeant, except his earlier attempt to make the Mynah bird say anything had been a failure. 'So you saw Mr Clarke, the Aberbach headmaster?' he asked now, absently smoothing the feline head.

'Yes. He was still at the school when I got there at five. He wasn't shedding any tears over Gibbon, but he wasn't giving much away either. Not at the start, at least. He agreed the boy was asked to leave the school without being actually expelled. That was to save his mother pain.'

'From what you said, it seems it was more to save Mr Clarke's face, boss.'

'That's true enough,' said Parry, who had already given Lloyd a brief account of what he had learned at the house in Hereford. 'When I said Mrs Gibbon had told me

191

about the attempted rape of the woman teacher, Clarke opened up a bit more. Said the woman had been against giving evidence to the police. She just wanted Gibbon chucked out of the school.' The chief inspector swallowed some pie, before adding: 'Clarke then said Gibbon was a cunning young swine, a crook, a womanizer, and a bully who never got caught in the act. When I asked him how the boy managed to live such a charmed life, he said he'd no idea. On the two abortions Mrs Gibbon mentioned, he said he'd never heard of either. Said they'd probably happened at Gibbon's previous school.'

'When he couldn't have been more than fifteen, boss.'

'Which in turn suggests the girls involved might have been below the age of consent.'

'Except there isn't one for abortions, boss,' said Lloyd with feeling.

'Clarke did say Gibbon bragged a lot to his classmates about how attractive he was to grown women, as well as girls. Seems Gibbon once told someone he'd slept with a French mistress at the school. The woman had already gone to a new job by the time this got to the headmaster. He didn't follow it up.'

'But he didn't give you chapter and verse on the bullying and the rest.' This came as a resigned comment from the sergeant, not as a question, and before Parry could reply he completed: 'He wouldn't, of course. Did he seem a generally weak sort of character to you, boss?'

'Yes. And very lucky to have got a headmastership.'

'And to have kept it,' said Lloyd pointedly. 'We all thought as much at the time of the Peter Absom investigation. And he had nothing new to offer on that, of course?'

'Afraid not, Gomer. Except he said, if Absom did commit suicide – and he's pretty certain he did – it's possible it was because Gibbon and others had been making the lad's life a misery. He stressed, though, that the boy died in the holidays when Gibbon was no longer a member of the school.'

'Oh, yes. Typical of Mr Clarke, that is. At the time, he never mentioned to us that Gibbon even existed. And I'd remember if he had. I interviewed him twice in August,' Lloyd offered bitterly, while smoothing the cat with unconscious vehemence. 'Too anxious to protect his reputation for keeping good order and discipline. If he's half right about Gibbon, the boy should have been in detention years ago. So, what's next, boss?'

Parry drank some beer before replying. 'Well, assuming Gibbon was pushing drugs, we need to find that red-headed motor-cyclist fast. He may not have been Gibbon's only supplier, but he's the only one we know about. We also need to know where Gibbon stored his stuff. Was it bulky enough for him to have needed a place outside the college, for instance? And who was he supplying? Nobody, according to our information to date. So how did he organize protection for himself that good, because it still seems to be working for him even when he's dead. And did he really run a used-car business from the college car park? If he did, it's not that important in itself, but it could lead us to people who were involved with him on other things.' He picked at one of his front teeth. 'Trouble is, I'm sure his mother knows more than she's told me so far.'

'Well, we know how he kept Sara and Bronwyn happy,' said Lloyd. 'He paid them well. By the way, they'll be taken down to Cardiff Central nick tomorrow, to go through the mug-shot albums. To try to identify the motorcyclist. The other student we know Gibbon was paying off was Alwyn

Bowen, the fat boy who did his homework for him.'

'But wasn't Bowen vague about the form of the payments? What did he say? That Gibbon let him listen to his CDs.' Parry chewed on a piece of steak for a moment before adding: 'Doesn't sound like much of a payment, does it? So was he giving Bowen drugs? Get someone to see that lad again, will you? Find out for sure if he really was at home last night, as he said. The girl students' stories need going over again, as well. I mean the three in room twenty-eight. And is there anything on Oscar's yet?'

'Yes, boss. We've checked the membership list with the total cooperation of the manager. He's only too pleased to help on that because of the drug raid last week, where nothing was found. He wants to go on proving he's Mr Clean.'

'Except the Drug Squad say they're sure there was a tip-off before the raid,' Parry observed cynically.

'That may be, boss, but we now know Ifor Jenkin is a full club member, not a temporary one. Has been for two years. And Freddy Gibbon was made a member on November the twentieth last year. Both had credit-card details listed on their membership forms. We're checking through the credit-card receipts to find out when they were last in the dub. Afraid it wasn't last weekend, though.'

'Unless they were there and paid cash? Get the manager to extend his heartfelt cooperation by showing a picture of Gibbon to his staff,' said Parry.

'That's being done already, boss. We've also got Gibbon's credit-card number from the membership form, so we can have a check made on whether it was used any-where else at the weekend.'

'Good. Interesting to see if your Mr Clean lets any of his staff give us any really useful information. Like who Gibbon and Jenkin brought to the club.'

'Perhaps they went with each other, boss.'

'That'd be useful information in itself. And since Gibbon was a member, Jenkin can say it proves his point about it not, being an all-gay club.' He pushed his nearly empty plate to one side, then pulled his quarter-full beer glass towards him. 'You know, Gomer, the angle we haven't studied enough yet is revenge. Someone with a record like Gibbon's must have had enemies, or at least people who were waiting to do him down. And by that I don't necessarily mean kill him.' He sniffed. 'In fact, let's also work on the possibility that murder might not have been intended. That it was a mistake, an accident, or literally an overkill. Then think of–'

'Dr Newsom-Pugh really wanting him out of the college, boss, despite needing more students there, not less,' the sergeant interrupted, in the spirit of the suggestion. 'He said it was because Gibbon wasn't learning enough. But that could have been a touch of Mr Clarke's strategy, couldn't it? That he had worse reasons he couldn't tell people about.'

'And Mrs Newsom-Pugh is the college's French mistress, of course. French mistresses being a Gibbon speciality,' Parry contributed with a dour expression.

'Right again, boss. But if one of those two did for Gibbon, my money'd be on the lady. In a fit of jealous rage. Probably when she learned he was sleeping with someone besides her. I can picture her in a fury, can't you?'

'Vividly, but don't get too carried away, Gomer.'

'Well, perhaps that's a bit far-fetched.' The sergeant reached across to Parry's plate and removed a sliver of meat which he presented

197

to the sceptical cat on the end of his finger. 'But if Gibbon was having a bit of hanky-panky with Mrs Newsom-Pugh, that gives her husband a better reason for getting rid of him than the ones he's mentioned to us. Rid of him in both senses, too.'

'And while we're considering older women,' said Parry, 'could there be other reasons why Miss Strange made no secret of her deep dislike for Gibbon? Could there be jealousy there, perhaps? And I don't mean of Sara Card, though even that's conceivable.'

Lloyd shifted in his seat, temporarily upsetting the cat. 'You mean because Miss Strange may be lesbian, and fancies one of the girl pupils Gibbon was having up to his room?'

'Yes. Josephine Oswald, for one.'

'I thought of that, boss. It's ... it's possible, yes,' Lloyd admitted, with evident reluctance. 'We know she was in the college all Sunday, of course, like the Newsom-Pughs. Mark you, Mr Jenkin wasn't far from the place last night either. He could have been in and out again, easy.'

'Yes, and Gibbon could have had some kind of hold on Jenkin. Something worth money to Gibbon, which could land him in blackmailing, too. Except, I still think Gibbon's body was taken to the college after death, but there's no evidence yet to prove it. Difficult to transport a dead body on a motorbike, of course, but not impossible. And whoever dropped it at the bottom of the tower had to be there at some point.' Parry paused for a moment. 'I've been wondering about Debby Thomas's opinion of Gibbon,' he commented next. 'Amusing and good-looking, she said, do you remember? The kind of boy who broke girls' hearts.'

'And wouldn't worry about making them pregnant,' put in Lloyd, with a deepening glower.

'That's right. So why was she so tolerant? You know, it might be worth seeing her at home, when her ex-policeman boyfriend's there. To gauge whether he thought as highly of Freddy as she did. Want another beer?' Parry was finishing his own.

'No thanks, boss. The boyfriend, Colvin Russell, he was only a detective constable in the Met. I was having him checked out anyway, for interest.'

'Good. And while we're searching for Gibbon's enemies' – Parry leaned across the table – 'I'd like to see a job history on all

199

college staff, teaching and otherwise, who've joined, say, in the last two years. I'm sure Mrs Newsom-Pugh couldn't have been the celebrated French mistress in Aberbach, but someone from there could have followed Gibbon to the college. Or been here when he arrived last term, which might have revived an old grudge.'

'The most recent member of the teaching staff is Emlyn Harries, the English tutor, boss. He slept there last night, and he was the first to reach the body this morning, of course. But he's just come from teaching abroad. New Zealand, I think he said. So no old grudges there.'

'Good. All the easier to check up on him, then,' said Parry, with a tolerant beam while rising from his chair. 'Want a word with the Toucan again, before we go?'

'No, it's a definite nontalker,' said Lloyd, confident he had a way with animals – except he shifted the half-sleeping cat off his lap too energetically, and it snagged a claw in his trousers.

11

'So say in your answers that, at the start, none of the three most interested parties took Bonnie Prince Charlie's seventeen forty-five rebellion seriously. Not the French, who were supposed to be financing it, and didn't to any degree. Not the English, who treated it as a pretty harmless French diversion. And certainly not the Scots. Some Highlanders rallied to the cause, but the Lowlanders were actually joining up in droves to fight against it.' Cynthia Strange glanced at her wristwatch. 'Right, we'll do the Battle of Culloden. Moor and its unspeakable aftermath next time. We're a minute or so early, but that means you can all get your coffee while it's still hot. See some of you later this afternoon for tutorials.' She smiled, gathered her papers to her bosom, and stepped off the podium to exit ahead of all but one member of her assembled class, Mair Daltry, who had moved quickly to hold the door open for her.

It was close to ten fifteen on Tuesday morning. Miss Strange's first class of the day had been fifteen students strong. The modern history group was always the biggest, the subject being accepted as probably the easiest A level. The lesson had been given, as usual, in one of the basement lecture rooms.

'Shall I check that Josephine's all right, Miss Strange?' asked the dark, long-haired Mair who was wiping her nose as they emerged together into the corridor.

'No, don't bother, Mair. I'll do it. You go and get your coffee. You look as if you could do with the lift.' Morning coffee, like tea in the afternoon, was freshly brewed, and a good deal more palatable than the machine versions permanently available. 'I have to go up to my room anyway,' the tutor went on. 'Oh, and when you come for your tutorial, don't forget to bring back the Robert Walpole biography I lent you.'

'Yes, miss. Thank you.' Mair wiped her nose again. It was usually a rather attractive nose, like the rest of its owner's slim and well-proportioned body, but today it was fiery-red and sore looking. The girl seemed scarcely to be recovering from the condition that had kept her in bed all of Sunday.

Miss Strange made a mental note to air her own room thoroughly before the four o'clock tutorial – and to keep a window open a little, whatever the outside temperature. She had avoided colds and flu so far this winter, but the sniffling Mair was clearly a mobile germ disseminator. That was one of the reasons why the tutor had stopped Mair going up to see Josephine Oswald, who hadn't shown up for the class just ended. Probably she had developed a cold as well: no point in letting Mair give her a secondary infection. Except that increasingly throughout the lesson, Miss Strange had been uneasy about the guileless Josephine, and the uneasiness had now grown into a foreboding. It was silly to feel that way, she had told herself. If anything had been going to happen to Josephine it would have been while Freddy Gibbon had been alive, not after he'd died – and he'd have been the cause. Her distaste for Gibbon hadn't decreased one iota since his demise.

'Could you spare me a sec, Miss Strange?' asked a female voice behind her.

The tutor turned about, to be confronted by the elfin Detective Sergeant Mary Norris, who was emerging from a door now adorned with a notice that declared THE FREDERIC GIBBON INCIDENT ROOM.

'Actually, I'm in a bit of a hurry. Nobody's seen anything of one of my pupils this morning, and I'm worried about her. I was going up to see she's all right.'

'Then I'll come with you. Which pupil is it?'

'Josephine Oswald. No panic, really. I'm getting to be a regular fusser, I'm afraid.'

'That's the girl from Brecon. The one with the room next to Freddy Gibbon's. I've met her.' The sergeant fell in beside the other woman as they both ascended the stairs. 'Did you know we're holding a news conference in ten minutes,' she added conversationally. 'Outside in the car park.'

'Aren't you needed for it?' asked Miss Strange.

'No. Not enough rank,' the sergeant smirked. 'We were wondering, can you tell us whether you knew Gibbon offered things for sale? On the cheap? To people in the college?'

'He never offered me anything. What sort of things?'

'Anything from cigarettes to used cars, and ... and other things.'

'Other things meaning drugs?'

'Possibly.'

'That doesn't surprise me. But no, he never offered me anything. And if he'd offered me drugs I'd have had him before the principal, and out of the place bag and baggage in double quick time.' Miss Strange tackled the last few steps up from the basement with renewed vigour, her movements fuelled, it seemed, by righteous indignation. 'Mark you, I always suspected he was crooked. On the make.'

'Seems like you may have been right, Miss Strange. The other thing we were wondering was, did you ever come across him before he came here? I mean, you aren't from Aberbach or anywhere around there?'

'No. North Wales. Wrexham. My parents still live there.'

'And is that where you worked before you came here?'

'Only for a year, a long time ago.' By now they had passed through the main hall, soon to be filled with chattering, hurrying students and staff in search of refreshment, and were scaling the grander second flight of stairs again at a rush. 'My last job was in Buckinghamshire,' Miss Strange continued. 'Posh girl's school there, catering for the daughters of the great and the good. Why do you want to know?'

'Freddy Gibbon's past is catching up with him. We'd like to talk to anyone who taught in any of his previous schools.'

'Of which there would have been quite a few, I expect.'

'Yes. How did you know?' the sergeant questioned sharply.

'I didn't.' The response had been just as prompt. 'Just guessed.'

'Well, you're right. But none of them were girls' schools, of course.'

'Much as it would have suited him, probably. I mean if some of them had been.'

'Yes. He seems to have been one for the girls, all right. You told Sergeant Lloyd you saw Sara Card coming out of his room one evening. It was only the once, was it?'

'I only saw her there once, yes. But he was in Josephine's room one evening, and one afternoon, when I'd gone up to see her ... about work.' She had put a good deal of emphasis upon the last two words, then added: 'Both times were close to the start of this term.'

'Do you know what the two of them were doing in Josephine's room?'

Miss Strange hesitated. The pair had just completed their third set of stairs and were breasting the last narrow flight into the tower, so her pause could have been ascribed to excusable exhaustion. 'It looked as though they'd just been talking, but Josephine seemed a bit embarrassed both times. That was almost certainly because the door had been locked, and had to be unlocked, by Gibbon, before I was let in. Josephine would never have locked the door herself when a boy was with her. I wouldn't be surprised if she hadn't been aware he'd quietly locked it. She's such a pure, innocent child.'

'But that's all they were doing? Talking?'

'Well, I couldn't see through a wooden door, could I? God knows what he might have been planning on before I arrived. I remember there was a shuffling noise the second time, before the door was opened. I asked then why it was locked. Josephine reddened but said nothing. He said the catch was loose. That it kept flying open with the wind.'

'And was it loose?'

'It was a bit, yes. Now then, it's the first room along,' Miss Strange provided breathlessly as they got to the top. She led the way down the corridor, then tapped on the door. 'Josephine, are you in?' There was no reply. She tried the handle. The door yielded immediately. 'Oh dear, we are a sleepy head this morning, aren't we?' The portly tutor beamed, nanny like, as she advanced heavily towards the recumbent figure in the bed, face to the wall. She peeled back the duvet and shook the still shoulders quite roughly. 'Wake up, young Josephine. You've missed... Oh my God.' When the girl's body didn't stir, the woman's eyes had turned to the bedside table. 'We need a doctor, quick. She may have taken an overdose of ... paracetamol, is it? Could be a whole package, and something else as well.'

But the sergeant had taken in the situation and was already issuing emergency instructions on her radio.

The girl, clad in a plain blue nightdress, was lying in the foetal position, her back to the newcomers, hands clutched tightly together under her throat, her face and arms white as parchment. There were empty strips of a paracetamol and codeine remedy lying on top of their outer packaging on the crowded tabletop. Beside those there was another shorter, two-tablet strip, also empty, but unlabelled.

'Ambulance is on its way. And they're contacting the village doctor,' said the policewoman a moment later.

'I can't find a pulse,' Miss Strange anguished.

'Let me try.' Mary Norris knelt down beside the bed, fingering first the girl's wrist, then her neck. 'There is a pulse, but it's faint, very faint. Let's get her up. One each side. Gently.'

There was a small movement in the girl's closed eyelids as, both women supporting her, they swung her body round, then lifted her on to her feet, one of her arms over each of their shoulders.

'Josephine, can you hear me? Try to walk, love. Move your legs. We're holding you.' But the student was unresponsive, her body still utterly limp. 'Making her throw up could help,' the sergeant offered with more confidence than she was feeling.

'Well, let's try,' beseeched the desperate Miss Strange.

'Into the loo, then,' the policewoman directed. When they got there, on the other side of the corridor, she leaned the girl forward, pulled down on her lower jaw, and thrust a finger through the partially opened mouth as far as it would go. 'Hope for the best,' she mumbled.

Hope was fulfilled – almost instantaneously, and with great gusto.

Fifteen minutes later, the still only blearily conscious Josephine Oswald was being transferred by stretcher to a waiting ambulance at the front entrance to the college. This took place under the interested but fairly remote gaze, a hundred yards or more distant, of five reporters, two cameramen, and a clutch of senior policemen. A studiously relaxed Dr Handel Newsom-Pugh and his wife were also part of the group – he in a gaudily tasselled mortarboard, and red academic gown worn over his topcoat, she glamorously turned out in a fur hat, a black leather coat with mink collar and cuffs, and leather boots.

The news conference had already been under way when the ambulance drew up. After Parry and the principal had listened to a whispered message from Mary Norris, who had made an uninvited and very brief appearance at the chief inspector's side, he had announced that one of the girl pupils had a bad stomach upset and was being taken to hospital for observation, to be on the safe side. He had then added, in a tone as inconsequential as he could command, that the event had no bearing on the murder investigation. This was corroborated by vigorous head-nodding from the principal, and was close enough to the truth if it had to be defended later.

From what Mary Norris had just told Parry, whoever had killed Gibbon, it clearly couldn't have been Josephine Oswald. The chief inspector had judged, too, that to have admitted more about what had really happened at this point could have been prejudicial to his main enquiry. It would also have been unfair to the girl and her parents, risking the possibility that her name and her still only apparent suicide attempt might have been announced through the lunchtime news bulletins and the evening papers.

It was still unfortunate that Josephine's plight had been discovered at the exact time when journalists had been assembling to view the site of the murder at Modlen College, and to be updated on the progress of the police investigation into it. Nobody regretted this more heartily than Newsom-Pugh, who had been reluctantly persuaded by his wife to treat the occasion as a sound public-relations opportunity – not the un-mitigated disaster it would become if news of a further potential catastrophe had leaked out.

Miss Strange had decided to go with Josephine to the hospital, in company with Mary Norris, who had slipped into the ambulance while the reporters were being shown the spot where Gibbon's body had been discovered.

Meantime, Gomer Lloyd and Alison Pope were examining the girl's room upstairs. Besides the empty pill strips, the bedside table had been accommodating a nearly empty glass, a half-consumed bottle of still Malvern water, a closed bible, a prayer book opened at the burial service, the empty wrappings of a milk chocolate bar, and an unsealed envelope addressed to 'My Mother and Father'.

'I expect the chocolate was a last treat,' said Lloyd, recalling the hearty breakfasts proverbially offered to condemned prisoners on execution morning.

'Or the only way she could get down all the other muck, Sarge,' the detective constable responded more prosaically. 'Wonder what was in this other pill strip,' she added, dropping it into an evidence bag.

'Something worse than paracetamol, I expect,' said Lloyd, adding: 'Thoughtful of her not to have stuck down the envelope. Saves any hassle with lawyers saying we shouldn't have opened it.'

Earlier on, Sergeant Norris, holding the envelope by a corner, had withdrawn the contents – a single-sheet letter – with the aid of a pencil. After scanning the sheet, she had bagged it, and the envelope, before hurrying down to speak to Parry.

Lloyd, in turn, was now reading the letter through the clear PVC evidence bag. The words were in a spidery handwriting and read:

Dear Mummy and Daddy,

I cannot go on without Freddy. I don't expect you to understand, but he was everything to me. He loved me, and I loved him, more than life itself. I am having his baby. If he had been alive, I would have had an abortion as he wanted, even though I hated the thought of it. But since he's been taken from me, there's no place now for me on earth either.

I don't know what Freddy kept in the window seat, and I don't want to know. I don't have a key to it, but perhaps what's in there could help the police find out who killed him.

Forgive me for hurting you. But you have Claire still, while I have nobody.

Your loving
Josephine

'Claire's a sister, I expect, Sarge,' said Alison, who had already read the letter.

'And the parents' favourite, judging by what Josephine's written. Sad that.'

'You mean if she felt unwanted?'

'That's right. Which was very likely just her imagination. Often the case. Kind of jealousy. Teenage kids can be funny.' Lloyd rubbed an open palm across his moustache. He was kneeling now on the other side of the room, running his hand over the window seat. 'So we need to get this open.'

The seat was a feature not exactly replicated in Gibbon's own room next door. It was quite narrow, running the length of the two-light window, and was covered by a long blue cushion with a deep valance hanging down to the floor. The sergeant had already removed cushion and valance, revealing what was, in effect, a built-in wooden chest, its lid secured by a smallish but serious padlock.

'Doesn't seem we can get at the screws in the staple,' Lloyd pronounced ruefully. 'So it'll mean breaking the wood. Pity. Nice bit of seasoned oak.'

12

'Regular treasure trove it is, too, boss.'

'And shows he had a finger in a lot of action. All of it crooked,' Parry responded with some bitterness to Lloyd's comment.

It was half an hour later. The two were with others in the basement incident room going over the contents of Josephine Oswald's window seat, now laid out on a table before them.

Earlier, Mrs Watkyn had been sent for and asked if she could supply a spare key to the padlocked seat. She couldn't, and went on to disclaim all knowledge of both the padlock and its hasp and staple fittings. She had further insisted, in a scandalized voice, that the items must have been attached to the seat since the Christmas holidays without college permission, and hadn't been noticed because of the covering valance. After this she had stormed from the room tight-lipped. This sequence had led Parry dourly to surmise that her outrage had been overtaken by irritation, because she had

215

unintentionally almost confirmed that the area was never cleaned.

Eventually, DC Alf Vaughan had opened the seat lid by cutting through the metal hasp with a hacksaw, something which he had achieved without damaging the wood underneath, and which earned a commendation from Gomer Lloyd.

The aptly described treasure trove had mainly been stored in an oblong, old-fashioned, black enamelled deed box, eighteen inches long, and nine inches in width and depth. The box had also been locked, but this time the fastening had been no obstacle to the dextrous Vaughan. He had coaxed the ancient lever open with the miniature set of cracksman's tools carried in his pocket, and surrendered to him early in his career by a burglar anxious to establish grounds for mitigation.

When the contents of the box had first been disclosed, three rubber-banded wads of used ten-, twenty- and fifty-pound bank notes in a large envelope had been the immediate focus of attention. The value of the notes had come to exactly five thousand pounds – not so substantially less than the total of five thousand, three hundred and fifty pounds credited to Frederic Gibbon in two building society pass books in his name found in the same envelope.

A small jewellery case covered in navy-blue velvet had yielded in turn a pair of emerald earrings, a double string of graded pearls, and an impressive diamond and sapphire ring.

A two-pint-sized, screwtop glass preserve jar had contained more than five hundred ecstasy tablets, identified by the heart design embossed on them. Also in the jar was a transparent plastic bag of white powder, twelve ounces in weight, pro-visionally assumed to be heroin, and a three-inch-square block of what was just as surely cannabis resin. The ecstasy tablets had been packaged in crimped strips that matched the smaller of the empty strips found on Josephine Oswald's bedside table.

A second, smaller envelope had disgorged two different, and new-looking, Chubb keys with tie-on travel labels attached to each. The labels had addresses written on them in capital letters, with sets of four-digit numbers added underneath.

Finally, a film supplier's standard yellow folder had disclosed five coloured photo-graphs, and a folded photocopy of a press cutting.

Crushed into the window-seat space, alongside the deed box, there had been a zippered canvas holdall with leather handles. This was half filled with easily recognizable dried Liberty Cap fungi – otherwise known as magic mushrooms.

It was the quantity and variety of the drugs that had been unexpected, and not so much the final proof they provided that Gibbon was trading in them – something broadly assumed since the interview with Sara Card and Bronwyn Tate. This was partly the reason why the photographs had caused a greater stir. One was an upper-body shot of a shirt-sleeved Ivor Jenkin, with a shorter, younger man. The two appeared to be embracing passionately. The second man's face was half buried in Jenkin's partly bared chest, while his arms were around the tutor's neck.

The dated press cutting was of a magistrates' court report taken from a two-and-a-half-year-old edition of a North Wales weekly newspaper: it also featured Jenkin.

Three other photographs showed Kate Unwin and Abby Kennedy, full length and both naked, entwined together on a bed in amateurish, and very staged, erotic poses. A fourth shot had Kate Unwin similarly engaged on the same bed, but this time with a naked man. Although her partner's face was out of the picture, the pleasure he was experiencing was evidenced by the state of another reactive and prominently exhibited part of his anatomy.

'Looks as if Freddy didn't have time to get to his building societies last week, sir,' said DC Alison Pope, who had counted the notes. She was watching Parry examine both the pass books.

'Yes. Last deposit made ten days ago,' he replied. 'He was probably careful about turning up too often with armfuls of cash. Bit of a risk keeping that amount here in a tin box, all the same. He may have other accounts, too. Do we know yet how much is in the Aberbach bank account?' This was the bank to which the insurance company transmitted Gibbon's monthly allowance. Parry had got the name and address from Mrs Gibbon, but the branch had been closed by the time he had left her the previous evening. He was reasoning now that Gibbon had kept the account there partly to give him an innocent reason for paying regular visits to the town – to supply old drug customers and to recruit new ones.

'We should know how much is there by

this afternoon, boss,' Lloyd affirmed.

'Good. I suppose he needed these large lumps of cash handy here to pay suppliers.' Parry had been eyeing the pile of bank notes as he spoke. 'And, by the look of it, the man on the motorbike wasn't the only one of those. Gibbon's weekly turnover seems to have been more than the thousand pounds or so the girls were taking to Cardiff.'

'That's if they were telling us the truth, boss.'

Parry nodded. 'Maybe the motorbike man was just one supplier he didn't want to meet himself.'

'So he'd have had plenty of cash with him at the weekend, boss. A working weekend, no doubt,' said Lloyd with a glower.

'At least as much again as we've got here probably, yes. Anyway, the chances are he'd have had enough on him to invite robbery, and even murder if he resisted, certainly by the sort of people he must have mixed with.'

The bank notes and the drugs had already been put in labelled evidence bags by DC Lucy Howells, a quiet, mature brunette with a pretty, dimpled face, who was married to a sergeant in the uniform branch. She was one of the Unit's regular exhibits officers, sitting in on the meeting now because she never let material evidence she had logged go out of her sight unless it was signed for, or placed under lock and key.

'The pattern of successful drug dealing is right here, isn't it?' Lloyd put in next, waving a hand over the bags. Some years before, he had done time with the Drug Squad. 'Most likely he began trading in mushrooms, the easiest drug to start with in this part of Wales. And the cheapest. You only need one grower contact.'

'And worked his way on from there, as his capital increased,' Parry agreed. 'Trading his customers up through the soft stuff to the hard, but keeping all his lines of merchandise going, probably because he was still bringing in fresh buyers.'

'Especially since he was working with schoolchildren,' said Lloyd. 'It's no wonder he was keen to get to a private college where the kids have more money.'

'And where no one seems ready to grass on him, even after he's dead,' Parry added, shaking his head slowly.

'But against what his mother told you, sir, it looks as if he'd given up selling cars, perfume, liquor and cigarettes, and taken up burglary and blackmail. Busy operator, even so,' said DC Vaughan.

'His mother didn't think his car business amounted to much,' the chief inspector corrected. 'As to the other stuff, it could be, of course, he stored his stock somewhere else.'

'The blackmail looks certain in the case of the maths teacher, doesn't it, sir?' Vaughan put in. 'About the girls—'

'I've just noticed, the background to this Jenkin picture could be the dance floor at Oscar's,' Lloyd interrupted, studying it more closely than before. 'And the press cutting says he was fined and put on probation for soliciting young men in a public swimming pool. That was nearly three years ago. Lucky he didn't get time for it.'

'Luckier still he ever got employment as a teacher again,' said Parry, thinking that either Newsom-Pugh was careless over his staff recruiting, or else that Jenkin had been clever about covering up past discretions – except, it seemed, from Freddy Gibbon.

'I don't believe the bed in the other pictures is the one in Gibbon's room, sir, or any of the ones in the girls' room,' Alison offered. 'Too plush. More like a hotel, perhaps.'

'Or somebody's home,' Parry suggested,

picking up one of the shots. 'I'd say from the look in their eyes they were stoned out of their minds, and doing whatever he told them to do. The man in the shot with Kate Unwin is Freddy, is it?'

'I think so, sir,' said the detective, uncertainly. 'It's ... it's his build, all right, but with his face covered ... I mean, there's nothing much to–'

'It's him all right. Identification shouldn't be a problem. Anyway, young Miss Unwin will need to tell us who it is, won't she?' Lloyd broke in, covering what he rightly took to be the female officer's embarrassment. 'I expect Abby Kennedy took that picture. Or their other roommate, Mair Daltry, although she's not in any of the shots.'

'I'd guess he had blackmail in mind with the bed pictures, too, not a first attempt at entering the porno business. It's difficult to tell with this character, though,' Parry observed. 'On the other hand, they could have been performing as payment for drugs. Or maybe he just needed a hold over them. As for the jewellery, he may have been fencing it, but it's more likely he nicked it himself, and didn't know how to get rid of it.'

'The cars his mother said he traded could have been stolen too, couldn't they, sir? If so, they'd have to have been sold for cash,' Lucy Howells suggested. 'That might be one reason for the size of the bankroll he had here. More than he'd have needed for other things we know about.'

'Or don't know about yet,' Lloyd offered glibly.

'The jewels couldn't belong to his mother, could they, sir?' Vaughan questioned.

'No. Too expensive, by the look of them,' said Parry. 'But let's show them to her when she's here today. She may know something about them, but I wouldn't count on it. You're meeting her, aren't you, Alison?'

'Yes, sir. Eleven twenty-three at Cardiff Central. I'm taking her to the hospital to do the identification, then bringing her here. She's seeing the principal, and she wants to pick up some of Freddy's things.'

'Good.' The chief inspector looked at the time. 'And we should know soon if any of the jewellery is on the stolen property list.' Polaroid photographs of all the items had already been transmitted to police headquarters. 'Assuming these two keys open street doors to the properties on the labels, and the numbers are the codes to their alarm systems, then either they've been burgled or they were about to be.'

'Sorry, sir.' A suddenly confused DC Alison Pope produced a fax sheet, one of several she was holding. 'We've had a report that the properties are private homes, with no burglaries recorded at either since nineteen eighty-nine.' This had been something it had been easy to check swiftly.

'When Freddy Gibbon would really have been too young to be involved. Or would he?' Parry grinned. 'Well, give him the benefit of the doubt. We should have heard something on the code numbers too, by now. That's if they are code numbers. Stir them up, can you, Alison?'

'Yes, sir.' She slid off the empty desk she'd been perched on with DC Howells, and moved down the room to speak to the team's communications officer, a male civilian. One of the addresses on the key labels had been in Penarth, the other in Llantwit Major, both communities close to Cardiff. Local police had been instructed to contact the householders in both cases.

'So how much of this was young Josephine Oswald in on?' questioned Lloyd, fingering one of the evidence bags. 'Beats me we didn't find a key to that padlock anywhere in her room.'

'Except it bears out what she wrote in her suicide note, Sarge,' said Lucy Howells.

'Possibly she wasn't involved in anything important,' Parry conjectured. 'I'd say she was Freddy's lackey, his dogsbody, useful for routine jobs. And he went to bed with her when he felt like it ... or, more likely, to keep her happy.'

'Meaning she wasn't the great love in his life, like she wrote he was in hers,' Lloyd agreed.

'If she'd been the love of his life, it was an out of character relationship, wasn't it, Gomer? But as for his letting her in on the real action, I'm not certain. She's too ... ingenuous, which in his book should have spelled unreliable. But it was in his interests, perhaps, for other people to go on thinking of her as ingenuous, so he could use her room as a store, and her as a front, an errand girl, with no one realizing she was that close to him. Which is the clear message we've been getting about her from every-one.'

'Well, her room was certainly safer for storage than his, boss.'

'Exactly. But it could only have been in term time. He wouldn't have left important

226

stuff there through the holidays. Apart from lack of accessibility, when the college was officially closed, Mrs Watkyn insists all the rooms are given a complete clean every holiday. So the seat padlock would have been noticed if it had been there since last term. Always supposing Mrs Watkyn's idea of a complete clean is just that. No, he's got to have another storage place, and according to his mother, and my look at his room, it isn't her house. Incidentally, are we checking the rooms of Sara Card and Bronwyn Tate?'

'All in hand, boss.'

'Good. He could have been using them in exactly the same–'

'I've got the information on the Penarth house, sir,' interrupted a flushed Alison Pope, and looking as though she'd been there and back herself. 'The numbers on the label make up the alarm code. No break-in reported, as we knew already, or missing items noticed either, not till now. But after checking her and her husband's things, the wife, that's a Mrs Anderson, said a ring and a pair of earrings are missing. Seems there was plenty of other good stuff that wasn't taken, though. Much better stuff, too. Anyway, she described the missing things in detail, and they fit with the ones we've got here.'

'Things she didn't wear often, were they, Alison?' Parry speculated.

'Well, the Andersons went skiing, sir. Over the New Year. To Klosters, she said. She hadn't taken any jewellery with her, and there'd been no reason to take out the earrings or the ring since they got back. Or ever, by the sound of what she told me. She never wears them much because they're old-fashioned.'The keen detective paused before adding: 'They sound like pretty rich people, sir.'

Parry chuckled. 'So Freddy got lucky. That's assuming he did the burglaries himself. Or it could be we're underestimating him, and he could calculate accurately what Mrs Anderson regards as old-fashioned, and puts at the bottom of her jewellery drawer. Was it a drawer or a safe, did she say?'

'Not a safe, sir. She said they're fully insured and the burglar alarm is foolproof. She wanted to know if it was one of her cleaners we'd caught with the stuff.'

'Hmm. In the circumstances, a fair guess, I suppose, unless you're one of rich Mrs Anderson's innocent cleaners. So what about the Llantwit Major address?'

228

'No one at home, sir. But the house has a burglar-alarm box on the wall. Local patrols have contacted the key holder. The owners aren't away or anything, so the house is being checked every half-hour till someone comes home.'

'It'll be the same story. The numbers will be the code to the alarm. The key will fit the front door, and the one or two missing items will be small, with nobody noticing they're missing till we tell them. But why did he operate that way? I mean, why take so little, and not even the best stuff? Unless the idea really was not to have the thefts noticed for long periods.' Parry paused. 'Anyway, figuring how Freddy got hold of those keys and numbers may give us a lead to his killer.'

'You don't sound too sure, boss.'

'I'd rather have had a lead through the drugs. People keep telling us he was a loner. Well, that's a dangerous thing to be in the illegal drugs business, a lot more dangerous than being a burglar or a blackmailer of schoolteachers ... or schoolkids. And more so if our loner was barging in on some important trader's patch.' The chief inspector looked at the loot on the table again, then gave an optimistic smile. 'Still, we've got a breakthrough of sorts, so let's get to work.'

13

'He kept stuff in Josephine Oswald's room. Ma Watkyn just told me. The police have found it. Oswald told them herself probably, stupid bitch,' Abby Kennedy uttered angrily. She was standing with her back to the window of the large bedsitter she shared with Mair Daltry and Kate Unwin. It was after lunch and she had left the refectory later than the others.

'You shouldn't say that if she's dying,' Mair admonished thickly, pushing hair from her face with a half-clenched fist. She had been coming through the bathroom door as she'd caught Abby's words, her fingers clasping a fresh wodge of tissues. Still ailing, and looking it, she slumped into an armchair.

'Well, she isn't dying,' Kate Unwin announced dismissively. 'When I saw her on the stretcher, she was playing Ophelia, but rescued from fate in the nick of time.' Like her room-mates, she was doing *Hamlet* for A levels. A normally confident, bouncy redhead with a well-developed body, she was academically even less promising than either Abby or Mair, but made up for it in other ways, not least by having the wealthiest father and the biggest spending allowance of the three. Lying on her covered divan bed with coloured cushions stacked behind her head, she was turning the pages of the latest edition of *Hello!*. But the magazine was occupying her hands not her thoughts. 'Mind you, she looked bloody awful,' she added, but not in an overly sympathetic tone.

'They told Ma Watkyn she was in a pretty bad way when they found her, but she's come round in the hospital,' said Abby. 'They could be lying, of course. I mean, if it was something worse than food poisoning she got at the weekend. But in any case, I never want to eat in Brecon again.' The speaker was short and dark with a snub nose, and darting, very deep grey eyes – at the moment, very indignant deep grey eyes. The feeling behind her words so far implied that she might even have preferred it if things had gone the other way for the hapless Josephine.

It had been at the instigation of the always calculating Inga Newsom-Pugh that Mrs

Watkyn, a natural gossip, had been nominated by Dr Newsom-Pugh as the best college disseminator of information on Josephine Oswald. Although the housekeeper had been trusted with the truth of the matter – and had been canny enough to have guessed it anyway – she valued her job and the survival of Modlen College too much not to put over the 'party line' version of events to enquiring students, and to make it sound credible. She had thought that the titbit about some of Freddy Gibbon's belongings being found in Josephine's room was harmless enough embellishment. It even had the additional advantage of being true, although she had no knowledge of what had been uncovered as a result.

'So what if he had prints of the photos in her room?' Abby demanded, making it plain that this subject was more important to her than Josephine Oswald's survival.

'But he told us he'd put them all with the negatives in his bank,' protested Kate, and sounding as if she'd believed him.

'He told us a lot of things,' Abby snapped, moving to a chair opposite Mair's, and lighting a cigarette. Smoking was strictly forbidden for students at the college – but so were a lot of other things, and Abby

232

indulged in most of them.

'But if they are in his bank, who'll get them now?' Kate pressed, because the thought had only just occurred to her.

Mair looked up. 'His mother, I should think. In the end, anyway.'

'Oh, bloody marvellous,' the redhead exploded, turning several pages of the magazine very fast with her eyes screwed up.

'It'll be better than the police getting them,' said Abby, also frowning. 'His mother won't want to show them to anyone, will she? Not if she knows he'd taken nearly all of them, and is in one of them. We should tell her that. And that he'd promised to give them to us at the end of term. She ought to keep his word for him.'

'I don't think you can count on any of that,' Mair cautioned. 'And I wish you'd put that sodding cigarette out, Abby, it's bunging up my sinuses.'

'Hard cheese,' Abby replied, but she did as she'd been asked all the same – which was unusual for her.

'Freddy was murdered,' Mair continued, in a dogged tone. 'So the police are into everything. They'll probably see his bank stuff before his mother does.' She paused. 'I still think you should have told them, or Miss Strange at least, as soon as he started blackmailing you. And definitely when they interviewed you yesterday.'

The other two girls exchanged glances before Abby answered petulantly: 'Yes, you would think that, wouldn't you, Mair? Except you weren't in any of the pictures.'

'Which was just luck anyway,' Kate chimed in. 'Just because you weren't with us at Abby's house that weekend.'

Mair shrugged. 'I wouldn't have been so bloody stupid as to let him get me that paralytic,' she said.

'Oh, for God's sake, none of it was that serious,' Kate protested, again with a brief look in Abby's direction. 'You've never seen the pictures, Mair. A lot of people would say they were just done for a ... a bit of fun. A joke. And it wasn't real blackmail. We didn't have to give him money. Only ... only do things for him.'

'That's right,' Abby agreed, clearly also trying to impress Mair with Freddy's still hard to define virtues. 'What was it he used to say? That he was just helping us shed our middle-class hang-ups.' There was something of nostalgia in her voice, but, again, it was difficult to decide whether the sentiment was natural or feigned.

'And you believed him about giving you the photos and the negs at the end of term?' said Mair soberly.

'Yes. And so did Kate, didn't you, Kate?'

'Sure. And, anyway, what else could we do about them?'

'I've told you what you should have done about them,' Mair replied in a prissily reproving way.

'Well, we didn't take your advice, did we? In any case, you had a lot of fun with Freddy too.'

'Not after he'd tricked you into posing for dirty pictures at the end of last term.'

'Only because you were fazed about not being included,' Kate insisted – quite accurately as it happened.

'That's crap,' answered Mair, but knowing it was true.

'Oh, for God's sake, let's stop the bitching,' said Abby. 'Freddy played one dirty trick on Kate and me, and made us pay for it in ... in different ways. But we didn't hate him for it. I mean, we wouldn't have done him any harm, would we, Kate?' She looked pointedly at the girl on the bed as she completed: 'Not on purpose. Not at all really.'

'Of course not,' Kate replied.

There was an uneasy silence for a moment – as if a more specific and important denial needing making: but it wasn't.

It was Kate again who said: 'Can we find out if Freddy told Josephine Oswald about Saturday night?'

'Only if anyone knows a good medium,' said Abby with a snigger, and producing a shocked look from Mair who continued: 'Look, she couldn't have been there, could she? Even if she'd wanted to be, which she would have, of course. She was picked up every Saturday by her awful father, and taken home. I don't think Freddy would have told her about it, knowing she'd fret because she'd have needed to be there with him, not because she'd have enjoyed it. And he wouldn't have wanted her there, in any case. No way. He never let her in on things like that. She was his weekday worker mouse. He called her that to her face. It used to make her purr every time.'

'Mice don't purr,' Mair corrected, gently and painfully blowing into some fresh tissues.

'Well, that's still what she did.'

'So why didn't he call her his worker pussy?' asked Mair, the word 'pussy'

236

emerging through her blocked nose as 'puddy'.

'Because she looks more like a mouse than a cat. And being called his pussy would have made her blush all over. Anyway, he never asked her to the fun things, so it stands to reason he wouldn't have told her about this one.'

'That doesn't make sense. How could she have minded if she didn't–'

'It doesn't bother me if she knew a rave was happening,' Kate interrupted Mair's further pedantry. 'But it bothers me like hell if she knew *where* it was happening.' She pulled her legs up under her on the bed as she went on: 'It was in my house, for God's sake.' The Unwin home was an isolated, modernized farmhouse in unspoiled country on the Gower Peninsula, west of Swansea. 'Daddy would really freak out if he knew I'd had seventy kids to a rave in our barn. And there'd have been a lot more of them, too, if it hadn't been for the snow.'

'And with only three others from here, in the end?' Mair asked.

'Yes, well, you know Freddy didn't like too many from the college at his raves,' Abby put in. 'He said they were meant to spread things wider. A lot of the kids this time were at the last one Kate and I were at. In Caerphilly, after New Year. He gave out the venue for this one then.'

'Worse luck,' moaned Kate. Allowing her house to be used had been one of the bigger 'favours' she had done Freddy.

'But this was much better than Caerphilly,' Abby announced.

'Except with that girl passing out—'

'A girl passed out?' Mair cut in on Kate.

'No, sort of fainted. Didn't last,' Abby corrected quickly. 'Isn't that right, Kate?'

'Yeah.' Except the immediate response had sounded uncertain before the putative hostess of the weekend's main event continued: 'But that's not what everybody thought when it happened. Thank God she didn't go into a coma. Kids on ecstasy have done that, and died sometimes.'

'Well, she didn't, did she?'

'Was everybody on ecstasy?' asked Mair. She was becoming less and less envious at having missed what might have been the most fun party of the year, since it might yet turn out to have been the most notorious one instead. The day before, though, she'd still been too low to have been interested in asking for the details of what had happened – which matched with the time when the

238

others had been unusually diffident about supplying them in any case.

'A lot were on ecstasy. All those who weren't on something else,' said Kate dismissively, her normal confidence returning. 'And like Abby said, the girl only fainted. She didn't have to be shipped to hospital in the glare of TV lights. Like it could have been here this morning with bloody Oswald. Come to think, was that just a pathetic try for attention? Because those TV reporters were here?'

'I don't think she'd have known about them in advance,' Mair offered.

'Maybe,' Kate agreed, but diffidently. 'Except I still wouldn't put it past her. Makes you think, too.' She paused. 'I mean, if it had been different at my house on Saturday. What if my parents in Cape Town had seen pictures of Abby and me on TV, being arrested, or something, after an acid party where someone had croaked? That would really have made their holiday, wouldn't it?' Abruptly, she lowered her head and began turning more pages of the magazine.

'But it didn't happen that way, so I'm not fretting. And you shouldn't either. We're in the clear,' said Abby, meaningfully emphasizing the last sentence. 'And if the police get the photos, we'll just say they were done for a joke.'

'So what if they find out Freddy was with you from Saturday afternoon till late Sunday morning.' Mair dampened Abby's affected euphoria.

'Which they won't. And no one's going to tell them, either,' Kate insisted, looking up. 'I've talked to the three from here. They haven't told the police they saw Freddy at the weekend, and I'm positive that'll go for anyone else who was there. Nobody wants to be involved with anything Freddy was doing since he left here Saturday. Not any more than we do.' She quickly lowered her gaze again to hide her sudden, inexplicable feeling of shame over her last words – the more so because she'd been telling the truth.

Mair sensed that the glamour of being one of Freddy's girls had quickly evaporated for the other two after Freddy's death. For her, it had done so long before that, though for most of the previous term she'd been just as crazy about him as the others. And she had to admit to herself that Abby could have been right about that other eventful weekend when she hadn't been with them.

It had been because of her mother's birthday. If she had been at Abby's house then, she knew she just could have been talked into the drugs session – and the porno pictures Freddy had taken afterwards. It would have depended entirely on how persuasive he'd been. And Freddy had been more persuasive than anyone else, she had known in her whole life. It was only later she had realized that he had been more cruel than anyone else, too.

What the others had done that weekend had sounded to Mair like a glorious, soul-free party when they told her about it afterwards. At the time, she had regretted not being there. It was when Freddy had come the heavy with the photographs that Mair had seen through him, and she certainly hadn't bought the idea that he was just helping Kate and Abby to shed their hang-ups. Ever since, she'd been nearly certain that Freddy was going to make them pose for more pictures – that he was aiming to enter the pornographic picture trade. She still wasn't sure that this hadn't come up at the weekend just passed, and if it had, what Kate and Abby might have done about it.

'And kids who came to the rave can't be mixed up in Freddy's death, because everybody except you two left before him?' Mair continued now.

'That's right. And he was OK when he left us too,' Kate responded, with unconcealed eagerness. 'He had to get the sound system back by noon. He left in time for that, and that's the last we saw of him.'

'So I don't know why you didn't come clean and tell the police he was with you till Sunday morning. There's really nothing to hide,' Mair argued.

'And have to say what we were doing with him Saturday afternoon? Like buying magic mushrooms,' said Kate. 'And lifting jewellery from a house in Llanelli on the way back. That'd sound marvellous, wouldn't it?'

'But you wouldn't have had to say anything like that.'

'Of course we wouldn't.' It was Abby who was answering Mair's point. 'But it could have complicated things, making up what we did do. So we decided it was better saying nothing.'

There was another brief silence until Mair asked: 'Did the burglary take long?'

'Five minutes,' said Abby. 'Like always, Freddy had the front-door key, and the alarm code, and he knew exactly where the control box was. We all went up to the bed-

242

room. He took just pearls again. We had to choose them for him. It was dead easy. Easier than the last time you were with us.'

Mair would have preferred not to be reminded that there had been a time when she had taken part in similar escapades – and enjoyed the thrill. 'You just took more pearls?' she asked, implying either failure or disappointment.

'Because they're harder to trace than other things,' Kate replied defensively. 'Freddy was shopping to order this time, too. He knew there'd be three sets of pearls to choose from. That's why he wanted us there. To make sure he was taking the right ones. They were worth twenty thousand, and he was going to get six thousand for them. Well, that's what he said.'

'If he had time to get rid of them,' said Abby, then bit her lip.

'Well, if he didn't, whoever killed him got them probably,' Kate offered with a frown.

'And that could be why he was murdered, couldn't it?' said Mair.

'That's what we think,' Abby answered promptly, her eyes on Kate.

Mair was staring in the same direction. 'And did Freddy say any more about nicking something of your mother's, Kate?'

'He had a look at what was on offer.' The reply came in a matter-of-fact voice. 'What she hadn't taken to South Africa. He said he'd go halves with me on a really naff necklace Mummy never wears, and probably wouldn't notice she'd lost for years. But I wasn't sure.'

'But I told you before, you'd have been daft to let him take anything of hers,' Mair insisted.

'Why? It'd be replaced by the insurance, wouldn't it? Anyway, it won't happen now, will it?'

'So how much did Freddy charge for a party ticket?' Mair asked next, changing the subject.

'Twenty-five for a single,' Abby supplied. 'No reduction for doubles, but with cola, burgers and one reefer included. Other stuff extra.' They all knew that the extras on offer were hard drugs.

'Use of the barn loft was free as well,' Abby put in with a smirk.

'So with the extras he'd have had well over two thousand on him in cash?' Mair had done a quick calculation.

Kate shrugged. 'Most likely. I think he needed it for something Sunday afternoon. And he'd had to pay more for the mushrooms than he expected on Saturday.'

'Some of the kids must have known he was loaded,' Mair commented. 'I still think the police should be told about the rave.'

'Well, what you think and what's going to happen don't match, do they? Like, otherwise, all of us could go to gaol. And I mean all of us. Understood?' said Kate, far more aggressive than before, and making her words a threat not an order.

Mair hesitated. 'Fine with me,' she said, regretting that her earlier involvement with some of Freddy's activities put her at the mercy of the other two.

'So nobody tells the police anything,' Kate went on. 'The rave had nothing to do with Freddy's murder. It couldn't have. But if it gets out he was at my house, we're in trouble.'

Mair nodded, and wiped her nose again.

Kate looked wide-eyed at Abby, then went back to her magazine. They'd achieved what they'd planned.

Except, at that same moment, some other, more public-spirited citizen was telling the police quite a lot about the event they were so keen to forget.

14

'This picture was taken without my consent,' insisted Ifor Jenkin, with stolid belligerence, and as though he had thus absolved himself from the necessity of further interpolation. The photograph Parry had given him was still in his hand. He was grasping it in a way that suggested he wasn't going to let it go again either – although Parry had already cautioned that the police held other copies.

'Or, presumably, the consent of the person with you, Mr Jenkin,' the chief inspector commented rather than enquired.

'Of course.'

'Unfortunately, consent isn't usually needed when it comes to taking photos, sir.' It was Lloyd who had responded this time – affably, and with sympathy in his tone.

'Well, it ought to be. It's a ... a flay ... flagrant invasion of privacy.'

'Quite so, Mr Jenkin,' Parry agreed. 'But you confirm it was taken in Oscar's?' he continued. 'Two of our officers think they recognize the decor.' Gomer Lloyd being one of them.

'I suppose so ... yes, it was taken there.'

It was two fifteen. The three men were in Jenkin's room, seated around the fireplace. The maths tutor had been there reading when the two policemen had entered a few minutes before this.

'And you feel strongly that, in certain circumstances, this photo could damage your career, sir?' the sergeant questioned, conscious that he sounded like a health warning on a packet of cigarettes. He and Parry were both in chairs half facing Jenkin.

'You could go a ... a bloody sight further than that. In any circumstances it could lose me my job at Modlen College.'

Parry cleared his throat. 'Because it suggests...'

'That I'm gay,' Jenkin supplied abruptly on the inspector's purposeful hesitancy. 'Something that wouldn't and shouldn't bother most people, but it's guaranteed to send my present employer into a fit of ... of bluestocking prejudice and ... and narrow-minded disapproval.'

'Dr Newsom-Pugh doesn't employ members of the gay community, sir?'

Jenkin exhaled breath noisily. 'Or approve

247

of them, either. And that goes for his impeccably Aryan wife as well. Has he seen the photo?'

'No, sir.'

'So is there any reason why you have to show it to him?'

'None at all that I can think of, Mr Jenkin,' said Parry. 'At the moment, it's a piece of possible police evidence in a murder enquiry.'

'So it stays confidential?'

'It remains as possible evidence while it can be called for in court, sir. If it isn't called for, we return it to the owner, or his or her lawful heir. In this case, that'll be Mr Gibbon's mother.'

'Why won't it be given to me? I've paid for it. Through the nose. And why would it be used in court?'

'Whether it is or not would be up to the prosecuting counsel, sir. Also on the identity of the person being tried, I expect,' the speaker completed judiciously.

'For murdering Gibbon, you mean? Well, that's not going to be me, I can tell you that. I hated his guts, with good reason, but I had nothing to do with his death. Couldn't have. I've told you already, I didn't get back here till nine on Monday morning.'

'We've explained where the photo was found, sir.' said Lloyd. 'Can you tell us why it was in Mr Gibbon's possession, and what he was doing with it?'

'Yes, I certainly can. The bastard took it himself. In Oscar's, with one of his fancy cloak-and-dagger cameras. And what he was doing with it was blackmailing me.'

'He used it to extort money from you? Is that what you meant when you said you'd paid through the nose for it?'

'I paid him a thousand pounds for that picture. That was just before Christmas. He said he'd given me all the prints, as well as the negative, the bloody liar. And that's why this is legally mine, and any prints you've made from it.'

'I take your point, Mr Jenkin,' Parry said, 'but it might be hard for you to prove ownership. I don't suppose he gave you a receipt for your money.'

'Well, what do you think?' Then, in response to Parry's still expectantly raised eyebrows he added: 'No, of course he didn't give me a receipt.'

'I see, sir. Well, I'm afraid, in any case, whoever owns the photo, for the foreseeable future it's Crown evidence.'

'You'd have done better to go to the police

249

when he first threatened you, sir,' put in Lloyd.

'Oh yes, and lost my job as a result? He told me if I went to the police he'd deny everything, and push a copy of the photo under the Newsom-Pughs' door.'

'So this particular job was that important to you, sir?' asked Parry.

'Yes. Isn't your job important to you, Chief Inspector?' The reply had been quite spirited, but the speaker's general de-meanour was evidently becoming too deflated to match the forced pugnacity of the words.

Parry smiled and leaned forward in his chair. 'If you lost your job here, would you have that much difficulty finding another?' he pressed with good reason, while ignoring the other's question.

The tutor was silent for several seconds. He'd put the photograph on the table beside him, and was rolling the hairs of his beard around the forefinger of his left hand. 'There are reasons why I want to stay on at Modlen College,' he answered finally, in a quiet voice. 'It ... it suits me.'

'The ... the young man with you in the picture, sir,' asked Lloyd. 'Would that be Mr Lawrence Pritchard, the one with the flat in Rumney?'

'That's Larry, yes. And he was nineteen this month,' Jenkin responded, swiftly this time – and protectively. He had understood the begged question lurking behind the expression 'young man'.

'And that's the same Lawrence Pritchard who was a catering-trade student, working in the college kitchens from the beginning of last year through to December, sir?'

The tutor looked surprised. 'Off and on, yes. He came on government-sponsored work experience at the start. Then, after the summer, he got a regular place at a catering college.'

'And got day release from them to go on coming here till Christmas, sir? Is that how it worked out?'

'That's right. He's doing the same now at a Cardiff hotel.'

'Is that so, sir? Seems as if he's doing well.' The sergeant beamed like a benevolent uncle expressing pleasure at the progress of a young family member.

'He is. And deserves to. How did you find out he'd worked here?'

'Oh, just through college records, sir. We're going over the whole staff list for the last two years.' Lloyd made a note as he went on. 'So Larry would have been seven-teen when you first came across him?' he commented, fixing a guileless gaze on Jenkin.

'When he came here, you mean? I suppose he would have been. For a few weeks. Before his eighteenth birthday. I didn't ... I didn't actually speak to him till the summer term. Gave him a lift up the hill one day, on the pillion, from the bus stop in the village,' he added carefully.

'But you became friends from then on? So when did Mr Gibbon take the picture, sir?'

'In November.'

'And did he try to blackmail Larry as well?'

'Not so far as I know... No, I'm sure he didn't.'

'Or Larry would have told you, I expect,' said Parry, taking over the questioning again. 'And you've been here two years now, Mr Jenkin. Your previous post was at a comprehensive school in North Wales. Can you tell us why you left there?'

Jenkin hesitated. 'The usual reason. The job here was better paid.'

'Indeed? So you didn't leave because of a court case involving you and some youths at a swimming pool?' He raised his hand to stem the other's burgeoning protest. 'Perhaps this will refresh your memory.' He nodded at Lloyd, who passed Jenkin a photocopy of the local-paper cutting.

A miserable Jenkin looked at the piece without reading it – or needing to. 'You got this from Gibbon's box too?'

'Yes. That was part of the blackmail, was it? He threatened to show it to Dr Newsom-Pugh as well as the photo?'

The tutor crumpled the paper into a ball, then, leaning forward, he pressed his tightly clasped hands between his knees and continued speaking with his head bent. 'I never did what I was accused of in court. It was a fit-up. The magistrates knew it too. There were two charges made against me. The serious one was dismissed for lack of evidence, and I was only made to pay a small fine over the lesser one.'

'And put on six months' probation, sir,' Parry added lightly, as though this was of little consequence.

'Yes. But both charges should have been dismissed. Some boys ganged up on me. They'd dreamed up a story between them. It was malicious. It's they who should have been prosecuted.'

'Why weren't they, I wonder, sir?'

'Because of their ages, probably. They'd conspired to get me because they didn't like me. Because I'd failed two of them in mock exams. My headmaster was very sympathetic, and really ashamed at what the boys had done to me, though he couldn't say so openly. Proceedings should have been taken against them.'

'Knowing their actions were malicious, sir, you didn't think of going to appeal, then bringing proceedings against the boys yourself?' asked Lloyd.

'Of course I did. But I was advised not to. By my lawyer. He said it'd only prolong the ordeal, and the publicity, with no ... no guaranteed result. Even though I was innocent, you can't really win in the kind of situation I'd been forced into, can you?' Jenkin swallowed, then looked up at both policemen, almost furtively, his expression more beseeching than questioning before he dropped his gaze again.

'Was there a lot of publicity, sir?'

'Only in the local paper. Nothing beyond. But that was bad enough. Still, nobody down here, for instance, knew what had happened to me. If I'd sued the boys, my lawyer was sure the case would have got in the London papers, making the whole thing much worse for me if I'd lost.'

'Probably good advice, sir,' put in Parry, and meaning it.

'I had to resign my job, of course. My headmaster explained he'd have had no alternative but to dismiss me otherwise. In any case, I couldn't have faced going on there. The head gave me a reference, though, saying I was good at my work.'

'Without mentioning the ... the court proceedings, sir?' Lloyd questioned, and unable quite to hide the surprise in his voice.

'Yes. Because he believed I was innocent.' Earlier, the speaker had seemed close to despair, but now he was rallying. 'That was how I got the job here. Through that reference and the ones from my two earlier posts. And I'm safe here ... except ... except it'd be difficult if I had to leave. You see, the head of my last school retired last year. If I had to change jobs, checks might be made through his successor. The new head, or more likely some admin secretary, could rake up the old stuff – about the court proceedings. It could be on file at the school still. And yet I never did anything to those boys.'

'We understand, sir,' said Parry. 'And, as

you mentioned, you've felt safe here. That was despite the fact Freddy Gibbon had been blackmailing you?'

'I've felt safe since he stopped blackmailing me, yes. I mean, that was all over. I'd paid him.'

'To be precise, you told us you'd paid him for the photo, sir. What about the press report?'

'Oh, of course, it was all one. He approached me with both things. I gave him the thousand pounds in exchange for all his copies of the press report, plus the negative and the copies of the picture. He swore he hadn't kept any copies of either.'

'But we all know now he had, sir, don't we?' said Lloyd in what sounded like a genuinely shocked tone of voice.

'So he was a liar,' Jenkin exploded, moving about in his seat.

'Blackmailers often are, I'm afraid, Mr Jenkin,' Parry observed levelly. 'They're also noted for not keeping their word. So he hadn't approached you again, sir, recently, very recently, demanding more money?'

'Certainly not.'

'But his asking you whether you were going to Oscar's again, on Saturday, in the car park, that doesn't sound as if he regarded the business as closed. On the contrary–'

'I've said already, whoever told you about that was lying as well. And Gibbon wasn't asking me for more money either. I may have been bloody stupid, but I ... I trusted him.'

Parry leaned forward in his chair. 'If we find out later he did ask you for more money, I should warn you, you'd be better off in the long run telling us now, sir. A lot better off.'

'And I tell you, he didn't. So far as I was concerned, the whole dirty business was over. So he kept those copies because he was a swine, a liar and ... and a cheat. But I wasn't to know that, was I?' He looked helplessly from Parry to Lloyd before going on. 'All right, so I was being naive. Maybe he planned to come after me again with the picture or the report ... or both. But if he had, then ... then I swear I'd have gone to the police straightaway.'

'Although you didn't before, sir.'

'No, but I nearly did, and I would have next time. If there'd been a next time. But there wasn't, I swear to God there wasn't. And I swear I never did anything to hurt Gibbon physically. I had no reason to, did I?

I keep telling you, for me it was all over and done with.'

'Yes, you've made that quite clear, sir,' Parry completed, aware that he needed more evidence if he was going to arrest Jenkin for the murder of Freddy Gibbon.

'It was worth the extra for the blue, wasn't it, Doreen?' asked Vi Mills, wife of the landlord of the Prince of Wales at Brynglas, but her words were well short of conclusive.

'Oh yes, every time, love. It'll go perfect with the white blouse and hat. You'll look smashing,' Doreen Fowler, barmaid at Brynglas's premier pub (there being *one* other), replied with the support she knew her companion badly needed. 'Back to David Morgan's for those shoes, then, is it?'

'Oh, I'm still not sure.'

'I am. And Eddy said to go the whole hog. No stinting.' The two turned left out of Marks & Spencer into crowded Queen Street, part of Cardiff's throbbing pedestrianized precinct. They were stepping carefully, although there was little snow or ice left on the treated surface.

Vi seldom needed to shop for clothes in Cardiff – which is another way of saying she seldom bought new clothes. But there were family nuptials pending in April, and Eddy, her husband, had said she should get a complete new rig-out. He had sent thirty-three-year-old Doreen with her because he trusted her taste – which was livelier than Vi's – as surely as he mistrusted his own, at least when it came to choosing anything for his wife to wear. He only wished he had ever known what was wrong for her before she bought it: so did Vi.

Caroline, Eddy's niece, was marrying a boy from a well-to-do Clifton family – Clifton being what Vi called the tonier part of Bristol. Both the girl and her prospective husband were university graduates, and both had good jobs in industry. It'd be a well-dressed 'do' – church service with choir, and the reception in the best hotel in Milford Haven, where the bride's parents lived. This meant that the men in the family were expected to hire morning suits, which was fine with Eddy, because it put everyone on a par. When it came to the women, though, the bride's mother, Eddy's sister, was always dressed to kill, whatever the occasion (she'd married money to start with, never letting you forget it either, according to Vi), and Eddy was determined

259

she shouldn't be ashamed of her sister-in-law – or her brother, who she usually referred to grandly as being 'in brewing', as though he was on the board of Brain's, not just running one of their pubs.

'The shoes were very nice, of course. Ever so comfy too, as soon as I put them on. Almost like they were made for me,' Vi agreed grudgingly, as they went through the automatic doors of the wide, modern arcade of St David's Centre. This would lead them down to David Morgan's department store, below the covered market in The Hayes. 'And you're sure they'll go all right with the suit?'

'Better than anything else we've seen. Far better.' Surreptitiously, Doreen glanced at the time.

They had been in Cardiff for nearly three hours, buying the blouse and hat at C&A, and the light wool suit and some underwear at M&S. Vi had grudgingly agreed on the unbudgeted undies to be on the safe side, in case, as Doreen had cautioned, she had an accident or had to see a doctor in Milford Haven: Vi was even keener on propriety than she was on thrift. Allowing another half-hour to buy the shoes, and get back to Eddy's VW, where they had left it in the

Westgate Street car park, Doreen reckoned she wouldn't be home till five, and she had a still-to-be-confirmed blind date at six. She was divorced, childless, and lived with her mother in Bridgend.

Vi was hesitating before the window of Salisbury's handbag and shoe shop as they passed it, eyeing a pair of medium-heel court shoes similar to those she had tried on at Morgan's, but five pounds cheaper. 'Doreen, you don't think–'

'Look, that's him!' Doreen cried suddenly, clutching Vi's arm, and single-mindedly propelling her down the centre of the fairly crowded main aisle.

'Who?' Vi questioned, still casting a querulous eye back at the shoes, while also being careful to protect the single bag Doreen had assigned her to carry. It had the precious white hat in it.

'That tall, hunky dreamboat who met Freddy Gibbon in the bar. The one I've had to describe for the police.'

'Go on? Where is he?'

'Just ahead. With a redheaded boy in a leather jacket. There they are, but they're moving ever so fast. He's in the camel-hair overcoat – see him?' Doreen, who had eyes for nobody else, nodded over the heads of the people. 'But we'll never catch them at this rate.'

'Well, I still can't see him. And what are we going to say if we do catch him?' Vi was doing her best to keep up the pace, but failing dismally.

'We'll say who we are, and tell him the police would like to talk to him.'

'Oh, I don't think we should do that. Say who we are.' Self-preservation ranked even higher than the proprieties and thrift in Vi's well-conducted, ordered life. Something told her now that giving her name to a big man wanted by the police might be asking for trouble. 'Why don't we just see where they go?'

'And lose them after? No, no, that'd be silly.'

'But you don't know what he might have been up to. Perhaps if we see a policeman we could–'

'Don't be daft, he's straight as a die, and ritzy with it. He'll want to help the authorities all right, I know he will, as soon as he's told.' The last time Doreen had seen this paragon, she'd been furious with herself for not getting his name at least. That was when they'd been chatting over the bar at the Prince of Wales – and when he'd

262

unguardedly mentioned his *ex*-wife, which for Doreen was like being given a handful of free National Lottery tickets with the first winning number guaranteed.

'Well, tell you what, give me the other bags, and you run on and catch him, if you want,' said Vi, too exhausted to carry on at the rate they were going.

'Right. Take the bag with the suit. If I don't catch him, I'll see you outside Morgan's main entrance.' Doreen thrust the larger of two bags into Vi's arms, and hurried on ahead.

Even at the speed she was now moving, it was unlikely Doreen would have caught the couple had they not stopped on the pavement, in the open air, a few yards beyond the arcade exit. As she came close to them, she hesitated for a moment, tidying her hair, collecting her breath, and deciding what she should say. It was then that she overheard a snippet of what the younger man was saying – pleading with his companion over something, and using his first name.

'Excuse me for interrupting,' said Doreen, addressing her hero over the other's shoulder, 'but I saw you in Brynglas with Freddy Gibbon–'

It was the bespectacled runt in the bomber jacket who reacted first. He had rounded, terror-stricken, to confront Doreen. Then in an almost reflex, and superbly coordinated, triple movement, he swung the crash helmet he was carrying at her head, thrust his knee hard into the other man's groin, and sprinted off at lightning speed.

The big man, taken more by surprise than even Doreen had been, was left breathless, doubled up with pain, and with watering eyes registering total outrage and astonishment.

Doreen had jumped backwards, and while her prompt defensive movement had saved her from being hit by the helmet, it had propelled her into Vi who had just come puffing up resolutely behind her.

Vi had even been at the point of waving to the man she realized she also knew, when she had needed to move back sharply to avoid collision with the retreating Doreen. In the process, she stepped straight on to a slither of hard ice.

So it was Vi who fell first, and, reaching out for help, brought Doreen down on top of her – at the same moment as a piercing screech of brakes emanated from very close by.

'Oh, my white hat!' cried the despairing

Vi, aware she was sitting on that prized object, and for the moment oblivious to the pain in her coccyx. It was in the ambulance later she came to wish fervently that she'd been wearing her new undies already.

15

Shortly after leaving the maths tutor, Parry and Lloyd were in the incident room, digesting two important pieces of fresh information. On the face of it, neither of the new developments did anything to strengthen the case they were building against Jenkin – although they did nothing to weaken it either.

'This Len Patel, he runs a one-man disco sale-and-hire outfit in Swansea, sir,' DC Alison Pope was explaining. She was seated with the two men at one of the small tables. 'He saw Freddy Gibbon's picture and rang the local police.'

'When was this?' asked Parry.

'He first saw the picture last night on the telly, but only for a sec. He didn't make the call till noon today. That was after he'd seen the picture again, in the *Western Mail*. Said he needed another look to be sure it was who he thought it was, sir.'

'And he's certain now?'

'Yes, sir. He's been interviewed by Swansea CID, and I've just talked to him on the phone. Freddy was in his shop at one thirty Saturday afternoon. He hired two turntables, a mixing board, a tape deck, some speakers, laser lights and a load of recorded music. Said it was for a private disco he was running that night at a house on the Gower.'

'He gave an address for the party?'

'Afraid not, sir. Said he'd forgotten the name of the house, but knew how to get there.'

'Except Freddy must have given this Len Patel an address of some kind? People don't hire out equipment without one, surely?'

'That's right, sir. He said he lived in Hereford, and put his mother's address on the hire form. It was the same as the address on his driving licence, of course. Mr Patel asked to see that.'

'Did he bring the disco stuff back after the party?'

'Yes, sir. Just after noon Sunday morning. In good working order. He'd had to leave a deposit of six hundred pounds, in cash, because it was a last-minute booking. But he got that back in full. He'd paid the hire fee in cash as well, in advance.'

'How much was that?'

'Two hundred and twelve pounds, sir. I've checked the addresses of all the kids in the college. Only one actually lives on the Gower. That's Kate Unwin, who told us she went home for the weekend. Abby Kennedy went with her. So if the disco was in one of the students' houses it was most probably Kate Unwin's.'

'So things are building up fast for Miss Unwin and Miss Kennedy, aren't they?' Parry commented.

'That's right, sir, what with the photographs as well. And remember Miss Unwin's car was parked Sunday night next to the space Freddy's car was in the next morning.'

'You haven't approached her yet, or Abby Kennedy?'

'No, sir. Thought you should know about the disco first.'

'Right, we'll decide who should see the girls shortly. But what's this about Freddy having a mobile?' This had been the second item of information. 'Nobody here knew he had one?'

'No, sir. Not officially, anyway. They're forbidden for students at the college, so he'd have kept it out of sight,' DC Pope replied, adding: 'But it's another Brownie point for Mr Patel. He noticed a mobile lying on the front passenger seat of Freddy's estate when they were loading up on Saturday. Since he wasn't a hundred per cent happy about Freddy–'

'He said that?' Parry interrupted.

'Yes, sir.' The detective constable looked up from her notes, 'He wasn't comfy with not knowing where the disco was happening.'

'But not uncomfy enough to refuse a fat deposit and hire fee?'

'That's about it, sir.'

'Can't blame him there, boss,' said Lloyd. 'Lot of competition in the disco-hire business.'

'Mr Patel had already written down Freddy's car number, and when he wasn't looking, he memorized the number of the phone as well. It was labelled on the front. The mobile's registered in Freddy's name, we've checked. He's had it since last October.'

'Have you asked for a log of his calls over the weekend, in and out?'

'Yes, sir, and where he was when he made and received them. The phone company know he's been killed. They're treating it as a priority. We should have all the information within an hour.'

'Good. When we've got it, ask them for the same data going back to the time he got the mobile. We'll be happy to wait longer for that, but not too much longer,' Parry completed, with a grin.

'Will do, sir.' DC Pope gathered her papers.

'Oh, hang on, Alison. Did you do the identification with Mrs Gibbon?'

'Yes, sir. She didn't come here after all. Not after I explained we've sent a lot of her son's things to forensic. She's coming again next week, with her car, to take back what's available then.'

'But you showed her the pictures of the jewellery?'

'Yes, sir. None of it was hers, and she'd never seen any of it before.'

'As we'd guessed. So she didn't see Dr Newsom-Pugh either?'

'No, sir. She talked to him from the hospital, and the bursar too, Miss Thomas. It was about the fees for the rest of this term. They're being waived. That pleased

Mrs Gibbon a lot.'

'And you didn't ask her about Freddy's mobile?'

'Afraid not, sir. It was before we'd heard from Mr Patel. I left her at the undertakers. Shall I call her at home and ask if Freddy left any old mobile accounts in his room there?'

'Good idea, yes. It's not likely though. I went over the room yesterday. It was like a shearing shed. She told me he hardly ever used the place. Well, I don't see how he could have done. There were mounds of wool everywhere, and hardly anything of his. One or two bits of old clothing in the wardrobe and the chest of drawers, plus a few books, but no personal papers.' He paused. 'So she went to the undertakers? You'd told her they can't release the body yet, had you?'

'Yes, sir. She wanted to make the arrangements for when they can. She wants the body cremated in Cardiff, not taken to Aberbach or Hereford. Funny that, in a way. She ... she seemed quite cheerful. In the circumstances. Nice lady, I thought.' The detective constable got up, and, with her usual overlong strides, moved off in the direction of her desk at the far end of the room.

'So what do you reckon on the two girls,

boss?' Lloyd asked, producing a fresh tube of peppermints.

'That they were with him Saturday night at the disco, whether or not it was at the Unwin house, and that so far they've just been too scared to tell us, probably.' Parry sniffed. 'I could be wrong, but I have the feeling it doesn't go much deeper than that with those two.'

'And not nearly as deep as it goes with Mr Jenkin,' the sergeant offered.

Parry nodded. 'Yes, he's a different kettle of fish. We know now he had more than enough motive to murder Freddy Gibbon, and probably enough opportunity as well. As to means and method, we're in the dark, of course. Pity we can't get a more exact description of the weapon used for those stab wounds.'

'Well the view now is that it was a thin steel rod with a smooth *or* lightly serrated edge, and a pointed end, boss. So it could have belonged to a butcher, a plumber, a doctor – well, to almost anyone, couldn't it?'

'Including a motorcyclist? Something from his tool kit?'

'Except even if it was, it doesn't get us that much further with Mr Jenkin, or the method of murder, does it, boss? We'll have his tool kit examined all the same,' Lloyd added, making a note while sucking hard on his peppermint.

A more formal report had arrived at lunchtime from the pathologist. It had shown that the two-inch stab wounds had penetrated the fatty subcutaneous area at a downward angle of only fifteen degrees from the surface, which was why they hadn't caused damage to any organs: Gibbon had been well fleshed in most areas. The report continued that he had died of causes still undetermined, but that he had been dead for a minimum of two hours before he had been dropped into the basement area of the college. No corresponding maximum time limit had been offered, although the contents of his stomach showed that he had consumed buttered toast and raspberry jam, followed by chocolate cake, approximately three hours before expiring. Thus, as was often the case a more accurate time of death could be determined if, in turn, it could be established when he'd had that last meal. Tests on his mucus membrane had indicated that he had probably inhaled a quantity of heroin approximately an hour before death.

Parry rubbed the skin hard above his right

eyebrow. 'I don't believe those stab wounds are irrelevant to the murder. They obviously didn't cause his death, but they must have been involved in some way.'

'Bit extreme to have been love blows of some kind, boss?'

Parry grinned. 'The same thought occurred to me, Gomer. I mean, they must have caused a fair amount of bleeding at the time, rather than pain. And they could hardly have been accidental, could they?'

'You mean, like he could have been fooling around with other people he'd been drugging with, boss?'

'It's possible, I suppose. Assuming he wasn't ... chasing the dragon on his own. That's what people who smoke heroin call it, don't they?'

'That's right, boss. And they're not usually serious heroin addicts. Well, not at that stage. More likely to be weekend trippers. When they get serious they inject, and the report says there were no needle marks on his body.'

'Of course, this is the first evidence we've had that Gibbon was on drugs himself,' said Parry.

'And pushers don't usually indulge either, the bastards,' the sergeant replied bitterly.

His special detestation of drug dealers was well known.

'Which, like you said, Gomer, suggests he could still take it or leave it.'

'Hmm, heroin's serious stuff, boss.'

'I know. OK, let's forget drugs and the cause of death for a second. There's no doubt in my mind Freddy was still blackmailing Jenkin.'

'But Mr Jenkin isn't going to admit it, is he, boss?'

'No. And why should he, since it'd put him centre frame as the killer? But the way he was talking, he'd have done anything to stop his relationship with Larry Pritchard getting out.'

'Because of his job here.'

'That, and because of possible criminal charges. I'd say the liaison started when the boy was underage, and Freddy could have had proof of it. We need some digging on that one.'

'And on why Mr Jenkin left that last job, boss. If he was as innocent as he says–'

'Which he might not have been,' Parry cut in. 'Sounded as if the beaks had been ready to give him the benefit of the doubt over the worst of two charges, but not over the lesser one.'

'Fair enough, boss. But those boys probably were conspiring against him. And the reason his lawyer advised against suing them could have been in case it unearthed evidence that strengthened the second charge, or worse, did the same on the first one.'

'Meaning it could have unearthed more boys,' Parry agreed. 'Which was also the reason he didn't want to stay in the area. There's nothing yet to show Jenkin was ever involved with Freddy previous to here, is there?'

'In Aberbach? Don't think so. Easy enough to check on the records.'

'Easier still to do it on the spot, Gomer, and to check other things at the same time. What was the name of the boy who hanged himself?'

'Peter Absom, boss. Freddy Gibbon was at the same school.'

'Yes, and Absom was on drugs. Was he gay?'

'Two of his classmates told me they thought he was, yes, but it didn't come out at the inquest.'

'So let's find out if Jenkin had anything at all to do with the school, or Peter Absom. If he did, that means there's a possible connection with Freddy earlier than their meeting here.' Parry paused. 'I don't want to have Jenkin in for formal questioning yet. Not until there's enough evidence to nail him, assuming it exists.'

'You're pretty sure he did it, boss?'

'In all respects except one, Gomer.' Parry pressed his lips together before adding: 'And that is, would he have had the guts?'

'Like, if he was seriously provoked?' the sergeant countered.

'Agreed. But who can tell.' Parry sniffed. 'On his own admission, he was back in Cardiff Sunday evening. After that, young Larry's his sole alibi.'

'The lad looks timid from the photo, boss.'

'Timid, but I expect well briefed in what to say if questioned. We've got the address. I want to see him after we've talked to–'

'Sorry, sir.' Detective Sergeant Mary Norris had appeared suddenly, flushed with hurrying. 'I've just come back from the hospital, with Miss Strange. Mr Oswald, Josephine's father, he's here too. Arrived at the same time. We ran into the principal in the hall. They've gone into his study. Dr Newsom-Pugh has asked if you could join them, sir.'

'How's the girl?' Parry asked, getting up.

'Pretty well recovered, sir. Her mother's taken her home – in a private ambulance. And ... and she wasn't pregnant after all.'

'My daughter's a virgin. I could have told anyone that, without doctors or any so-called suicide note. And, by the way, the note in question was confidential. It was addressed to me and my wife. So I need to know why it's been read by half the South Wales police force, and the Lord knows who else. But we'll come to that after.'

The very Welsh, compact, florid Mostyn Oswald delivered words in sharp bursts, like machine-gun volleys. He took a breath while still fixing Parry in a stare that remained more grieved than simply angry. He was far from the father who the chief inspector had been prompted to describe earlier, on the basis of received reports, as too cautious to get his car out of a one-inch Brecon snowdrift. This character looked as if he could have shifted it out by manpower, single-handed, despite his modest height. His broad head was bald on top and shaven that way at the sides. While his face was hairless too, he had a boxer's crooked nose, and pointed ears set flat to his head. As he spoke, the heavy shoulders, and sometimes the bulging arms and fists, moved to punctuate his phrases. He sat well forward and bolt upright on the armless chair he had chosen, his trunk never touching its back, the buttons of his waistcoat and jacket straining for release.

'I'm afraid, sir, I can only–' Parry began

'Let me finish, will you, Mr ... Parry? I was going to say you don't have to take my word on Josephine being a virgin. The hospital doctor, gynaecologist, confirmed it an hour ago. Her present plight's been brought on partly by her vivid imagination, and partly through overindulgence by her parents. I see that today, where I'd not seen it before. She's lived an overprotected life. Never been exposed to the temptations commonplace to most young women these days. And till now, she's been none the worse for that. Brought up to fear God, and to respect her mother and her father, like the commandments bid us, and just like her brilliant older sister at her age. We should never have sent her away to school. I see that now, as well. Here she was mentally and physically open to the assaults of the devil, and no one ready to defend her.'

Dr Newsom-Pugh seemed to be erupting in his seat. 'I really must protest at that last remark, Mr Oswald,' he spluttered.

'No, he's quite right,' put in Miss Strange. 'I was responsible for Josephine's moral wellbeing. I should have twigged the extreme depth of her innocence. We can only be thankful that Freddy Gibbon did better than me, or anyone else in that respect, much as I disliked him.'

'What d'you mean?' demanded both the principal and Oswald in broken chorus, but concerted protest.

'I mean he obviously played her along. Made her think she was enjoying sex with him to the full, for instance.' She ignored the hiss of Oswald's breath as she went on. 'God knows what they did together, but it was nothing that impregnated her, or, it seems, even severed her hymen.'

'But it could have been something worse,' Oswald exploded, the gimlet eyes now fixed reproachfully on Newsom-Pugh. 'Something much worse. Something degenerate, disgusting and ... and unnatural.'

'I doubt if it was anything that really disgusted our sensitive virgin. If it had, she'd have turned away from it,' the history tutor returned with a beatific and disarming smile. 'You know, I think Gibbon probably did respect her moral hang-ups more than

279

you did, Mr Oswald, no doubt for his own selfish reasons. Pity, in a way, he didn't remove those hang-ups. She's obviously kept her innocence in a lot of contexts, although it might be more appropriate to call it her dangerous ignorance. There are plenty of young men who'd have taken more advantage of her, much more.'

'But how could–' Mr Oswald began.

'Please hear me out,' Miss Strange insisted in a voice that had briefly become as stentorian as his. 'From what I knew, and what I've been learning about Gibbon,' she continued more quietly, 'I didn't believe there was anything at all to commend him, the more so since we learned he allowed her access to ecstasy tablets. Well, I now think we've found one small, mitigating something. He used Josephine as he used others in his workforce, but he also humoured her, don't you see? I think she was excited about her phoney pregnancy. No doubt that was dreamed up through her missing a period for some other reason. Such things do happen. Or because she purposely forgot she'd had a period. That happens too. Gibbon probably had a plan to simulate the abortion. A harmless pill, I should think. Only the unexpected happened. He was killed. No fault of his, clearly, but that *really* left her unprotected. Hence today's outcome. But, mark this, I think the suicide attempt was genuine. She must have loved him madly.'

There was dead silence for several moments.

'Perhaps there's something in what you say, Miss Strange,' Oswald offered in the tone of a seer who'd not only met his match, but was ready to acknowledge as much. 'A good deal perhaps,' he added, any lingering reservation now gone from the voice. He looked at the principal again who was remaining curiously – if sensibly – silent. 'Josephine's not coming back here, I can tell you,' the girl's father now pledged, then turned to Parry. 'And if the police need to interview her again, it'll be in my presence, if it happens at all. I'm taking legal advice on that.'

'I don't think we'll need to see her again in the near future, sir,' the chief inspector replied, relying on it that the resourceful Mary Norris would already have gleaned all the information likely to be forthcoming from the girl. 'And over the ... the alleged suicide attempt, that'll be in the hands of the local health authority, of course.'

It was Miss Strange who offered: 'Could I

very respectfully suggest, Mr Oswald, that the next person to interview your really very talented and sensitive daughter should be an experienced counsellor, and not in the presence of anybody else? Josephine once told me you're a celebrated lay preacher. Stick to that, and your butcher's shop. I'm sure you're super at both callings. But do get her some sound professional advice.'

The woman's earnest entreaty had shifted Parry's thoughts back dramatically to where they'd been before the present interview had started. He had been wondering then who might possess a butcher's steel other than a butcher: now the question had become superfluous.

16

Emlyn Harries heaved himself from the water, at the same time twisting his body around, in an attempted macho flip, to land close beside Detective Sergeant Mary Norris on the pool edge – except that one of his hands slipped and he nearly ended up back in the pool. 'Whoops,' he uttered shamefacedly, and rubbing a hurt elbow. He took the opportunity that sympathy might betoken to shuffle himself even closer to her than he would have been before.

Mary Norris was seated overlooking the shallow end of the pool where she had perched herself a few seconds earlier. Like Harries, she was healthily exhausted, and, also like him, pleased that they continued to have the whole pool building to themselves. She could have gone straight through to the changing room before he'd had a chance to join her, but she hadn't – and not, she had to admit to herself, for any reason at all connected with her job.

'That's the modern crawl you do,' she said, her feet, like his, dangling in the tepid water. 'I've tried it. Too complicated. But you left me way behind, especially with that somersault turn you do.' They had both been doing unbroken, multiple lengths of the pool in silence, except for gasps of controlled breathing, and with the earnest dedication of fitness addicts.

'It's not a difficult stroke once you're used to it. The opposite really. The turn's a doddle, and quite showy with it,' he grinned. 'I learned both last year from a real pro in New Zealand. Ex-Olympic swimmer.' He reached for the towel behind him, and started to dry his hair – awkwardly, with one hand.

'Here, let me help you.'

'Thanks.' He dipped his head as she took the towel from him, and applied it to his hair, vigorously.

'Of course, I'd forgotten you were in New Zealand till Christmas,' she said. 'Sorry, that wasn't a hidden question. I'm off duty. There, that should do.' She gave him back the towel as she added. 'I shouldn't be here, not really, except I love swimming, and Miss Thomas said yesterday I was welcome to use the pool.'

'And why shouldn't you be here? Very few of the inmates ever come. In fairness, very few of them could at four forty on a weekday. I just have a free spot at this point every Tuesday. But the place will be just as empty this evening. Seems to me the pool's kept heated just so Dr Newsom-Pugh can take exercise as a private right, with me admitted as a special privilege. Or to check the water's clean enough for him.'

'And it's the only sport available?' she asked.

'No. There's ping pong, but the table's warped, and the rubber's coming off the bats. We concentrate here on work, not play. I think it salves the principal's conscience that swimming's on offer, but it wouldn't be if he weren't an aqua fanatic himself.' He smiled down at her, which gave him another chance to consider her figure, which he found altogether delectable. 'And why do you say you shouldn't be here?'

'I'd have thought that was obvious.' She shifted her body, but no further away from him, pulling at the bottom of her black, single-piece swimsuit. 'The college is the scene of a crime, and I'm on the investigating team. So no shop, please. Otherwise I'll have to leave, or start calling you sir.'

'One gets the idea from TV that detectives never go off duty till the murder's solved.'

She wrinkled her nose and watched her toes wiggling in the water. 'For sergeants and constables, that can be because of the money not the dedication. We get paid overtime, if the funds run to it, which they often don't. Not that ambitious officers wouldn't do it out of dedication when needed, of course,' she completed, with mock primness.

'Like the best kind of teachers. And obviously you're ... dedicated.'

'Oh, but ambitious as well. I intend to rise

to dizzy heights in the force.'

'But right now the overtime helps?'

'That's right. But I finished today at four – well, half past, after briefing my opposite number on the next relief. We do have normal knocking-off times like everybody else.'

'Oh well, illusions are made to be shattered,' the English tutor chuckled. 'Seriously, if money's short–'

'It always is these days in the police force. Speak to your Member of Parliament and your local councillor about it,' she interrupted in a serious voice.

'I will. I was going to say, if money's short, it must be tempting to cut corners. I mean, do the police high-ups declare a case closed if it goes on too long without a ... a solution?'

'I'm not a police high-up, so I wouldn't know,' she replied carefully, 'but we don't give up easily, and unsolved cases are never closed. They're just ... unsolved.'

'Quite right too.' He nodded his approval. 'By the way, I heard on the grapevine that Gibbon didn't die here after all. Must say, it didn't look that way when I first saw the body. Straight case of death through a very nasty fall from a very great height. But then it was thought to be suicide, whereas now it's murder.' He began doing arm exercises to keep his damaged elbow supple as he ended: 'And I'm not fishing for confidential information. Couldn't care less really.'

'You mean about how he died? That it was murder?'

He stopped doing the exercises, but raised one straight leg, then, frowning, splashed it gently back into the water. 'No, not quite that. I meant, if he wasn't killed at Modlen College, his death wasn't anything to do with us. And since he appeared to have a pretty active life outside the realms of academia, and none of it very savoury, the sooner the college is shot of involvement with him, the better. Wouldn't you agree? I did say that to your Mr Lloyd when I talked to him again this morning.'

But without asking DS Lloyd any leading questions, thought the sergeant, who had read the report. Then she said aloud: 'Do you think there were people here who knew about the ... the nature of these outside interests? Presumably *you* did, for a start?'

'Only by elimination. I mean, he didn't seem to have any inside interests, which is what he was here for. I was supposed to teach him English, but he wasn't learning

287

anything, despite my undoubted abilities as a gifted instructor,' he smirked, and examined his elbow again as he continued, 'but he seemed pretty busy always. And rolling in lolly, even though he was supposed to come from a modest background. He wasn't ever in college when he didn't absolutely have to be, and very often not then either. I gather drug trading's been mentioned, and bullying, and ... and blackmail.' There was a distinctly interrogative bias in the last phrases.

'Who was he supposed to have been bullying?'

'I thought you'd know that. Perhaps he wasn't.'

'And if I knew—'

'You'd hardly be telling nosy tutors.'

'And you'd never come across him before you came here?' she asked conversationally, and appearing to ignore his last comment. 'I mean, you didn't teach him anywhere else? In Aberbach, where he came from, for instance, or at one of his other schools?'

'And he'd a few of those, I know,' he answered. 'Turfed out of most of them, too. But no, I never actually met him before I came here. Mr Lloyd asked me that as well.'

'Did he?' She had known as much already,

although, this time, while the question had been exactly the same, the answer had been slightly different, less guarded than Lloyd had reported. And was it reasonable to suppose, she asked herself now, that Gibbon might have told Harries he'd been effectively expelled from other schools? DCI Parry had said that Gibbon's past history had been kept under wraps from everyone at the college, and Harries wasn't even what they called Gibbon's course tutor. 'It's just that I don't believe blackmail's been mentioned,' the woman sergeant added. She knew for certain that it hadn't been, except to the one man who'd been blackmailed, and he wasn't likely to have told anyone else. 'Who told you about that?'

He shrugged. 'Can't remember. Just a bit of exaggerated, unsourced gossip I picked up, I expect. You get a lot of that in schools.'

But more amongst the pupils than the staff, surely, the sergeant was thinking as she questioned: 'He wasn't blackmailing you, was he, sir?'

'Certainly not.' The answer had been unusually prompt. 'In any case, I've led a totally blameless life. And why have I suddenly become a sir? Blotted my copy-book, have I? Oh hell, and just as I was going to ask you out to a modest dinner tonight, to enjoy the supreme pleasure of your off-duty company. If you come, I promise I'll give you my whole life history if you want, unless you fall asleep listening to it. Please come.' He had swivelled himself on to his knees, and was clasping his hands together in comic supplication.

Mary Norris picked up her towel and got to her feet. 'I don't think I'd fall asleep in circumstances like that,' she replied, a touch archly. 'And it all sounds irresistible, but sorry, Mr Harries, I'm already booked for this evening. See you around, though.'

He jumped up. 'Same time, same place tomorrow, perhaps?'

She hesitated. 'Perhaps.' Her evening date, a girlfriend, could easily have been put off. As a woman, Mary Norris would certainly have accepted the English tutor's invitation because she found him more than just dishy. But because of her position on the case, she'd just decided that there was a bit more to be explained about Emlyn Harries before she could afford to be seen having a cosy dinner with him – and, in the process, possibly spoiling her professional reputation and future. All the same, she still hoped the explanation would prove he was as blameless as he made out.

'Josephine Oswald fantasizes,' said Parry, as he moved the Porsche along the fast lane of the motorway. Not that, when this lane was compared to the other two, it made a great deal of difference to the speed at which they could travel: it was five thirty, and rush hour.

'A lot of people fantasize, boss,' Lloyd observed philosophically, levering himself up a little in the seat, and tugging at the front of his trousers. 'But she took it to extremes, didn't she? Had to have a phantom abortion to match the phantom pregnancy, of course. Or perhaps Gibbon dreamed up both for her, to keep her happy?'

'Happy?' Parry questioned.

'In a way, yes. Or fulfilled.'

'But the suicide was no fantasy,' the chief inspector insisted. 'Miss Strange is convinced it was genuine, and I think I agree with her. What that girl had swallowed should have been lethal. She'd had two ecstasy tablets on top of the other stuff, and I wouldn't mind betting that was her first experience of drugs.' He rubbed the tip of his nose with his left forefinger. 'I wonder if

Gibbon had given them to her before the weekend, saying they'd induce an abortion, expecting her to think the sensation she'd get meant she was aborting?'

'And expecting her to be dead when he got back Sunday, you mean, boss?'

'Because he had no more use for her? No, he hadn't reached that stage. Not with his stuff stashed in her window seat.'

Lloyd scowled. 'No doubt she's naive enough to have believed anything he told her.'

'Including some bizarre ideas on how babies are conceived? How could a girl be that ignorant in this day and age?'

'Easy, boss. I remember another boy telling me the facts of life when we were both eleven. I said there must be another method because my parents wouldn't do anything so daft. We were strict chapel, too, like the Oswalds.' The sergeant chuckled to himself. 'A girl brought up like Josephine Oswald might be just as badly informed, even today,' he completed.

'Oddly enough, her father agrees with you, Gomer. Only he figured Gibbon had introduced her to what he called unnatural practices.'

'And he was probably right, boss. And

apart from all that, it was bloody risky giving her two ecstasy tablets, and leaving her on her own with them.'

'Except she didn't take them at the weekend,' Parry replied. 'Perhaps they were for someone else, and she misunderstood his instructions. And you can never know for sure with failed suicides, whether they were going for real or just for attention.'

'Well, she certainly got all the attention she could have been craving in the end, boss. But would she have been counting on someone going to her room? I mean when she didn't show up for the first class this morning? Nobody did, I know. Not till it might have been too late. That was a risk she must have been ready to take. Fatalistic, like?'

'If it was a risk she thought she'd get away with, it very nearly cost her life. She could easily have been dead when Miss Strange and Mary Norris got to her. They saved her all right. The method they used was frighteningly unorthodox, but it worked that time.' Parry's response had been delivered firmly, while he continued to concentrate on the arc of windscreen that an overworked wiper was keeping clear. There had been a short flurry of snow, too wet to settle, but enough for the vehicle ahead to be throwing up a spray of sticky gunge.

The sergeant's free-range eyebrows rose a fraction. 'You said Josephine's older sister is the family favourite. Like we guessed from the suicide note.'

'Yes. Claire. She's not merely bright, she's brilliant. Her father was singing her praises as I walked to his car with him. She's a doctor, married, living in the States. Just been made a consultant at a Chicago hospital.'

'Ah, and the not so brilliant and neglected Josephine's at a crammer for backward students. The poor girl's probably been playing second fiddle all her life. So that's it in one, is it, boss? No murder link there, though.'

Parry pulled a face. 'Except ... except there's the possibility the father just could be involved.'

'Because he happens to be a butcher, is that it?'

'Linked by the so far circumstantial connection between those stab wounds and a butcher's steel,' Parry extended the point almost lightly. 'Yes, it's pretty tenuous, but we can hardly ignore it, at least until we're told the weapon definitely wasn't a butcher's steel.'

'Interesting combination, lay preacher and butcher, boss. The spirit and the flesh, like.' Lloyd folded his arms over his bulky overcoat and the seat belt, before adding: 'So you think Mr Oswald could have known about Gibbon and Josephine?'

'He says categorically he didn't. But he would, wouldn't he, if he'd murdered Gibbon? Incidentally, he's much more relieved about Josephine's survival than he is angry about the rest of what's happened. He's also shrewder than I'd given him credit for at the start – and very much a realist. Told me, when we were alone, that he'd fully expected he might be one of our suspects.'

'Go on?' said the sergeant in surprise. 'But he doesn't know about those wounds, and what they might have been made with, does he?'

'No. Just assumed we'd have him on the list, if we got the idea he'd known about Gibbon and his daughter all along. For that reason he accounted to me for his movements on Sunday, without being asked. We sat in his car talking for nearly half an hour. It's partly why I missed our four o'clock update. That and having promised to go back and see Newsom-Pugh.'

'No matter. I've got notes here on everything, boss. Is the principal worried?'

'Yes. About the college's survival, chiefly. Wanted to know if there was anything we could do to lessen the bad publicity they're getting.'

'Thinks we're a social service, or a public relations company, does he, boss?'

'Something like that. I think his wife's behind it. Anyway, I've made the right noises.' Parry hesitated. 'Going back to Josephine's father, he said he was with other people nearly the whole of Sunday, running chapel services, or doing things with his wife and daughter. That's except for an hour or so from seven in the evening. That was when he was visiting an elderly sick member of his congregation who lived alone.'

'Well, that should be easy enough to check, boss.'

'It would have been if the lady in question hadn't died unexpectedly at breakfast time yesterday morning. He volunteered that as well. It was part of the reason he was late bringing Josephine back to the college.'

'So what he called an hour or so Sunday evening could be anything up to the time it'd take him to drive down here from

296

Brecon, and do for Gibbon? And no one to say he wasn't on local good works, boss?'

'It's possible. He'd have needed more than two hours for that, always supposing he knew where Gibbon was. But that's possible too, if he'd been having him followed.'

'He didn't say he'd done that, boss?'

'No. And he'd already sworn to me he'd never even heard of Gibbon till this morning.' The chief inspector rolled his tongue along the inside of his closed lips as he turned off the motorway for central Cardiff. 'May be a long shot, Gomer. Too long, probably. Jenkin is still our ... our front runner.' He straightened a little in the driving seat. 'So, anything yet on Gibbon's mobile calls?'

'Yes. He only made three through the whole of Saturday and Sunday, boss. The first at five past one Saturday afternoon. That was to Mr Patel's disco hire. At the time, Gibbon was in the phone company's grid cell that covers the motorway, halfway between the college and Swansea. The other calls were to his mother. Both made p.m. Sunday. Neither was answered. Probably he didn't know she was away. The first was at ten to three, and he was then where we'll be in a minute – at the top of Northern

Avenue, moving south towards the city.'

'So he could have been going where we're going?' But his comment was also prompting him to go over in his mind all the other people involved in the case who lived on the west side of the city.

'Possible, boss,' the sergeant agreed as he continued: 'The final call was two hours later, made from the centre of Bristol. So he was alive then.'

'Not necessarily, if someone else was using his mobile. His killer, for instance.'

Lloyd stroked his moustache. 'That could be true enough. Except, would the killer have known his mother's number? It's not likely Jenkin would have, for instance. And she's not in the Hereford phone book yet. Hasn't lived there long enough.'

'No, I suppose if the calls were to his mother, the chances are it was he who made them,' Parry agreed. 'So let's assume he was alive at five on Sunday night. Did he have his mobile switched on all through the weekend?'

The sergeant shook his head. 'Afraid not, boss. Only when he was making the calls.'

'Damn. Just our luck.' They both knew that if a mobile phone is switched on, whether it's in use or not, its location in the cellnet is continuously logged by the operating company which stores the data for accounting purposes. 'Perhaps he never gave the number to anyone, so he never expected incoming calls, or wanted them.'

'That's what we figured, boss. Anyway, he was in Bristol at five, but we don't know why.'

'At a guess, picking up or delivering drugs. Or arranging a disco for next weekend.'

'Right. And why was he trying to contact his mother, boss?'

'To get her to do something for him. That's the usual reason according to her. You know, it's strange about her...' Although Parry had begun to add something about Mrs Gibbon, he was diverted by the need to flash his lights at a slow-moving Ford Sierra, ahead in the fast lane, whose driver was determinedly reluctant to move over and let the Porsche through. When he resumed the conversation, he had changed the subject. 'I gather the forensics on Gibbon's Sierra estate give us nothing new, Gomer?'

'That's right. Like we saw before it was taken away, the car was clean. Very clean – and relatively empty, as if it had just been done over and tidied inside. There were the usual bits of debris, but no blood traces anywhere, for instance. The rear compartment produced some wool fibres. The kind you'd get shedding from a travelling rug. But no rug. And a rug's a common enough accessory in passion wagons. That's what my older brother used to call estates, when we were young,' the sergeant finished with a nostalgic grin. Parry assumed he'd meant when he was over eleven years of age, or else the innocent, chapel-reared Gomer wouldn't have understood his brother's meaning.

'So, did we get anything out of the lunchtime customers at the pub today, Gomer?'

'Nothing, boss. A few recognized Gibbon from his picture. But most of them had seen that on TV or in the paper anyway. Nobody remembers seeing anyone with him. We'll try again tomorrow. We'll have that photofit of the other man ready by then. Mrs Mills and the barmaid weren't there at lunchtime today. Gone to Cardiff on a shopping spree, Mr Mills told me. No, I'm afraid it hasn't been a good day for identifying people.' Lloyd had produced his notebook, and was flicking through the pages to find the right one. 'Which brings us to Sara Card and Bronwyn Tate, the two domestics. They never picked out the bloke they've been meeting at the station. They spent a long time in Cardiff going through our rogues' gallery, probably because it was time they'd been allowed off work. Anyway, it wasn't all wasted because I arranged to have their rooms searched while they were there.'

'Without their permission?'

'Wasn't needed, boss. Mrs Watkyn was present throughout, like she was doing an inventory on the fixtures and fittings, which she's entitled to do any time, only she had DC Pope with her, giving her a friendly hand, like. Didn't take long, and nothing was found. No drugs. Nothing. If there had been anything, I expect they'd have got rid of it before Mrs Watkyn brought them to see us yesterday.' He cleared his throat. 'Next important point, when you were seeing the principal and Mr Oswald, DS Norris and DC Pope interviewed Kate Unwin and Abby Kennedy separately, but in their own room.'

'What about the third girl who shares it, the one with the perpetual cold?'

'Mair Daltry? No. She was having a tutorial. Mary began with a shock tactic by showing them the nude pictures. Both girls were frightened out of their lives by that. They said Freddy had promised no one else would ever see the photos, if they did whatever he told them to. He swore the photos were kept in a box at his bank, and he'd hand them over to the girls at the end of this term.'

'A con we've heard somewhere before,' Parry put in. 'Did doing anything he asked involve sleeping with him?'

'They both say it didn't, boss. That he only really cared that way for older women. They both said he got them high on drugs and booze before the photo session, that at the time it was supposed to be a lark. It took place at Abby's house, when her parents were away one weekend, at the end of last term.'

'So who took the shot of Gibbon and Kate Unwin engaged in that convincingly intimate lark?'

'Abby did. The Daltry girl wasn't there, or involved, but Abby said she knows about the photos. Mair used to be soft on Freddy, but went off him last term because of that and other things.'

'So he's since been blackmailing only the other two?'

'Yes. But they gave different versions of how. That was after each girl had been told we knew all about last weekend's disco at Kate's house.'

'Which we didn't.'

'True enough, boss. But it was a good guess. The actual disco was in a barn on the paddock behind the house. Anyway, Abby said Gibbon's been making them work for him, helping to set up these weekend discos. Seems they were fairly regular events, and good little earners in their own right.'

'More like a way of extending his illegal drug franchise,' Parry put it.

'The girls won't confess to anything about drugs, boss. Not yet, anyway. It was Kate who first admitted he made them help him with some house-entering, though only because Mary Norris bluffed her into thinking we knew a lot more about that than we did, and she was dim enough to fall for it. Later, Abby had to admit the same, of course. Seems he always had keys to the houses, knew the alarm codes, and when the owners would be away. Usually he only took one small, valuable piece from each house in the hope the loss wouldn't be noticed. And he knew the specific piece he was taking in advance, like he was under orders.'

'And the girls had to go with him to be sure he got the right piece, because he knew nothing about jewellery?' asked Parry.

'Yes, boss. This was usually at weekends,

but once or twice on week nights when they weren't supposed to leave the college. Once Abby accepted Kate had given them away over the burglaries, she admitted she thought he was doing it in partnership with someone else.'

'The someone who was providing the keys, the information, and the orders, and, at a guess, works for Centurion Protection, the alarm company,' put in Parry, tapping his fingers on the steering wheel as they waited at a road junction for the lights to change.

'Yes, we're working on that, boss.' Lloyd was flipping through some pages in his notebook, moving it closer to the car's map light. 'There's a lot more to the report on the girls,' he added, 'but it doesn't help us over what happened to Freddy after Sunday morning, since Mr Patel saw him alive and well later than anyone who was at that disco, including Kate and Abby.'

'They've been told they can now be charged with illegal entering and burglary, have they?'

'Yes, boss. But Mary Norris advised them that if it comes to that, they can plead duress by Freddy Gibbon.'

'Because of the lewd photos? Yes. And

they're cooperating, so there's mitigation. Hmm. So were there other students from the college at the disco?'

'Yes. Two lads and a girl, boss. But they'd agreed with Kate and Abby to keep shtoom about it.'

'And presumably we'd already interviewed them?'

'Yesterday, boss. But they were seen again immediately after we were through with the other two who say they watched Freddy leave Kate's house with the disco gear just after eleven thirty on Sunday morning, and they swear they never saw him again. Kate said they hadn't told us about the disco because she didn't have her parents' permission to hold it. They're in South Africa. Mary made Kate and Abby account for every minute of their time Sunday. They seem to be in the clear. They went to see an aunt and uncle of Abby's in Swansea at teatime, watched some TV there, had supper, left for the college at nine, and checked in with the duty tutor, Mrs Newsom-Pugh, at ten to ten. The aunt and uncle have confirmed the time they left. The other three students were together in one car, stayed Sunday night with the parents of one of them in Neath, left at seven thirty in the morning, and rolled up at the college after the body was found.'

'Did Mary check if anyone at the disco quarrelled with Freddy?'

'Yes, boss. All five of our group said nobody did. That it went without incident, excepting for a girl who passed out at one o'clock after drinking too much. She recovered quite soon. Only I'd guess it was drugs not drink she was suffering from, or both.'

Parry nodded as he changed gear. 'Alwyn Bowen, the farmer's son, was he one of the three others at the disco?'

'No, boss, but DC Vaughan saw him as instructed. From nine on Sunday night, he and his dad were taking it in turns tending a cow that was on the point of calving. They were at it till six when the vet came. Bowen then had breakfast with his mum before he left to drive to the dentist at eight thirty. He says his mum and dad will vouch he was at the farm all night. Funny lad, though. Alf Vaughan says he didn't seem to mind whether he was being believed or not. Like the time you and I interviewed him.' The sergeant had returned to squinting at his notes. 'Two other points,' he went on. 'Miss Thomas checked Jenkin's CV for us. He's never worked anywhere near Aberbach. Always in mid or North Wales before he came here.'

'That's probably accurate,' Parry commented, without sounding pleased about it.

'And finally, boss, about the jewellery in Gibbon's possession, only the earrings had been reported missing.'

'Doesn't mean the other stuff hadn't been stolen, of course,' commented Parry. 'Probably just not missed yet. So who owned the earrings?'

'Another lady in Penarth.'

'But not the owner of the house there that Gibbon had a key to?'

'No, boss. But it could be one of the other houses the girls broke into with him. We're checking on that with them. We know already it's going to be protected by Centurion.'

'What about this Centurion company?'

'We know them, boss. Been going eight years. Clean record up to now.'

17

'The police searched the rooms of Sara Card and Bronwyn Tate today,' Inga Newsom-Pugh announced casually, although this was not at all how she was feeling about the event. She slipped the divided omelette out of the pan, half of it on to each waiting warm plate.

'I wasn't told,' her husband responded in an affronted voice. He had just come up to their suite from his study, and was sitting at the small table close to the diminutive kitchen at the rear of their sitting room. The kitchen had been a conversion made from part of the oversized lobby. In term time, a substantial lunch was the couple's main daily meal, which they took at what Newsom-Pugh referred to as the high table in the college refectory – though the members of the teaching staff who sat there still had to fetch their food from a service counter. Only soup and salads were provided in the refectory in the evening, and the Newsom-Pughs sometimes fended for themselves at that time of day – or, more precisely, Mrs Newsom-Pugh cooked them something light. Cooking was not permitted in other college rooms.

'I'd guess they didn't need to tell anyone, darling,' she countered, bringing the plates to the table, which was already laid with cutlery, glasses, a wooden bowl of mixed salad, and an open bottle of white wine. 'I found out because nominally it was Mrs Watkyn who did the searching, except it was actually done by one of the policewomen. Mrs Watkyn told me, of course. They didn't find anything.'

'Well, one of you should have alerted me immediately. The police mustn't be allowed to take advantage.'

'Except they can if they want.' She sat across from him at the table, took her napkin from its ring, and poured herself some wine – he had already consumed the better part of a glassful, and was busy helping himself to salad. His mind was much too preoccupied for him to be conscious of her needs. 'Cynthia Strange told Mrs Watkyn this morning they have the right to search every room in the place, because illegal drugs have been found here,' his wife completed. In a way, it helped her to share the information with him, even though she could scarcely share the reason for her deep disquiet.

'And what does Cynthia Strange know about such things? She teaches history, not law,' challenged Newsom-Pugh.

'She knows a good deal. There was a drug search in her last school. It included body searches. No one was spared, apparently. And that included all the teaching staff.'

'All the teaching staff?' The principal of Modlen College was horrified at the implication. 'But here that would be outrageous.' He didn't explain why it should be more so at Modlen College than it had been at one of England's finer private girls' schools.

'Well, it's certainly not the sort of thing that impresses parents if they hear about it. But the woman sergeant who went with Cynthia and the Oswald girl to the hospital said it was less likely there'd be a full search here. After all, they're looking for a murderer, not a glue-sniffer. It's a pity Sara and Bronwyn were so involved with Freddy Gibbon.'

'I don't know what you mean by that. One could hardly be a member of the college without being involved with the wretched boy in some way – some probably innocent way. We really must protect our young people from being put upon.' It was the children with fee-paying parents he was thinking about, not other domestic servants – though good examples of both species were becoming increasingly difficult to attract these days.

'Cynthia got the impression a few more rooms might be searched, but that'll be the end of it.' This had become Inga Newsom-Pugh's favourite wishful thought, always provided that the search didn't include the principal's apartment.

Her husband lifted a forkful of omelette towards his mouth, but kept it there, fixing it with a steely gaze as though he'd spotted salmonella lurking between the prongs. 'Who's said anything about more rooms? Oh, the woman sergeant, I suppose. Which rooms?'

'Who can tell, darling? Cynthia and Mrs Watkyn have put the word out unofficially to students and staff. After that, only dim-wits will have anything incriminating in their rooms, or on them.' Or those who had any control in the matter, she thought to herself bitterly.

'We have a surfeit of dimwits,' he

pronounced dully – and unguardedly for him – before his lips at last closed over the omelette.

On balance, having to admit the low mental capacities of the average pupil affronted Newsom-Pugh much more than the thought that they might all have been smoking pot behind his back. He ran his own crammer – which he insisted on calling a sixth-form college – because no university faculty or board of school governors had ever seen fit to offer him an appointment and salary matching his own estimation of his academic worth. Even now he remained a disappointed man, stalked by the certainty that if it hadn't been for an unexpected family legacy five years before this, he would still be on his own, tutoring backward students in Latin, Greek and Welsh in return for an hourly pittance.

And the early commercial success of Modlen College was definitely something that belonged in the past, like its once impressive record of academic achievements. There was too much competition nowadays, forcing down fees and profits. A drug scandal on top of the murder could presage total disaster, especially if it exposed an indeterminate number of students with a drug habit started, and fed, by the establishment's own and known rotten apple.

'Ice-cream or cheese?' Inga asked, as she took away their empty plates.

'I'm sorry? – oh, cheese, I think.' The choice had hardly registered.

While Inga was apparently busy in the kitchen getting the cheese and preparing coffee, once again she anxiously reopened drawers there, despite having been through the selfsame motions earlier with every drawer and cupboard in all three rooms, plus the bathroom. This searching had begun late on the previous Friday evening, but not then in any urgent way. It hadn't been feverish, even after Freddy's death, but it had become close to maniacal a few hours back, when she had learned about the police search of the servant girls' rooms. Since then she had taken to seeking out possible overlooked crannies wherever she was in the suite by herself, just as she was doing now, even though she had given the whole place a top-to-tail turn-out before lunch, albeit to no purpose. While she had persuaded herself that if the police searched here too, their methods could be no more exhaustive than hers, there was always the chance that they had the means to be in some way more scientific about it. The experienced Cynthia Strange had mentioned the possible use of trained seeker dogs without realizing the turmoil this had engendered in the mind of her listener.

As Inga returned from the kitchen, she said: 'Cynthia told me police search staff as well as student rooms because, once students know a search is on, that's exactly where they hide drugs, rather than waste them down the loo.'

'Because they believe staff rooms will be overlooked?' Her husband sounded even more affronted than before.

'Exactly. Here that would have to mean the staff sitting rooms used for tutorials, wouldn't it?'

It was as she'd been seeing Freddy to the door of the suite, at five o'clock on Friday, that he had murmured something about leaving her 'the rest of the goodies'. She had missed or ignored his ensuing words because she'd still been in a seventh heaven, embracing him passionately. They had spent all of the previous hour in the bedroom. She thought he had meant that he had left some ecstasy tablets on the bedside table. That's where they had been when the two had been in bed. But he could have put them any-where while she'd been in the bathroom by herself – or in the bathroom itself, when he'd gone there too.

During the time that Freddy had been with her, Handel had been in his study downstairs, as he was invariably at that time of day, and without fail on days when she was giving tutorials in the suite. She had, of course, still taken the precaution to bolt the door to the corridor.

As a lover she had found Freddy irresistible, and incredibly satisfying. Their couplings had been rapturous, uncom-mitting, and sufficient in themselves – or this was how she had conveniently rationalized her otherwise unconscionable attitude since his death. She had argued that they had given to each other in equal measure, with no obligations, no depth beyond the physical one, and not the remotest thought that their illicit association could or needed to endure. Each had been convenient for the other's pressing, passing need: that was all. This explained why she had been so little affected by what had happened to Freddy – except for her irritation over his carelessness with the ecstasy tablets.

But then, Inga Newsom-Pugh was as self-centred and uncaring by nature as her now departed paramour had been.

Her husband watched her as she poured the coffee. 'Bowen was supposed to have been close to Gibbon, wasn't he?'

'Yes, Handel. Is that important?'

'And he was here for a tutorial yesterday at four?'

'Sure.' She simulated a startled reaction. 'Oh, my God, you mean he could have hidden something in here ... or ... or in the bathroom?' She had avoided mentioning the bedroom: in any case, the bathroom was through the bedroom. Even so, he could scarcely be imagining she'd been to bed with the yokel Bowen as well.

'It's possible,' he replied to her question. 'It must have been after everyone knew the police had interviewed Sara and Bronwyn for the second time. Bowen's not stupid. If he had drugs in his possession he might have assumed a search could be made. Of his locker, for instance, since he doesn't have a room in college.'

What should have been Inga's delight that he had taken the bait she'd laid was stillborn by her awareness of the searching way he was appraising her reactions.

'He asked if he could use the bathroom in the middle of the tutorial,' she said, naturally still needing to milk the opportunity to blame Bowen if drugs were discovered in the suite. 'Of course, I said he could. Well, what else could I have done? It never occurred to me...'

'Quite. Bowen was here for a tutorial with you on Friday at the same time, wasn't he? With you and Gibbon?'

It was her guilty state of mind that now panicked her into believing he must know something – otherwise, why would he be harping back to Friday?

'Oh damn!' she cried, jumping up from her seat, and unnecessarily dabbing at the front of her skirt. She had purposely spilled some coffee, though only over her napkin. She now hurried to the kitchen in the pretence of mending damage – anything to avoid answering the question.

The Friday tutorial had been the second that Freddy had ordered Bowen to cry off by pleading a migraine attack. He had also made Bowen stay out of sight in Freddy's own room until after the session was over. Freddy had promised Inga that Bowen wasn't aware she was party to the subterfuge on either occasion he had used it. When she'd expressed doubts about Bowen believing the disclaimer, Freddy had banished them by insisting he had ways of making Bowen believe anything: except Freddy wasn't around to do that any more.

'They wouldn't have left anything here on Friday, would they?' she questioned ingenuously on her return to the table.

'I suppose not.' Newsom-Pugh seemed to be watching her even more intently than before. 'But they were here, then. The two of them.'

Her stomach heaved. His intonation had suddenly made her sure he suspected Bowen hadn't been at the tutorial. It had been the way he had emphasized the word 'two' – and the way he had put the point as a statement, not a question.

'Yes,' she lied, and with all the assurance she could muster, hoping, praying there was no way Handel could know the truth – unless Bowen himself had told him, and she didn't see why he should have done. So Handel could only be imagining he knew something. 'But there simply was no reason for them to ... to push drugs down the sides of our chairs on Friday, for heaven's sake,' she protested. 'Bowen could have done it yesterday, of course. You don't mean you've found something? Some drugs? Why didn't you tell me?'

Now it was she who was waiting for his reaction. If he'd come upon the ecstasy tablets – and she was better prepared now to accept that he might have done – he'd have to tell her. And pray to God if he'd found them it was since the Bowen tutorial yesterday.

He shook his head slowly. 'I've found nothing ... nothing tangible.'

'Then I think we should look, don't you?' But what did he mean by tangible?

'If you think it's worth it, my dear.'

He was staring at her in the same deeply penetrating way as before. It was at this point that she began to sweat, and for a new reason.

At first, Inga had figured that if he had come upon Freddy's 'gift' to her, he wouldn't have known what it was, nor where it had come from, and, in any case, that he would have told her. Now she wasn't so sure. And had he afterwards leaned on the hapless Bowen to find out if he'd been at the Friday tutorial, and if so, had he got the truth? If he had, then it was anybody's guess what action Handel might have taken. One thing was certain, she couldn't ask him.

319

Before this, the notion that her husband had killed Freddy out of jealousy would have seemed utterly preposterous. Now, wallowing in her guilt, it was beginning to seem utterly real, as, for the first time, she realized he could have had the opportunity as well as the motive.

Handel had made her tell the police that they had been together the whole of Sunday evening and night, discounting only intervals of a few minutes or so. But this hadn't been strictly true.

It had been Handel's idea to prevaricate in this way so that, he'd said, they wouldn't be bothered by further tiresome and demeaning questions. But in this way, so much was overlooked.

Handel's reported 'ten-minute' swim before Sunday supper had taken the best part of an hour.

The short distance between the pool house and where Freddy's body was found was only patchily lit and scarcely ever observed.

Freddy could have returned to the college and gone swimming too, or been enticed to do so by Handel for some compelling reason.

Handel was strong and fit – far more so

than people guessed. In a swimming pool, his element, he could have overpowered men much younger than himself, including Freddy – and like everyone else, she still didn't know exactly how Freddy had died.

Dead bodies removed from swimming pools didn't need to be stripped since they were close to that state already.

'Nice place you've got here, Larry. You don't mind if we call you Larry, do you?' Detective Sergeant Lloyd enquired with a beam, after he and Merlin Parry had identified themselves, explained the purpose of their visit, and been shown into the main, room of the basement flat at their own suggestion.

'No, I don't mind.' Larry Pritchard, friend of the maths tutor at Modlen College, was a short, dark, wiry youth with pale cheeks, dry lips that he kept wetting with his tongue, and long hair parted in the centre which was pulled back into a ponytail. He was dressed in a yellow T-shirt, and faded blue jeans. The shirt bore a sketch of a large rodent on the front. Unlike the creature depicted, the wearer looked undernourished, which, to Lloyd's way of thinking, was incongruous in a chef, even a trainee chef.

'Got your own bathroom and kitchen, have you, Larry?' asked Parry, also with extra affability.

'Yeah. And separate bedroom. We rent furnished. Want to see round, do you?' The offer had been nervous, and not exactly hospitable, but still with a hint of pride in the tone.

'No, no, we're just interested, Larry,' Lloyd offered. He had been standing in the open doorway to the bedroom, but now he turned. 'Mind if we sit down?'

'Yeah. No problem.' Then, because there *was* an evident problem, he stepped forward to move a load of magazines and sheet music from an armchair, which was part of a loose-covered, matching three-piece suite. The furnishings were adequate and not too worn, and in contrast to the stuff which was evidently the landlord's property there was the CD player, a new-looking portable TV receiver, a video tape machine under it, and an electric bass guitar set on a chromium rest in one corner. The fireplace housed a permanent modern gas appliance that was giving off a bright glow, as well as too much heat for the two visitors. While, like most basement rooms, this one probably lacked natural light in the daytime, with the curtains drawn, as now, it was cosy enough, the walls festooned with lively travel posters.

'So you're a guitarist, Larry,' said Parry taking the cleared seat while the sergeant moved round to the sofa.

'Try to be, yeah. I'm in a group. The Stoats.' He rubbed the inside of one wrist up and down over the illustration on the T-shirt, but as though he was attempting to obliterate rather than advertise it. 'We get a few gigs. Pubs mostly. Got one tonight.'

'Good for you. You get enough time off from college and the hotel for that?'

Pritchard shook his head. 'Not too much in term time, we don't. It's like ... easier in the holidays.'

'The gigs help with the rent, do they?' asked Lloyd.

'No ... that's covered.' But, judging by his frown, he had found the question perplexing. 'I'm saving for an American trip.' One of the wall posters promoted New Orleans, another Washington, and the biggest, San Francisco.

'Ifor covers all the rent then?' Lloyd's fresh query was styled more as a passing comment.

The youth's brow had knitted again at this reference to Jenkin, the first since, on the doorstep, the two men had explained their interest in the tutor. 'No. We ... we go halves. Sort of.' Pritchard, who was now sitting on the arm of the vacant chair, began rubbing the heel of one palm on his thigh, his trunk moving backwards and forwards in concert.

'But he doesn't get to stay here often?'

'It's more in the holidays. He was here Sunday night.' The response this time had been prompt, and delivered in a more confident tone than before. It was followed by a rapid tongue-moistening of the upper lip only.

'He told us about that, Larry,' said Parry. 'As we said, it's Sunday we'd like you to help us on.'

'Oh, yeah. Well, he'd meant to stay the night at his mother's,' Pritchard volunteered, again with no hesitation. 'Except the roads were bad so he came back early.' Both the last pieces of information had sounded rehearsed.

'When did he get here?'

'Around seven.'

'And what did you do in the evening?'

'Nothing.'

'Nothing?'

Pritchard shrugged, then smoothed the back of his hair with both hands down to the band of the ponytail. 'We had supper, played some CDs, watched a tape for a bit.'

'Can you remember what you watched?'

'A movie I taped in the week. *Emmanuelle Two*. Ifor didn't like it. After that I went to bed. He had schoolwork to do.'

'Did he go out after you went to bed?'

'No.'

'But you were in the bedroom and he was in here? How would you have known?'

Pritchard pondered for a moment. 'I was listening to music in bed. Till he stopped working. The door was open. And...' He swallowed.

'And what, Larry?' Parry pressed.

'I forget now what I was going to say. I'm not used to police.'

'Larry, there's nothing to be afraid of. This is just a routine visit to confirm some facts Ifor gave us.'

'OK.'

'So have you remembered what you were going to tell us just now?'

'No. It couldn't have been anything.'

Lloyd cleared his throat and leaned forward. 'Look, Larry, Ifor Jenkin is your friend, isn't he?'

'Sure.'

'So you'd like to help him?'

'Yeah, yeah.' The response had been more nervous than irritated, although it was that as well.

'Well, the best way you can do that is tell us all you can about his movements. That's from the time he got here Sunday night till the time he left – at what time Monday morning, was it?'

'About eight, I think.'

'You think?'

Pritchard moved his trunk from the waist up in a strained kind of roll. 'OK, it was eight ten, maybe eight fifteen. We were a bit late. Ifor was driving me to college on his bike.'

'And he was here the whole time up to then?'

'Yeah, like I said.'

'But the two of you saw nobody else during that whole time?'

There was a long pause as Pritchard studied the end of his Doc Marten boot, while again rocking himself on his perch. 'I didn't say that.'

'So you did see other people?'

There was more kneading of palm on thigh. 'We saw one other person. That's why Ifor wouldn't have gone out. Not if I hadn't been with him. And I'd gone to bed.'

'So who else did you see, Larry?'

'Ifor didn't tell you about Amin, then?'

'He may have, but you tell us, Larry.'

The youth looked more seriously out of countenance than he had since the start of the visit. 'Amin ... he was a friend of mine, before I met Ifor. He ... he sort of dropped in Sunday, about ten. Needed somewhere to sleep. Ifor wasn't keen on him stopping, but it was late, so we let him sleep on that sofa.'

'Is that what you forgot you were going to say just now?'

'I think so, yeah. It's what I forgot.'

18

'Why didn't you phone?' Parry asked, then kissed her again, for longer this time.

'Because I wanted to surprise you. And after that last phone call, it was too risky to ring. You might have told me not to come. I hurt you, didn't I?' answered Perdita Jones, stroking the hair at the back of his neck.

'Did you? I don't know. You certainly rearranged my whole life.'

'Oh, God, I'm sorry. Really sorry. It wasn't

meant to be like that. I thought you'd be ... well, proud of me.' She buried her face in his shoulder.

'I was, and sorry for us.' He smiled at her as he pressed her to him. 'You did take a risk coming down without warning. What if I'd been out on a case tonight?'

'But you weren't.' She looked up at him, her hazel eyes widening, while her fingers went to his lips to stop further protest as she went on. 'Or you could have brought a brunette home with you, but you didn't.' Perdita's hair was corn-coloured. 'Anyway, I was being fatalistic. At four thirty this afternoon I decided I could catch the five o'clock from Paddington and the six twenty-five back in the morning. I only just made it from the hospital, and obviously you were fated to be here fifteen minutes after me. I think fatalism works for us.' She took him by the hand and pulled him from the hall into the sitting room of his Westgate Street flat.

'I'm sorry, I should have called you at the weekend,' he said, as they flopped down together on the sofa.

'No, you shouldn't. I upset you. I was so bloody pleased with myself about being invited to specialize. Not that it was for certain in any case. I mean, I have to qualify first.'

'Of course you'll qualify. And it's not the specializing, it's the adding two more years before we can be together ... get married, whatever.' He checked the time. 'Do you want to go out?'

'No, I only just got here, and it's snowing outside.' She moved closer to him.

'I meant to eat. There's nothing much here,' he said. 'We could book at Quales, and probably make it before they have to send out a search party.' The snow really had been falling heavily again when he came in.

'No thanks. I came prepared. There's some Chablis in the fridge, and some caviar, and some probably tasteless out-of-season strawberries, oh, and some cream. The cream's organic. And I've made the trimmings for the caviar, hard boiled one of your eggs and grated it even. So I've been busy. No, I don't want to go out. I want to be alone with you, thanks very much.' She kicked off her shoes, and pulled her legs up on to the cushions. 'And I've got–'

'I've got news for you,' he broke in.

They had begun to speak at the same instant.

'That's what I was going to say,' exclaimed Perdita.

'Right, but me first,' he insisted. 'Listen, I'm sorry not to have sounded pleased about your offer. It's obviously a hell of a compliment. Anyway, after a period to reflect, I talked to Clive Gravely at home last night. Remember he used to be here? He's a detective chief superintendent now with Scotland Yard. They're going to have a vacancy for a DCI in three months. If I put in for it, he thinks I could get it. Right experience, right age, and so on. We worked very closely at one time, and he'll put in a word. Well, more than a word. It would mean losing the seniority I've got here–'

'Losing your next chance to make superintendent here, you mean?' she protested sharply, sitting, up straight. 'But that'd be awful. You're next in line.'

He shook his head. 'Nobody's that. But, yes, all things being equal, I should make it this time,' he offered quietly.

'But all things aren't equal. You're the best. And, anyway, you'd hate to trade Cardiff for London. So would I, permanently, I mean. Another year after I qualify is as much as I ever really wanted to face.'

'Don't you mean another three years that

you'll *have* to face?' he questioned. 'You told me specializing would mean at least an extra two years at St Mark's.'

'Well, that was true, but ... but something's come up.'

'Something nice or nasty?'

'Nicer than your needing to join the Met, darling, but I love you even more for that.' She took his right hand in both of hers and kissed it.

'Good. But is it nicer than your doing another three years in London?'

'Much. It's another strike for the fickle finger of fate. You see...' She swallowed, then began to speak very quickly. 'You see, and don't interrupt till I've finished, I found out this morning I'm ... I'm pregnant. That's why I'm here. And I know it wasn't intended, and so do you, but if we both agree, I'm going through with it. And after I qualify, if I qualify, I'll only do six months' internship in London before the birth, and when I'm ready to go back to work, I'll find a hospital place around here for a bit. And we'll have got married by then, won't we? And oh, my darling, I know, all of a sudden, that this is the most important, fulfilling thing that's ever going to happen to me, that I'd rather be the mother of our baby than the best gynae in Britain, so–'

'Wish I'd been a fly on the wall when Larry Pritchard's other friend, Amin, turned up on Sunday night, boss,' Lloyd exclaimed from the front passenger seat of the Porsche.

It was six forty on Wednesday morning, pitch-dark still, but the snow had stopped. Parry had already seen Perdita off on the London train – a reluctant and deliciously emotional parting for both of them – and had picked up the sergeant as arranged at Cardiff Central Police Station where Lloyd had left his own car. They were driving west on the A48, out of the city, and heading for the M4 motorway. 'Well, from the way Pritchard was talking,' responded the chief inspector, 'there was certainly no way Jenkin would have left them alone together for the night.'

'Right, boss. He didn't even want to tell us about Amin, did he? Must have been Mr Jenkin's instructions. Everything else was.'

'Possibly Jenkin told him to keep Amin in reserve. To be brought out if we pressed, or if we didn't look convinced enough with Larry Pritchard's sole testimony. Altogether too subtle an assignment for our Larry, I'm afraid. Still, perhaps he does a great salmon mousse or a fantastic *crème brûlée.*'

Lloyd looked doubtful. 'More likely a middling good cod in batter, I'd say, boss.' He sniffed. 'So instead of having one witness prejudiced in his favour, Jenkin had a second who was prejudiced in another way, but–'

'But not so far as it could affect us,' Parry completed for him. 'We've been in touch with him, have we?'

'Sure, boss. He was interviewed last night. Still works in the pizza place in Merthyr, like Pritchard said. They met two years ago when they were on the same youth-training scheme. As we expected, Amin doesn't like Jenkin, and he says the feeling's mutual, but he's sworn they were all three in the flat all night. Must have been a ball. Anyway, Mr Jenkin really has a well-orchestrated alibi over the murder.'

'Even though he was too jealous of Amin to admit to us earlier he even existed. People are funny. Even mathematicians with trained logical minds.'

'But that's about it, boss. Emotions being stronger than common sense.'

'Oh well. You gain some and you lose some, Gomer.'

'Hmm. You're taking the loss of our prime suspect very well, boss.'

Parry took a big breath, and let it out with a satisfied sigh. 'This morning I could even bear it if the Home Secretary pardoned every villain in the country. Well, almost.' There were limits to professional extravagance after all. 'You see, I'm feeling good,' he added, 'and there's a reason, but I can't tell you what it is. Not for a bit.' He stopped the car abruptly just short of a pedestrian crossing, and adroitly so, in view of the treacherous state of the road surface. With a generous show of bonhomie, he then motioned a single senior citizen, carrying a stick, to use the crossing – an individual who, in all conscience, had appeared too late to have expected the Porsche to stop, and who had not even indicated a firm resolve to cross the road in any case. In the circumstances, though, he did so now with a thankful wave to encourage this driver of the kind of car more commonly linked with speed than concern for the slowest movers.

'Fair enough, boss. Confidential information, is it?' Lloyd settled back in his seat.

'Not confidential, just tempting fate to let on about it yet. Tell me about the Mrs Mills episode.'

'Ah, well that's a rum one,' the sergeant began, while making a mental note to inform his wife, Gracie, that Perdita Jones was pregnant, but not to tell anyone else yet, especially Merlin Parry. 'Mrs Mills and Doreen Fowler, the barmaid, were shopping in St David's Centre yesterday afternoon, when Doreen saw the good-looking, tall bloke who'd been with Gibbon in the pub. He was with someone else. Short, younger chap with a limp, in a black bomber jacket, and carrying a crash helmet.'

'Sounds like Gibbon's drug courier.'

'Could be, boss. When Doreen caught up with them, and said something about having met the tall one with Gibbon, the young chap looked terrified, and hit out at him and Doreen with the helmet. Then he made a dash for it across the road – and ran straight in front of a bus. He died in the ambulance later. Pure accident, witnessed by six people. In the general fracas, Mrs Mills was knocked over and injured her back. Had to go to hospital as well. But here's the payoff. She'd already identified the tall bloke as Debby Thomas's boyfriend. At that point she didn't know his name, but–'

'Colvin Russell,' Parry interjected, 'the ex-copper from the Met.'

'That's it, boss.'

'So if it was that easy to identify him, why hadn't Mrs Mills done it before? Or anyone else from the pub?'

'Because she'd only seen him there once, during an evening visit he made with Debby Thomas, not Gibbon. Like Mrs Mills told us, Doreen never works evenings. Anyway, Mr Russell stayed to help look after Mrs Mills till the ambulance came.'

'Has anyone interviewed Russell yet to find out what he was doing with Gibbon?'

'Not yet, boss, but nothing's been done to put him on any kind of alert either. I thought you'd want to see him after we've looked at his record from the Met. We'll have that this morning, and it's going to include fingerprints. Incidentally, we now know he was with Centurion Protection before he joined Home and Corporate Security last October.'

'And it's Centurion who look after the houses that Gibbon's keys seem to open. Interesting. Are we finding out why he left the company?'

'DC Vaughan's got an appointment with their managing director this morning, boss. He's ex-fire service, and Alf Vaughan knows him from way back. So it'll be a confidential chat, like.' Lloyd was opening a new tube of peppermints as he went on: 'The identity tag with the key to the Penarth house had two thumbprints on it. One belonged to Gibbon. So far we haven't identified the other.'

'I can't believe it'll be Russell's, but if it is, we could have him for aiding and abetting at least.' Parry was silent for a moment, before adding: 'He and Gibbon could have had a scam going, with keys and alarm codes Russell lifted from his old firm. They might have needed an informer in the outfit still, to know when the property owners were away. Risky deal, even so.'

'Not if Russell thought having someone else do the burglaries would stop us tracing them back to him, boss. Perhaps that's why he hasn't been seen with Gibbon, not after those two meetings. Well, now he's going to wish they hadn't happened either.'

'After Gibbon's death, he should also have warned his girlfriend not to tell us they'd had him to tea at their house.'

'But he wouldn't have known about Gibbon's death, boss, not before we talked to her.'

'Hmm, not unless he did the murder himself. Or was involved in it.'

'That's possible, of course,' said the sergeant, nevertheless thinking his chief was moving a long way ahead of what existing evidence supported. 'Might have been awkard for him to explain to her why she shouldn't tell us about the tea party, of course. That's if she didn't know anything about their little setup, boss. Assuming they had one.'

'Hmm. If the motorcyclist with the limp is the same one Sara Card and Bronwyn Tate were contacting for Gibbon, then Colvin Russell has to be in the thick of it,' Parry asserted. 'Did he cooperate after he and Doreen Fowler were assaulted? Giving his name and address, and so on?'

'Yes, boss. Mrs Mills says he behaved just like a copper. That's till some real ones showed up after the bus accident, and before the ambulance arrived. I've spoken to the uniform sergeant involved. He says Russell didn't know the name of the dead man.'

'But Doreen and Mrs Mills said they were together?'

'Only Doreen actually saw them together, boss. And Russell himself said the chap was a complete stranger, who was asking him the best way to get to the M4.'

'From the arcade in St David's Centre? Odd place to be asking road directions from a total stranger. Russell should have thought up something better than that,' Parry commented drily.

'He said he couldn't believe what happened next, boss.'

'Then he must have lived a charmed life in the Met,' Parry offered, as woodenly as before. 'OK. Let's do the homework on Russell before we see him. He's become a promising enough suspect to make this outing irrelevant, hasn't he? Except ... except I still have the feeling we should have seen Mrs Absom before now,' he completed as he swung the car off the motorway on to the road that would take them up the Ebbw Valley to Aberbach.

'Time doesn't heal in such a case, Mr Parry. Not for loving parents, it doesn't. It just adds a bit of perspective. But you can't grieve for ever. We've accepted that. Otherwise you get maudlin.'

The quiet-voiced Howard Absom, stepfather of the dead Peter, and manager of a building society branch in the town, was seated with his wife on the sofa in the sitting room of their neat, detached house. This was on a newish development at the southern edge of the community. Nora Absom was holding her head high, and had her back squarely against the cushions, with legs crossed under a knee-length wool skirt. Her husband – a fair-haired, lightweight, with earnest eyes and a bony nose and chin – was leaning forward a little, but was as relaxed as his wife.

Sergeant Lloyd was already finding both Mr and Mrs Absom more rational, as well as more composed, than they had been when he had last seen them, six months before this. Nora Absom even seemed younger, and physically more attractive, while her husband was much more purposeful in his manner. In September, the exclusive function he had assumed to himself had been simply as support and comforter to his wife.

Parry put down his coffee cup, and smoothed the upholstered arms of his chair with both hands. 'I'm still sorry the enquiry into Peter's death hasn't taken things further forward, Mr Absom,' he responded to the other man's philosophizing.

'Did you expect it to?' asked the boy's mother, in a tone that was genuinely enquiring, not bitter or challenging.

After first glancing at Parry, Lloyd interposed with: 'I was on the case before the inquest, as you know, Mrs Absom, and to be honest, I didn't think we'd see more progress after it. There was very little to go on, and I gather nothing new has been uncovered since. Personally, I still find it hard to credit that Peter ... took his own life, just of his own volition. That's judging from what I'd learned about him, and thinking it over again since.'

'You think his suicide could have been caused by pressure from someone else, Mr Lloyd? That such a thing is possible?' asked Mrs Absom.

'It wouldn't alter a suicide verdict, Mrs Absom, but yes, I think there are cases where the victim is sometimes driven to it by strong outside influences. I think that could have applied in Peter's case.'

'And you now think he did take his own life,' Howard Absom stated starkly, his tone assuming there was no equivocation.

'On that, do either of you have a different view, Mr Absom?' Parry asked, not affirming or denying the stated contention.

While her husband hesitated, Mrs Absom offered: 'No, we don't. Not any more. And we also believe it would have been better if the jury had felt the same, and not left the verdict ... well, open. It's interesting that Mr Lloyd thinks the same. We don't believe there could have been ... foul play. Well, not what's usually meant by foul play. And we don't think it was an accident either.' She looked from Parry to Lloyd. 'I mean, how could anyone die, the way Peter died, by accident? So that only leaves suicide, doesn't it? And perhaps there *are* different types of suicide.' She brought her hands together on her skirt. 'I don't think Peter took his life because he didn't get top marks in two of his GCSEs. I think there was something else, or more likely, some*one* else involved. Probably the someone who gave him or sold him the drugs. You could call that power without responsibility, couldn't you? Well, I think that was what Peter was ... subjected to. Someone with power over him, who didn't accept responsibility for his actions.' The speaker seemed strangely relieved, even uplifted, after she had finished her summation – as though it was something she had wanted to say for a long time.

The chief inspector steepled his hands under his chin. 'Any idea who that someone might have been, Mrs Absom?'

The couple on the sofa looked at each other.

'We've been reading about the death of Freddy Gibbon,' said Howard Absom enigmatically. 'He was a bad lot, wasn't he?'

After a moment's silence it was Lloyd who said carefully: 'It's possible he was a bad influence at the school, but since Peter's death happened–'

'In the holidays,' Mrs Absom interrupted. 'So people didn't accept Freddy had anything to do with it. Well, we now think that may have been oversimplifying things. Only there's never been any way of proving it. So since there was no proof, if he wasn't involved, pointing the finger would have been cruel and unfair, wouldn't it? And we had to think of Freddy's poor mother, too. He'd led her a terrible dance, one way and another.'

'You know Mrs Gibbon well, do you?' asked Parry.

'Not well, no. Only to pass the time of day, really. We know her friend Beth Hooson better. Of course, everyone knows how Freddy Gibbon treated his mother. Most parents were sympathetic towards her. More because she was a widow, perhaps. Except a lot thought Freddy should have been expelled for some of the things he got up to. But Mr Clarke, that's the headmaster, he seemed to let him off lightly, time and again. Of course, it was common knowledge Mrs Gibbon was asked to take Freddy away from the school in the end, instead of him being expelled. Beth once told us, in confidence, the same thing had happened before, in other schools.'

'How close would you say Peter was to Freddy Gibbon?' the chief inspector asked next, his brow wrinkling.

'Being wise after the event, too close,' Howard Absom responded. 'We're certain Freddy used Peter.'

'In what way?'

'To start with, Peter was always doing Freddy's homework for him. One weekend, I remember, that meant him doing a whole mock A level exam paper. Peter was far better at A level work than Freddy, even though he was two years younger and in a lower form at the school. It meant Freddy was relying on Peter, of course, and we wonder now what Freddy might have done to keep things that way.' The speaker let out a long sigh. 'Of course, it might just have been a matter of loyalty. Peter was a very loyal boy. Or did Freddy give him presents –

money, or drugs even. We never suspected anything like that at the time. Peter didn't need money. He really lacked for nothing. Well, nothing within reason. We saw to that. Only, even if we'd suspected anything was wrong, I'm afraid there wouldn't have been any point in asking Peter about it. He kept everything very close.'

It was Mrs Absom who now broke in with: 'Peter was brilliant, of course, like his brother before him, while Freddy Gibbon was stupid. Well, at lessons, at least.'

'You never told us about the homework, and so on, sir, not when we were making enquiries after Peter's death,' said Lloyd, eyeing the last biscuit on the plate that Mrs Absom had brought in on the coffee tray.

'No. Nor when your colleagues went on with them after the inquest, either.' Absom had leaned further forward as he continued earnestly: 'That was really because Mrs Gibbon came round to see us two nights after Peter died.'

'She was the soul of sympathy. Very consoling, wasn't she, Howard?' Mrs Absom put in.

'Deeply so, yes,' her husband agreed, though his words sounded less forthright than hers. 'She said what a good friend

Peter had been to Freddy. How much he'd helped him with his progress scholastically. More than most of the masters, by all accounts. That's how she put it. She went on to say it was a pity Freddy hadn't been in Aberbach since the start of the holidays, that he might have been of help to Peter, if he'd been unhappy or depressed.'

Mrs Absom put a hand over one of her husband's. 'She did say, as well, that her son had been such a trial to her, but had promised to be more ... more worthy of her in future. That he was going to a new school. It was then she asked if we'd do what we could to keep Freddy's name out of the inquest on Peter.'

'That's right.' Absom took up the point. 'She said since Freddy hadn't been in the town for so long, and had turned over a new leaf, and ... and couldn't have affected Peter's death in any way, it'd be a weight off her mind if his name wasn't brought up unnecessarily.'

'But I understood it was brought up,' said Parry, glancing at Lloyd.

Howard Absom nodded. 'We did as his mother asked, out of feeling for her, you understand? But other people spoke about Freddy, didn't they, Mr Lloyd? You'll

346

remember that?'

'I do remember one or two passing references to him, sir. In the end, though, it was his having left the town that made him seem irrelevant to the main enquiry.'

'Do you still feel that was right, Mr Absom?' the chief inspector asked.

'No, I don't. We've learned a few more things about Freddy since then, especially in the last two days. In a way, I suppose we should blame ourselves that other young people weren't warned about him being a bad influence. For the future, I mean. You could say that was due to negligence on our part.'

'I think that'd be overstating it, sir,' Lloyd volunteered. 'It was soft-heartedness, more like. Towards his mother. And we found no evidence at all that tied Freddy in with Peter's death. Not directly.'

'Not at the time of his death, no, that's true,' Absom replied, but with uncertainty in his voice. 'And now that Freddy's dead as well, I suppose it's better for his mother, at least, that things weren't stirred up that didn't need to be.'

'I don't know if my other son would agree,' said Nora Absom. 'We haven't talked to him since Freddy's death was announced on Monday. He's very bad about keeping in touch. He's a lovely boy, all the same. Just busy, you see? He did some looking into Peter's death on his own when he was here at Christmas. Afterwards, he said he was sure Freddy Gibbon had a lot to answer for. Not just over Peter, mark you, because, like everybody else, he couldn't prove Freddy was involved in his death.' She looked across at the sergeant. 'Why don't you have that biscuit, Mr Lloyd? There's plenty more in the kitchen.'

'Oh, are you sure?' said the sergeant, affecting surprise. 'Well, if no one else wants it, Mrs Absom. Thank you very much.'

'And more coffee for you, Mr Parry?' Mrs Absom asked.

'Thank you, not for me,' the chief inspector answered, before enquiring: 'We understood your other son worked abroad. Is that right?'

'He did do, yes, but he's back here now. Got a very important new appointment. He starts at a Cambridge college this autumn. There was terrific competition for the post, so we're very pleased for him. And proud. Till he goes to Cambridge, he's doing different jobs to fill in.'

'I see. In case we need to talk to him, I

wonder, could you let us have his address?'

She shook her head. 'I'm afraid we've only got the address of Tom Brislow, an old college friend. He's at Bristol University. That's all Emmo's given us while he's all over the place doing temporary work. He uses Tom's flat as a hotel, almost. You'll be able to reach him through Tom all right, though. I've got the address and telephone number here somewhere.' As she'd been speaking, she had moved to a bookcase beside the fireplace, and now read out the details from an address book that had been lying on the top of it.

'Thank you, Mrs Absom,' said Lloyd, looking up from his notebook. 'And, sorry, I didn't quite catch your son's name. Emmo, did you say?'

'No, no,' she smiled, returning to the sofa. 'That's just what I've called him since he was a baby. Silly, isn't it? His proper name's Emlyn.'

'Ah, thank you. Emlyn Absom,' said the sergeant, writing it down.

'Not Absom, no. You see, Emmo kept my first husband's surname. Only Peter's surname was changed when I married Howard. We were told it'd be better for him. For Peter. He was such an insecure, fragile

349

little boy. He hardly knew his real father before he died, and the doctors said it'd help him to think of Howard as his daddy, as well as save him from having to explain his surname to people at school. I mean, why it was different from mine and Howard's.' She smiled gently at her husband as she completed: 'Emmo was eleven years older, of course, and stronger altogether. He and Peter were very close all the same. Emmo adored his little brother. He'd have done anything for him.'

'And Emmo's surname is?' the sergeant pressed, tolerantly.

'Sorry, I thought I'd said. It's Harries. Yes, his full name's Emlyn Harries.'

19

'The fact remains, Mr Harries, we weren't aware that you have a close connection with Aberbach. And you made no effort to make us aware,' said Parry, suppressing the anger he was still feeling.

'Well, I don't really have a close connection there. Haven't had for a long time.'

'A past connection then. Except with your parents living there still–'

'My mother lives there, yes,' the English tutor broke in, folding his arms and crossing his legs in one elongated, languid movement, 'but I haven't thought of Aberbach as my home for ages. I was teaching at a Manchester poly for a year before I went to New Zealand. My mother's second husband and I ... we ... we don't have that much in common. Nice enough chap. Kind to animals and all that, but not my cup of tea. Offered to help get me a job in his firm once. That was after I'd got my first degree.' The pursed lips, raised eyebrows and short, punctuating nod that followed the last intelligence left it to the others present to decide what opinion the academic whiz kid must have taken of a career in the building society movement.

'But you spent last Christmas with the two of them, sir,' offered Lloyd in a questioning tone.

It was ten thirty. The three men were seated at the table in the basement interview room. The policemen had come back from Aberbach at some speed. It happened that Harries had a free period after taking his first class of the morning. If he hadn't had, this would have made little difference to Parry's determination to see him immediately. The chief inspector had also declined to conduct the meeting in the relative comfort, and, for Harries, the relaxing familiarity of his own bed-sitting room – as the tutor himself had suggested when they had met in the college entrance hall.

The room was nearly as stark and official as a police station interview room would have been, which was the ambience Parry had needed. There was a state-of-the-art-looking tape recorder on a small table to the right of where the sergeant was sitting. Harries had earlier enquired, in a half-joking voice, whether the instrument was switched on. Lloyd had told him, in an unwaveringly solemn tone, that it was not, but that if it became necessary to record anything later he would be advised in advance

Harries shifted in his chair. He was on one side of the table facing the other two. 'It would have been a bit churlish not to have spent Christmas with my mother ... and stepfather, yes,' he said, in response to the previous comment. 'I got back to the UK the day before Christmas Eve, and I'd been away the best part of two years. Well, not counting a quick trip I made late last summer. That was to do with the interviews for my Cambridge fellowship. I stayed with my mother for one night at the end of it.'

'Would that trip have been before your brother's death, sir?'

'Yes, of course. Only a week or so before, though. That's why I couldn't come back again so soon.'

'I'm not clear why you couldn't, Mr Harries?' said Parry, staring at him unblinkingly. 'Remembering the gravity of the situation, and your being your mother's only surviving child.'

The unexpectedness of such apparently gratuitous and undisguised criticism prompted the tutor's head to jerk back, then forward again, in a reflex gesture of surprise. 'Well ... um, I suppose it wasn't literally that I couldn't have come over.' He swallowed. 'In fact, I've often wished since that I had done. But ... but, you see, apart from the expense, I'd accepted to be principal tutor at a four-week summer school in Christchurch. That's Christchurch, New Zealand. There was no way they could have found a substitute for me at such short notice. I'd already been a day late arriving because of the Cambridge trip. It was very awkward, and ... and at the time, I didn't really feel there was much I could do if I had been here,' he concluded, lamely.

'I saw your mother during that time, sir. She was inconsolable over your brother's death,' said Lloyd.

'Of course she was. So was I. But she had her husband to comfort her. If I'd been here, I'd still have been ... well, frankly the third wheel of the chariot. Meantime, I'd have been letting down a whole bunch of mustard-keen mature students, most of whom had given up their annual vacations to learn something hopefully of value. Do you understand what I'm getting at?'

Parry's expression and short silence could have indicated understanding or, just as easily, the opposite. 'As you know, there was a big police investigation before the inquest on your brother, Mr Harries. If you'd been here, you might have been able to help over that.' The chief inspector's words, like his manner, were still determinedly cool and wooden.

'Well, I question that, Mr Parry.' Harries, sounding more confident, tilted his chair back on its rear legs. 'According to my step-father, the enquiry was almost as heavy-handed as the one that came after the inquest. Sorry if you were involved, Mr

Lloyd, but that's what everyone seems to feel.'

'I was with the initial enquiry, sir, yes. We did our best with the evidence available. And I know nothing new came up after the inquest,' the sergeant responded, his face not as impassive as his boss's.

'Your mother told us you made some enquiries yourself into the matter at Christmas, Mr Harries,' said Parry.

'Because I thought somebody should, yes.'

'There's no record that you made yourself known to the local police at the time though.'

Harries brought the front legs of the chair down on to the floor with a thud. 'Because, according to my stepfather, everything they knew was common knowledge,' he said. 'And everyone had accepted by then that Peter committed suicide. Or had come to accept it. End of story.'

'That wouldn't have been entirely the case, Mr Harries. And a word with the police might have helped you and them,' Parry commented. 'Still, you didn't make your presence known, and that was that. For the time being at least. May I ask, did you take the view that your brother's death, was suicide?'

'No. Not then, and not now.'

'Even though your mother and stepfather seem to be resigned to it?'

Harries gave an irritated sigh, and ran a hand back through his hair. 'If they are, they're wrong. It wasn't suicide as I'd define suicide. If it wasn't something worse, it was aggravated suicide, and there's a hell of a difference.'

'As we've been explaining to your mother, sir, the law doesn't discriminate there. Not if suicide was intended,' said Lloyd.

'Well, it bloody well ought to. Peter was driven to what he did by someone else. Someone who should have been punished for it.'

'And who do you think that was, Mr Harries?'

'You know as well as I do who it was. Or ought to. It was Freddy Gibbon. In a way, he *has* now been punished, of course, which serves him right.'

'You have proof that he drove your brother to his death?' Parry asked.

'Of course I don't. Not copper-bottomed, send-him-down-for-the-rest-of-his-natural sort of proof. If I did, the police would have heard from me weeks ago. Well, in any event, quite soon after Christmas.'

'You could still have let the police have the grounds for your suspicions, sir,' Lloyd put in.

'Oh, yes? Telling them things they were aware of already, but had done nothing about? No, I pretty soon came to the conclusion that there was no future in trying to nail Gibbon over Peter's death, even though I'm positive he caused it. It was too late for that, even before I got back to the UK.'

'But you expected to be able to nail him for things he got up to here at Modlen College, is that it, sir?'

'That was the idea, Mr Lloyd, yes. Especially after a most extraordinary coincidence. On the very day I found out from my mother that Gibbon was here, I got a call from my jobs' agency saying the college urgently needed an English tutor. It was almost uncanny, and certainly too good an opportunity to ignore.'

'And you really believed that by coming here, Mr Harries, you could ... avenge your brother's death, in some way?' asked Parry.

Harries clasped his hands behind his neck. 'I thought I might be able to build up a dossier on Gibbon's various criminal activities, yes. Must sound ambitious to you, or crazy, even, but the challenge appealed to me. Otherwise I certainly wouldn't be working in this pathetic apology for a seat of learning, with its egocentric principal and his probably nympho wife.' He brought his hands down with a frown. 'On second thoughts, you'd better forget that last comment. I assume this talk is off the record?'

It was Parry again who answered stonily: 'We're interested in anything that relates to the death of Frederic Gibbon, Mr Harries, not extraneous gossip. Your mother told us you're just filling in with whatever work you can find till you take up your Cambridge appointment. You hadn't told her you were here. Was there a reason for that?'

The tutor hesitated. 'Yes, there was. I didn't want anyone in Aberbach who knew Gibbon was here to tell him who I was or ... or to think I was following him. I guessed early on the bastard had informants everywhere. It's true enough I'm marking time till the autumn, except I was offered more fulfilling temporary work elsewhere, including in Cambridge itself. The money's all right, here, but that's about all. And I'm not that hard up.'

'And you're something of an academic

high-flyer, Mr Harries?' said the chief inspector.

'Certainly not. It's just that I've been lucky enough to have landed a well-endowed research fellowship, starting in the next academic year. It means I'll be able to get on with two long-term projects. I can't do any of my own serious work in this place because there are no libraries. Well, there are at Cardiff University, but I'm not free at the right time of day to get down there to use them. I'm only staying here till Easter, in any case. Newsom-Pugh wants me to stay for the summer term as well, but that's not on now, for obvious reasons.'

'So you took work here solely to ... to build a case against Freddy Gibbon? A case involving what?'

'Drugs, blackmail, and his criminal domination of other people, all of which I'm sure he was engaged in for profit, apart from the kicks they gave him. In a way, the domination was the most brutal part of what he did.' The lucid answer had been expressed with great firmness.

'You think he dominated your brother to the extent he made him commit suicide?'

'I don't just think that, Mr Parry. I'm sure of it.'

'But you have no proof?'

'No, and I don't need any. Neither of you knew Gibbon. I did.'

'Do you know who he was blackmailing in Aberbach, sir?' asked Lloyd, who'd concluded that dominating other people would be a dead loss on a charge sheet of indictable offences: for a start, he'd suffered more dominating superior officers than he'd had holidays in Pembroke, and none of them had ever been prosecuted for it.

'Yes, but I'm not going to tell you. Not if it means I'll be sued if you make the information public. I can't prove anything, and now I don't suppose I ever will.'

'His victims could be persuaded to come forward, sir.'

'And advertise what they'd done to deserve being blackmailed? Don't be daft. Sorry, I'm not going to stir up that pot.'

'Could you tell us how you went about your ... your investigations, Mr Harries?' asked Parry, who was ready to let the refusal stand for the moment.

'By gradually becoming Gibbon's confidant. His friend, so help me.'

'Strange no one seems to know you were his friend.'

'Because I made sure they didn't. If any of

360

his victims had, they wouldn't have confided in me themselves. And it wasn't that difficult. I avoided being seen with him more than was absolutely necessary, but I gave him tutorials on his own, sometimes three in a week, quite often in my free time. The official reason for that was because he was more backward in English than anyone else. The tutorials were really just chats over drinks, of course. He wasn't interested in learning anything. I just pretended I admired his ... his free spirit. And I'm not proud of that, I may say.' The speaker shook his head over his own duplicity. 'Like a good many braggarts, he gave away a lot about himself when he'd had a few whiskies. I also covered for him – when he needed to be out of the college at times he shouldn't have been, and there were plenty of those. If he was missed for any reason, I'd let him say he'd been for coffee in my room, going over his reading list, that kind of thing. He was grateful for all that. I impressed on him that other staff members shouldn't know we'd become mates because that might spoil my usefulness to him. That appealed to him, because he thought it was my way of saying our friendship was more important to me than it was to him.'

'Did he offer you anything in return?'

'Yes. Very cheap Scotch. I don't know where he got it. I suspect it was stolen. I believe, in time, he'd also have offered me drugs. The other thing I did was try to keep a tag on people who went to his room. That wasn't easy because my room is on the floor below his, and the furthest from the staircase. I've been trying to get it changed ever since I arrived.'

'And this way, you got the information on him you wanted, sir?' asked Lloyd.

'Not all of it, but some of it, yes, and to my own satisfaction at least, if probably not to yours. Remember, I've only been here five weeks. It would have taken the rest of the term to ingratiate myself with him to the extent I really needed.'

'Are you sure of that?' challenged Parry. 'Was he really unburdening to you that much? Or was it wishful thinking on your part? In other words, were you just willing him into being your late brother's ... tormentor, to fit the role you'd created for him?'

'Certainly not. He as good as admitted to me he'd used Peter to a scandalous extent.'

'He told you that specifically?'

'Not in as many words, no.' Harries sighed

over the revealed weakness. 'It was when he told me why he'd had to leave Aberbach. That there'd been a lad there who'd idolized him, did all his work for him, but inconsiderately topped himself in the summer holidays, reflecting bad vibes on Gibbon. He was quite open about it. God, that made me see red, I can tell you, but I couldn't let him know it, of course. He said the lad had been bright, but mixed up, and a non-doer. In other words, a natural to be a disciple of one of the world's great doers. Doer and non-doer were Gibbon's favourite human classifications. Naturally, he always featured as a prince amongst doers himself.'

'Did he say he'd made a similar use of Modlen College's non-doers?'

'With the Oswald girl, and Alwyn Bowen, you mean? Yes, he did. And not just them either. For instance, there were the three girls in room twenty-eight, and the two domestic staff girls, Sara and Bronwyn. He even told me he had the principal's wife and the college bursar doing him favours.'

'Were the nature of the favours mentioned?' asked Parry.

'No, except for innuendoes implying that some of them were sexual.'

'And did you believe that?'

'I'm not sure. I thought it quite probable he was showing off again. He certainly claimed he was irresistible to older women. And one of the three students, Mair Daltry, had proved he was less so to young girls by going very cold on him. I don't know why because she point blank refused to tell me. That was around the time she ... she developed a crush on me, which, let me say, was in no way encouraged or reciprocated. A youngish, male tutor gets used to coping with that kind of thing. In the case of Mair, though, I did take advantage of what she was ready to tell me about Gibbon. Which is why I've known recently about some of the things he'd been up to at weekends. For instance, she told me yesterday about the disco he ran last Saturday at Kate Unwin's house. I'd certainly have told you about that, except she said the police knew already. But getting information on him that way was a lot easier than trying to follow him about, I can tell you.'

Parry sniffed. 'It's an interesting picture you're painting, Mr Harries, but so far, what you've told us doesn't really amount to an exposure of criminal activity on his part.'

'You might not think his activities were criminal, Mr Parry, but I do,' the tutor responded pointedly.

'Precisely, Mr Harries. And you had very little real prospect of getting hard evidence against him relating to your brother's death either, no matter how much longer you spent giving him extra tutorials or cultivating his ex-admirers. He was too spry. Grilling the ex-admirers might have been the more productive of the two strategies, and, in the case of girl students, no doubt the more agreeable. But we'll never know now how much more productive it might have been, shall we?'

'I had every hope that—'

'But hope wasn't enough, was it?' the chief inspector interrupted. 'And anyway, you've made it pretty plain you thought the law was too blind or too slow to nail Gibbon. Is that why you took things into your own hands?'

'What do you mean by that?' The answer had been shocked and strongly defensive.

'I think you know exactly what I mean, Mr Harries.'

'You think I did for the bastard myself? Good Lord, is that what you meant just now about revenge?' Harries had at first looked taken aback, now the hurt surprise was melting into mild amusement over the sudden and challenging change in the line of questioning. 'I'll freely admit I've thought about ways of punishing him sometimes, but my idea was always to bring him before the law if I could. For my mother's sake more than my own. No, murder isn't my forte, Mr Parry. And, anyway, I thought I'd already accounted for my movements at the weekend?'

'Hardly, sir. Not for the whole of Sunday night, you haven't. Is that why you've been enquiring about the progress of the case from Detective Sergeant Norris?'

'Of course not. Hell, did she really think that's what I was after last night? At the pool? Honestly, I was just chatting her up. She's very attractive.'

'She wasn't nearly so sure of your motives, Mr Harries, and neither are we.'

'Well, I tell you, Mr Parry, I never laid a hand on Gibbon, and if you want more detail on how I spent Sunday night I'll give it to you, and ... and produce more witnesses if you want.'

'The period that interests us is from ten on Sunday night till you and Dr Newsom-Pugh met in the pool at six forty-five Monday morning, Mr Harries.'

The tutor hesitated. 'Well, I could produce one important extra witness, I suppose, but it's complicated. I've already told Mr Lloyd, I was in bed from eleven till six thirty, which is pretty normal for a law-abiding citizen. Isn't that enough?'

'Oh come on. Mr Harries, we're investigating a murder. Who's this other witness?'

'If I tell you, and it establishes a ... an alibi for me, is that as far as it needs to go?'

Parry pouted before he spoke. 'You'll need to let us be the judge of that. I'm afraid, sir.'

'Well, I went to check whether Gibbon was back at ten, which he wasn't–'

'Sure, you went to his room, sir. You told me,' said Lloyd.

'Yes. There was a reason. Mrs Newsom-Pugh was duty tutor on Sunday, and if he was back, he should have reported to her by then. I was going to remind him. To earn a good mark with the management, as it were. Dr Newsom-Pugh would almost certainly have been with his wife at the time. Seeing Gibbon then would also have given me a chance to ask what he'd been doing over the weekend.' Harries cleared his throat. 'After I failed to find him, I ... I looked in on Cynthia Strange, in her room. We, er ... we had a drink, watched the end of a film on TV, and, well, one thing led to another, and I, er ... I spent the night with her. It's never happened before, and I don't suppose it'll happen again, but she was a bit low, and I've always known she fancied me so...'

'So you slept with her, and established alibis for both of you, sir,' Lloyd completed the tutor's long-winded admission for him, glancing at Parry as he did so.

'You realize we'll need to verify that with the lady, Mr Harries?' the chief inspector offered.

'Yes. She's ready for it, but not eager, I can tell you. I warned her it might be necessary, except at this stage I thought I'd be in the clear.'

'Which was overhopeful, since you might have realized we could get on to your Aberbach background at any point.' Parry sniffed before going on. 'You mentioned blackmail. Did Gibbon give you any real reason to think he'd blackmailed people, and if he did, who they were?'

'He didn't use the word blackmail, of course but he told me several times he'd collected dirt on a lot of people, first in Aberbach, then here. He put it in a way a malicious gossiper would, with hints and innuendoes. Only I also got the feeling it was gossip he'd already used to his advantage in Aberbach. That it wasn't just scuttlebutt, and that he was doing the same thing now here at the college. Same scenario, different players. He seemed to concentrate on people in the vulnerable professions, too. Notably teachers.'

'Did he name any of the people he'd collected dirt on in Aberbach, sir?' Lloyd pressed.

'Yes. But I don't think I can tell you who they were, can I? Not without wrecking possibly innocent lives? The same will apply to his victims here. You see, in any case, I'm going on intelligent deduction over what Gibbon told me. I could be wrong, which means I could be sued, doesn't it?'

Parry pinched the end of his nose. 'It means impasse, Mr Harries. With you withholding information that could affect the enquiry into your brother's suicide, as well as the one into Freddy Gibbon's murder, you would also be obstructing the course of justice.'

'But so far as my brother's concerned, not to any real purpose now, because the person who killed him is dead.'

Parry held up both hands, palms facing Harries, and smiled for the first time since the start of the interview. 'Look, why don't you tell us what you think you know? If we can get further with it, fine, if we can't, so be it. Either way, no recording's been made. We'll even forget where the information came from. Or, better still, put it down to brilliant detection on our part. There's really no sweat. All right?'

Harries hesitated. 'I suppose so.'

'Good. So, starting again at the beginning, who was Gibbon blackmailing in Aberbach?'

Harries looked at Lloyd. 'You must have met Clarke, the headmaster there?'

'Yes. Mr Parry has too,' the sergeant answered.

'Well ... he's married, with three children. Gibbon was sure he was also gay and a paedophile. He said Clarke had seduced my brother, and Gibbon had made him sweat for it. It was also why Gibbon was never expelled from the school, and why Clarke got him accepted here.'

20

'I saw Kate Unwin and Abby Kennedy separately this morning, sir, with DC Pope,' Mary Norris was reporting to Parry. He and Lloyd had returned to the incident room after the interview with Harries next door. Lloyd had already given the half-dozen members of the team present a rundown on what had transpired with the English tutor.

'And the house in Penarth where the earrings came from, was it one that Gibbon made them burgle with him?' Parry asked.

'Yes, sir.'

'I wonder if they'd already told Mair Daltry that?' the chief inspector mused with a grin. 'Harries has been pumping her for information without her realizing it. What you think he was trying on with you last night, Mary, except he swears in your case it wasn't what he was doing.'

'He says he was just chatting you up. Don't blame him either,' put in a beaming Lloyd approvingly, before taking a bite out of a doughnut.

'Well, I don't believe him.' The woman sergeant had reddened slightly as she went on: 'Still, it seems he's got an alibi for the time of the murder. Do you want me to see Miss Strange to confirm they were in bed together all Sunday night, sir?'

'I think you'd better, yes,' Parry replied. 'And tell her we're treating the matter as confidential. She's going to be embarrassed, I expect.'

'Oh, I shouldn't think so, sir. She probably regards him as quite a catch. Especially as he's so much younger than she is, and even if it was only a one-night stand.' The withering response had come in a miffed voice that the speaker hadn't troubled to mask. 'I'd say Miss Strange is more likely to be bothered about Dr Newsom-Pugh finding out what she and Mr Harries have been up to,' she added.

'Well, we can probably avoid that happening, can't we? Both parties have now been pretty helpful to us,' said Lloyd, sipping from a mug of coffee. His professional estimation of Harries had risen during the interview, even if his previous regard for Cynthia Strange had been somewhat blemished by what he viewed as moral turpitude. He was of the wrong generation to put the responsibility for that on her male partner – or even to share it between them. 'If Mr Harries had been given to the end of this term, he might have built a better case against Gibbon over his brother's death. Better, anyway, than the police have done so far,' he concluded.

'Well, that's still circumstantial,' countered Parry, 'but he wasn't doing badly with what he'd collected on Gibbon's activities here. Though what he's told us hasn't really got us any closer to knowing who killed him.'

'If we're back to Colvin Russell on that, sir,' said DC Vaughan, 'we've got his CV in from the Met, and I saw the managing director of Centurion this morning.'

'Good. Why did he leave them? Was he fired?'

'No, sir. They were quite satisfied with his work, but they didn't exactly part friends, all the same. He'd wanted more money. They couldn't afford to pay it. When he said he'd been offered more elsewhere, they thought he was bluffing, until he left them for a better job with Home and Corporate Security. The MD at Centurion thinks he got that by promising to shift a lot of their customers to the other outfit.'

'And has he?'

'Not many, sir, or not so far. Anyway, for his sake, I hope he can explain his thumb-print on one of the Centurion customer's house key we found in Gibbon's box.'

'It's definitely his print?'

'No doubt about it, sir.'

'What else did we get from the Met report on him?'

Vaughan unfolded the sheet of paper he'd been holding. 'He was born and brought up in West Wales, sir. In Carmarthen. Parents moved to London when he was fifteen, and he joined the Met at eighteen. He switched from uniform branch to CID eight years later, but was turned down three times for promotion to sergeant. He transferred to the Drug Squad at his own request, but failed to get moved up there as well. He left the police force and came back to Wales three years ago, after a divorce. The report goes on to say he joined Centurion, a private security firm, with a clean reference from the Met.'

'Right. We'll see him next. And have they identified the dead motorcyclist Russell was with yesterday?'

'Yes, sir,' answered DC Lucy Howells, who started to read from a fax. 'Through his driving licence, which is all he had on him, except for four hundred and twenty pounds. His name was Joseph Manuel O'Leary, aged twenty-seven, Irish citizen, but mother was Spanish. He lived with a common-law wife in a council flat in Milford Haven. Used to be a maintenance worker in the oil refinery there, till he was laid off two years ago. Since then he's thought to have been a motorcycle courier, but is currently registered as unemployed. He had two convictions for shoplifting. Probation for the first offence, fined fifty pounds for the second. A third offence, for possessing more than ten grammes of cannabis resin, was dismissed last October because of wrongly prepared evidence.'

'Hmm, so he got a smart lawyer as well as legal aid,' Parry commented drily.

'Possibly, sir. Sara Card and Bronwyn Tate identified him this morning from a photograph. They're pretty sure he's the man they've been meeting at the Central Station for Freddy Gibbon. And, of course, we know he also had a limp,' the detective constable completed.

'So Russell could be linked to him through Gibbon, boss, except Russell claimed he didn't know him,' said Lloyd

'Which may be difficult to disprove now,

of course, with both Gibbon and O'Leary dead,' the chief inspector responded.

'Another small point, sir, on a different subject,' said the conscientious Lucy Howells, shuffling the papers in her hands. 'The plane Mrs Gibbon and her friend Mrs Hooson were on from Tenerife. It was covered by our routine check on everybody's movements Sunday. Well, it landed at Gatwick at fourteen twenty-seven. It was late, but not nearly as late as she said.'

Parry frowned while flicking through his notebook. 'She was more disorientated by her stepson's death than she seemed, I expect. Better check it with her, though. Can someone give me the number of Home and Corporate Security?'

'Better to meet in the open air. Healthier for everybody, I thought, Chief Inspector,' said Colvin Russell affably, a wry glint in his eyes. Like Parry, he was almost too well protected from the elements. Despite the crisp snow on the ground, the sun was now shining in a clear blue sky. 'Can I take it you're not wired, Mr Parry?' he added.

'Of course I'm not wired, why–'

'Good. Because, if you are, after that denial, any tape you produce afterwards won't be admissible either way, will it? Not unless the laws of evidence have changed since I was on the force, or unless you're ready to arrest and caution me straightaway. That way I can always have you for wrongful arrest later.' The speaker guffawed loudly. 'Cigarette?'

'No thanks. And cut the cackle, will you, Mr Russell? We're meeting out here alone, because that's what you stipulated. I had my own theory why, and you seem to be confirming it.'

'Oh, come on, Mr Parry, I was just having you on. I told you on the phone, I had to be down here in the Bay estimating on a security job. Time is money in the private sector. You made it sound as if you needed to talk pronto, and I hate crowds, especially when I'm doing the police a favour.' He turned seawards, throwing open his arms, which prompted several short-sighted, circling seagulls to swoop in search of the food he might have been dispensing. 'Fantastic view, isn't it? The commercial potential of this area is unbelievable, or will be when they've hooked a few more big outfits. I've been inside all morning so far. Nice to get some air.' Despite the in-consistency between his words and his following action, he lit a cigarette behind cupped hands.

The two men were the sole occupants of an area fronting the white clapboard Norwegian Seamen's Church, a landmark in the heart of Cardiff Bay. The church dominated the end of a dramatic promontory, the ground around the building landscaped with stepped grass verges and terracotta tiling, though presently under snow. Erected in 1867, the church was now a noted survivor, since most older dockyard structures had disappeared, making room for open spaces like this one along the water's edge, with the new commercial buildings, museums, and hotels rising behind. The church itself had been returned to its original divine brilliance – though not to its original divine function: it was now a celestially disguised coffee shop, but a lot handsomer than most.

The huge expanse of water had once served as the natural outer harbour of the biggest coal port in the world. Now it was a manmade, fresh-water lake, for sailing and water sports, protected by a massive barrage. It was the key part of the re-development that accorded with the aims, not to mention the fervent prayers, of the

City Fathers – as well as those in charge of the deep-pocketed Welsh Development Agency.

'We need to know where you were from ten Sunday night to eight Monday morning, Mr Russell,' said Parry, who, like his companion, was now leaning on the rails above the lapping water, watching the gulls bobbing on the surface.

'Is that all, Mr Parry?'

'No, but it'll do for a start.'

'I thought Debby Thomas had given you the answer to that one already. We were home in bed. Well, home, and in bed from about half eleven.'

'No other corroboration?' But the widowed chief inspector was silently assuring himself that his own nights would soon be regularly vouched for again by a devoted partner – like most of the lucky people he seemed to interview.

'No, and normally there isn't other corroboration, is there, Chief Inspector? We both know that. One witness is enough. And any more would be kinky in a double bed, wouldn't it?'

Parry's face didn't react to the feeble witticism. 'I understand you were officially working that evening. Can you tell me what time you got home?'

'I could say that's my business, Mr Parry. But since you've had people snooping for information at the office already, I'll confirm I got back at four fifteen, two and three-quarter hours earlier than expected, and rang in to explain why to the duty operator at the company. I'd spent the afternoon checking on guards and general security at three of our major industrial contracts, but I got a bad migraine and had to pack it in. I'm management, not a wage slave. Inspector grade and above, like yourself. I don't clock on and off. I was on call all night, of course.'

'And were there any calls?'

'None, as it happens. They should have told you that at the office, too.'

'Fair enough, Mr Russell. Can you tell me next about your relationship with Frederic Gibbon?'

'Sure. Like Debby told you, we ran into him in Cardiff one Saturday, end of last year. She thought I'd find him amusing, so we had him back to the house.'

'How often did he visit you there after that first time?'

The ex-policeman blew out smoke slowly. 'From memory, a couple of times.'

'And how often did you see him alone? Like the time you arranged to meet him at the Prince of Wales in Brynglas?'

'Only twice, Mr Parry. And that was just social, when I happened to be in the area.'

'But you had business dealings with him?'

'Depends what you mean by business dealings. He robbed me of some valuable gear, if you can call that doing business.'

'Want to tell me about that?'

'Not specially, Mr Parry. Not yet. Can we get to O'Leary?'

The chief inspector's eyebrows lifted a fraction. 'All right, but we'll be coming back to Gibbon all the same. I gather you said at the scene of the bus accident that you didn't know O'Leary.'

'Had to, didn't I? The dealers know me, and he's got a wife to consider.'

'Common-law wife.'

'Same thing. The sort of people he worked for don't go in for niceties, not when they're extracting money owed. And they take their pound of flesh other ways if it's not there for the extracting, Mr Parry.'

'I don't follow?'

'You wouldn't do without me telling you. And that's why we're down here alone. O'Leary was a snout of mine. A good one.'

381

'When you were with the Met? The Drug Squad?'

'Then, and after. I'm still on close terms there, by the way. And if you want support for that, I can supply plenty.'

'The Met didn't supply any when we got your CV from them.'

'Well, they wouldn't, would they? Not in the ordinary way? But there's a detective chief super in Scotland Yard who'll tell you about me, if pressed. But he'd rather not be, if you follow me?'

'OK. Go on about O'Leary.'

'He looked like small fry, but that was one of his pluses. He was a cog in a drug distribution chain, working the length of the M4 west from London, and beyond to the Emerald Isle if required. His use to us was his tip-offs on wholesale deliveries into the country.'

'You mean he knew when they were being made, despite being just a cog?' Parry's doubts were evident in his tone.

'No, he never knew when, but he sometimes knew where a shipment had come in, or where it was being split for onward deliveries. He used his intelligence, see? And people used to trust him.'

'Until he shopped them?'

'Only when he knew the haul would be big enough, which wasn't often. He had his main living to think of, after all,' the speaker smirked as he went on. 'And as well as working for others, he ran a magic-mushroom business of his own. All in all, he couldn't have been making a fortune, which is why he was a grass as well. But his own business was growing.'

'Is that where Gibbon came in?'

'Got it in one, Chief Inspector.'

'And you introduced them?'

'All in the cause of improving official intelligence, yes. Gibbon was a young villain with future potential, and the more upward contacts O'Leary set in place, the more use he was to my old governor.'

'And what did you get out of it?'

'Lot of things, Mr Parry. But don't be like that, not unless you want my chief super to have words with your chief super.'

Parry stared hard across the water as he spoke, and without looking at the other man. 'Russell, you're no longer on the force, so stop behaving as if you were,' he uttered stonily. 'You may do a bit of intelligence work on drugs for the Met still, but you don't have any status down here. Give me straight answers and we'll make progress. I assume O'Leary was with you yesterday because of Gibbon's murder.'

'Right again, Mr Parry. He was scared stiff, and certain Gibbon was topped because someone figured he'd been grassing. O'Leary thought it'd only be a matter of time before the same someone reckoned he'd hit the wrong guy. That then he'd come after him. Trouble is, today, with the two deaths, one of the Mr Bigs in the drug business really could be looking for a connection, which is why I want to keep O'Leary's woman out of it.'

'What was O'Leary planning to do yesterday?'

'The two of them were going to Ireland. To lie low for a bit. Only I owed him some dosh. Four hundred quid. That was the reason for the meeting. Yes. I recognized the barmaid. When she called out to me, O'Leary must have thought she was speaking to him. That I'd walked him into some kind of ambush. Bloody shame. He died for nothing.'

'And it was nothing more complicated than an accident?'

'Couldn't have been anything else, Mr Parry. The driver was a shaking jelly after. O'Leary ran straight in front of the bus, slipped, and his head went under the wheel. I saw it. He'd have done better keeping his tin lid on instead of using it on me.'

'OK. Let's go back to Gibbon,' said Parry. 'You said he'd robbed you. Was that to do with drugs?'

'No. Debby happened to tell him I'd been on the Drug Squad. Later, when he and I were alone, he said, quite openly, he'd run a cannabis business in his home town, but his source there had dried. He went on about it was time harmless soft drugs were legalized, and didn't I agree. I said I did. Which was true. Then he asked if I knew of a contact for cannabis and magic mushrooms.' The speaker shrugged. 'That's why I put him on to O'Leary.'

'You put a schoolboy on to a drug dealer.'

'Mr Parry, don't come that again. I've given you the reasons. Anyway, he was pretty old for a schoolboy, and we're only talking mushrooms and grass.'

Parry breathed out heavily. 'All right. How did he rob you?'

'It wasn't drugs. It was those latch keys. The ones to some houses Centurion look after. The keys Debby's heard from the college housekeeper you found in his room. I did a daft thing. But if I tell you about it, it's so you can wipe it off the record. It's not relevant to Gibbon's murder.'

'Sorry, if it's illegal you know very well–'

'Except, keep listening, Mr Parry,' the other man interrupted testily. 'Keep listening and you'll hear something to your advantage – that'll likely help with your next promotion, amongst other things, and I heard that's pending. You see, I know who Gibbon was with Sunday night.'

'Then it's your duty to tell me.'

'Sure. Only there's still the matter of those keys. They're duplicates I had made before I left Centurion. When I was bloody furious with the management. You know how a man gets when he's being exploited? Fixated by it? Well, that's how I was. I was determined to get another job, and after that I was going to expose Centurion in some way with those keys, for being lax with their own security.'

'How were you going to do that?'

'Well, that's the point, Mr Parry. Once I got the new job, I cooled on the idea. I was going to destroy the keys, except I forgot all about them. That's when Gibbon must have found them, and nicked them. When he was at the cottage.'

'And you didn't know he'd got them?'

'Swear to God, Mr Parry. Not till he let on

386

to Debby on Sunday afternoon.'

'He was with you then?'

Russell paused. 'He was with Debby. Called in to see us both, he said. That was around three. She gave him some tea, and, not thinking, mentioned I wouldn't be back till seven. It was then he told her about the keys. Said I'd lent them to him to do some organized burglary, as he put it. That we were going to share the proceeds as a swop for me doing him a favour. That was him all over. He was bold as brass, a bloody liar, and always had an angle. I swear I never lent him those keys.'

'Did Debby know you'd put him on to a drug dealer?'

'Good God, no.'

'But she knew why you'd had the keys made?'

'Yes. And why I'd since thought better of doing anything with them. She didn't know whether to believe him or not, about me lending them. She said he should wait till I got home. That's when he asked if he could take a shower. A bit later, he called to Debby from the bedroom to look at something. When she went in, he was lying on the bed in my dressing gown. He had a string of pearls in his hand he said he'd just lifted from one of the houses. She went over to look at them. He pulled her down on top of him, rolled her over, and started to undress her. He had nothing on himself under the dressing gown. When she resisted him, he tried to rape her. He'd got half her clothes off when she grabbed the first thing handy, a big steel knitting needle, and for once I'm glad she knits in bed. She was jabbing at him with the thing, just as I got home. She screamed for help when she heard me slam the front door, got away from him, and ran out to the hall. He locked the bedroom door behind her. I shouted for him to open it. He called back he would, until I sussed he was getting out through the window. That's when I broke the door down. But he'd gone by then, half naked, but carrying the rest of his things with him, I expect. I'd have gone after him, except Debby was having serious hysterics, and I couldn't leave her.'

'That was quite an episode, Mr Russell,' said Parry, while debating whether the alternative scenario he had in his mind wasn't more credible than the one he had just heard. His version had the voluptuous Debby in bed with Gibbon – adding crumpet to the toast and chocolate cake – as she might have been many times before, and shattered by cuckolded Russell's un-expectedly early return. The stabbing could have been her desperate attempt to add credibility to her story, and the hysterics a delaying tactic to help Gibbon get away. At least the mystery of the 'plumber's probe' had been solved. He was also strongly inclined to believe that Gibbon and Russell had been in cahoots over the latch keys all along: otherwise there remained the question of how Gibbon found out when the householders would be away. 'So what happened to the pearls?' he asked.

'He got away with them. God's honour, we don't have them.' Russell lit another cigarette. 'Look, you can keep Debby and me out of any involvement with the bastard, can't you? It wouldn't be complicated.'

Parry made no comment on that. 'You were going to tell me where he went Sunday night, Mr Russell.'

The other man hesitated, dearly debating whether he should give away his only trading counter before he had got the im-munity he needed. On balance, he decided he had to risk it. 'He was going to Hereford, Mr Parry, to see his mother, about a friend of hers from Aberbach. Debby thinks her name was Beth.'

21

'We didn't know whether you'd be here or at the shop, Mrs Gibbon,' said Parry, as she showed him into her overfurnished sitting room. It was Wednesday mid-morning, the day after he had seen Colvin Russell.

'Beth's holding the fort there for me again, while I sort out some wools upstairs. They're needed urgently by some of my outworkers. Tell you the truth, I haven't nearly caught up since the holiday. Well, it's not surprising, is it, what with everything?' She blinked sharply behind the headlight spectacles, while vaguely motioning the policeman towards a flock of armchairs.

'Yes, we met Mrs Hooson when we dropped by at the shop.'

'You actually went there, did you? I didn't realize.' She sounded more discomforted than questioning.

'Yes. As I said, we assumed you'd probably be there. The place is well presented, by the way.'

'Well, thank you, Mr Parry. Nothing fancy,

and very small, of course, but it seems to be attracting the custom.'

'I had a quick word with Mrs Hooson while I was there. My sergeant, Sergeant Lloyd, he's still with her, going over a few points. The shop's a home from home for him. His wife's a dedicated knitter. I think he'll soon have her copying your best patterns,' Parry remarked, while settling into the same chair he had used on his previous visit. His hostess was already seated. 'Anyway, he'll be along here soon,' he completed, calculating that Lloyd would have set off on the mile walk from Edgar Street in the town two minutes before this, which is what they had arranged between them – to stop Mrs Hooson telephoning her friend without one or other of the officers being aware of it.

'I'll look forward to meeting Mr Lloyd,' Mrs Gibbon responded, but with tempered enthusiasm. 'It's about Freddy, then, is it? Don't expect Beth was much help to you there. I could have told you, she didn't know Freddy well,' she continued, as though she felt it her fault the policemen had been wasting their time.

'Partly about Freddy, yes. Though we needed to clear up something else as well.

391

About when that Sunday flight you were on landed. The one from Tenerife.'

Her face clouded. 'Very late, it was. We lost a day nearly.'

'We understand from the airport it touched down at two twenty-seven on Sunday afternoon, Mrs Gibbon. That made it only four or so hours late.'

She shook her head. 'Oh, no. They've got it wrong. Must be some other flight they've given you. It's a very busy place. I don't know how they cope. Well, they don't cope, do they, not if they're giving out wrong information?'

'I'm afraid the information is quite correct. It's been checked very carefully. That's why we're surprised it took you so long to get here. Two o'clock on Monday morning, I think you told me you arrived.'

'Did I? Then I'm certain that must have been when—'

'Only Mrs Hooson said she didn't bring you all the way here in her car,' Parry interrupted doggedly. 'She dropped you at Pontypool Station, and you got the train from there, while she went home to Aberbach. She thinks you'd have got here around seven thirty.'

'Is that right? Surely not?' Her hand went

to adjust the spectacles on her nose. 'Well … well, I suppose I could have got it wrong. And if you're sure that's what Beth said?'

'Quite sure, yes.'

'I remember it was dark and snowing. A terrible night. But wait, yes, it's all coming back to me now. I did get the train into Hereford, and a taxi to here from the station. And, of course, it was *two* in the afternoon we landed, not *two* in the morning when I got here. That's how I got mixed up,' said Mrs Gibbon, with the triumphant air of someone who had solved a very complex problem. 'You know, I've been so upset about Freddy, things have got muddled in my mind. So let's agree I was home by the time we said on Sunday, and no harm done. It's not important, after all, is it? Now then, a cup of tea, Mr Parry? Or coffee?' she continued briskly.

'Not for the moment, thanks all the same, Mrs Gibbon.' Parry produced a notebook as he went on, 'So you confirm that Mrs Hooson went on alone in her car to Aberbach after dropping you at Pontypool. And did she still come here later that night, or not?'

Mrs Gibbon looked mystified. 'But of course Beth stayed here Sunday night.'

'Eventually, you mean? Getting here, she says, a few minutes after midnight? But that wasn't from the airport, of course. And she wasn't alone, was she?'

'Oh dear, Mr Parry, I'm afraid I'm confused again. It's really been a terrible strain these last three days. Of course, Beth must have gone home after she dropped me. And then she drove here. To be ready to help me in the shop first thing.'

'So it was quite a trek for her, Mrs Gibbon? A double trek. Or even more than that?'

'Yes, but Beth's like that. Anything to help a friend in trouble.'

'Indeed. But were you exactly in trouble at the time? I mean when you arrived here first, alone from the airport?' Parry was affecting more interest than perplexity.

'But surely you know that well enough, Mr Parry? You of all people. The trouble over Freddy's...' Her hand went to her mouth. 'No, what am I saying? At that point, of course, I didn't know about Freddy. It was ... it was just the problems I was facing with the new shop. I told you about that. Beth had very kindly said she'd help me out there.'

'I see. And could you tell me, did Freddy

394

have a key to your garage?'

She frowned at the changed direction in the line of questioning. 'Er ... yes, he did. Why–'

'So that may explain something. We're assuming his car was in the garage when you got back here alone at ... at seven thirty. One of your neighbours told us there was no car in the drive when she passed with her dog around then. And, as you told me, the garage would have been empty otherwise, because your car was being serviced when you were away.' He smiled, and leaned forward a little. 'Freddy was here, wasn't he, Mrs Gibbon? With his car.'

She swallowed, and then removed her glasses, which she began polishing with energy, and a large white linen handkerchief, her narrowed eyes nearly closing altogether as she made the effort to follow the movements of her fingers. 'Really, I don't know what you're talking about, Mr Parry. Freddy here? On Sunday night?'

'Yes. We know he left Llanishen at four fifteen. He'd told the person he'd been with that he was going to Hereford to see you. He went to Bristol first, but we know he got to Hereford all right after that, and we know where the car went next. Measured against the petrol in the tank when we checked it on Monday, the car had travelled approximately sixty miles since its last refill, which is the distance between here and Modlen College, where it was parked.'

'Well, it's the distance between here and a lot of places, I should think, Mr Parry,' Mrs Gibbon commented with spirit.

The chief inspector leaned back in the chair. 'There are nine petrol stations open after six on Sundays on the road we thought he'd have taken from Bristol. Our officers called at all of them yesterday, with a picture of Freddy. The nearest one to here is less than a mile away. It wasn't doing much business at ten past six on Sunday evening. That's probably why the young woman on the cash desk remembered Freddy. He chatted to her, apparently, and she took quite a shine to him. It was the very last of the petrol stations we visited. That's usually the way,' he completed with a resigned grin. 'If Freddy had used a credit card to pay for the petrol, we'd have got our answer quicker, but unfortunately he was mostly a cash customer. The girl remembered that too.'

Mrs Gibbon fingered the man-sized wristwatch she was wearing. 'I'm sorry, Mr

Parry, but in spite of what you say, there's no way Freddy could have... Oh, that's the doorbell. It'll be your colleague, I expect. Excuse me while I let him in.'

The minute or so it took Mrs Gibbon to return, engrossed in conversation with the sergeant, had made a demonstrable alteration to her composure – or to her earlier loss of it. 'Do sit down, Mr Lloyd,' she said, with an ingratiating smile. 'And you must give me your home telephone number before you go. Your wife might like to knit for me. You see, I never miss a chance to recruit expert helpers. Miss Thomas at the college is one I enrolled last year. She likes really chunky knits. Wears them herself,' she went on, in benevolent vein. 'As I said, that's a smashing Welsh wool pullover you've got on. The natural colours are so much better than dyed, aren't they?' Then she turned her attention to the chief inspector. 'So sorry, Mr Parry. When I meet a kindred spirit I get quite carried away. Now, to go back to what we were saying, of course Freddy might have been here on Sunday. Then, when he found I was away, he could have left again, all without my knowing. If that's what happened, I'm deeply sorry I missed him. It would have been the last chance of seeing

397

him, wouldn't it? I might even have changed what...' She let a deep sigh complete the sentiment and the sentence.

'But, going back to Mrs Hooson's movements, she didn't come here directly from her home, from Aberbach, did she, Mrs Gibbon?' Parry questioned, in a contrastingly down-to-earth manner.

'How do you mean?' She bent her head to one side.

'That's right, ma'am,' put in Lloyd, opening his notebook. 'She got a bit confused when she was explaining that to us earlier, but she and I got it sorted in the end. According to her, you rang her from a call box in Brynglas at about quarter to eleven Sunday night. Asked her to meet you as soon as possible at the bus shelter there, and drive you back here. Which she did, and then spent the night. The bus shelter is ten minutes' walking distance from Modlen College. Well, you must know all that. Can you tell us how you got to be there?'

Mrs Gibbon looked down, and moistened her lips as she picked at the material on the chair arm, but she made no audible response.

'Had you driven Freddy's car from here to the college, Mrs Gibbon, leaving it there in the car park?' asked Parry. 'Mrs Hooson wasn't at all clear, but she was very nervous. She couldn't tell us what you'd been doing from the time she dropped you in Pontypool till she collected you in Brynglas. But we're still wondering if she was involved with you at all during that time? You see, we're now certain that Freddy's body was transported in the boot of his car wrapped in a woollen rug – the kind of travel accessory you sell in your shop. And Mrs Hooson admits you had such a rug, a large one, over your arm when she picked you up at the bus stop.'

'It was very cold, Mr Lloyd,' the woman uttered with what, in the circumstances. was absurd earnestness and irrelevance.

'Yes, ma'am,' said Parry indulgently. 'We also have to tell you that the pathologist now believes Freddy was asphyxiated. Smothered. The pathologist's conclusion was arrived at by elimination. But exhaustive elimination. Asphyxiation is a way of taking life that's virtually impossible to detect from internal examination. Or perhaps you know that? It's usually proved through ... subjective criteria – primarily contusions on the body, restraint marks and bruising, caused by the victim's struggles. There aren't many such signs on Freddy's body, but there're some – enough. The bruises are slight ones, because we think the person or persons who took his life were adept enough to keep them that way. The pathologist was also diverted at first, as we were, by the stab wounds to Freddy's stomach. They had nothing to do with his death, but they were the most serious evidence of assault, while not pointing anyone in the direction of asphyxiation.' The chief inspector paused. 'That method of murder, of a strong young man like Freddy, usually indicates the involvement of two assailants, and to one or both of them being women. We–'

'No. Beth wasn't part of it. She knows nothing about any of it,' Mrs Gibbon broke in dramatically. She was sitting up very straight now, and looking the chief inspector directly in the eyes. 'Beth got me home after it was over, that's all. I said Freddy had come here on his way back to the college. He'd been drinking, so I'd driven him the rest of the way, and missed the last bus to Cardiff, where I could have got a train to Hereford. Beth knows nothing about what happened otherwise. When it was an-nounced he'd committed suicide, I asked her not to say anything about my taking him back. That was to avoid either of us being involved. She agreed. She's a very ... very unquestioning, trusting friend. But I told her later to tell the truth if she was asked, except I never thought you'd need to ask her. Or to meet her even.'

'You're saying she wasn't involved with you in Freddy's death?' Parry pressed, but quietly. 'Despite his being so much stronger than you and–'

'It didn't need two. You see, I had my husband's handcuffs, and Freddy was ... he was incapable at the time. It was quite easy, and ... and I don't regret doing it. I took his life to save the lives of others. Young people like Peter Absom. Kids. I'm afraid what I told you I felt about him on Monday was only half the story, Mr Parry. It was how I'd felt before I knew for sure he'd caused Peter's death. Murdered him, as good as.'

'When did you know that for sure, Mrs Gibbon?' Parry asked.

'On Sunday night, when he told me, bold as brass. Told me that, and a lot of other things.'

'Freddy was here when you got home on Sunday, was he?'

She nodded slowly. 'Watching television in here, wearing just a dressing gown. He

401

seemed drunk to me, but he'd also had what he called a supercharged snort of horse. That's heroin, is it?'

'There were signs he'd ingested heroin before he died, yes.'

'I see. He knew I'd been away, but he'd expected me back by the time he got here. When I wasn't, he thought he'd got my holiday dates wrong, so he decided to stay the night, anyway. His speech was all over the place. He was saying crazy things. Bragging. He told me first he was giving up going to school – and on to university.'

'Even though that would have cost him his income from the insurance company?'

'That's right, Mr Parry. He said he was making too much money without it to be bothered. That he was on the way to being seriously rich as a major supplier in a vital industry, meaning drugs, of course. On top of that he said he had a string of young girls who did everything he told them. Then he said he'd set up a foolproof way of stealing untraceable jewellery, and that he had paedophile schoolmasters all over the country paying him whatever he asked not to inform on them. The list of things he was up to went on and on. It was ... sickening, Mr Parry. Nauseating. I told myself he was exaggerating, some of it, at least, except he was making it sound so convincing. At one point he blundered upstairs to his room, then came back with a lovely string of pearls, and a wad of fifty-pound notes. It was then he said he'd decided to let me in on the business. That we could both be rich, very rich, if I'd work for him, front for him, let him pretend he was living here, and use my shop as his business address. That was to give him respectability, till he bought a car showroom, which was his next plan, because trading in used cars was a way of laundering money. He also wanted me to get Beth to use her contacts in the trade to dispose of the jewellery.'

'Although she wasn't here then, Mrs Gibbon?'

'No, but he as good as ordered me to get her here to see him. I could have coped with that part, and the blackmail as well, probably. It was the drugs and what he'd done to Peter Absom that turned my stomach, much more even than the way he needled me about how I'd wasted my life running daft businesses that made no profit. He never mentioned the effort I'd made to bring him up properly, but he said what a fool I'd been to give him that insurance money I'd saved, on his eighteenth birth-day.'

'Why did you?' Parry interrupted.

'In the hope it'd stop him trying to make money dishonestly, I suppose. But it hadn't worked, had it? He said he'd bought his first big delivery of ecstasy tablets with that money. That it'd set him up.' She took out the handkerchief again and blew her nose before she went on. 'When I tried to reason with him then that drugs were evil, he just laughed at me. Said people were their own worst enemies. That if he didn't give junkies what they wanted, others would, soon enough. He was that brazen about it.'

'Was it then he told you about Peter Absom?'

'Yes. He said what an idiot Peter had been, that he'd been gay, and having an affair, as he put it, with Mr Clarke the headmaster. Then he admitted that he, Freddy, had introduced Peter to drugs, that the boy had been wet as water, a mess all round, ashamed of his sexual orientation, his drug-taking, the way he let his mother down. He also said Peter was petrified he'd be beaten up by other boys if he passed any more exams. Do you know that's what they'd been doing to him, a gang of them? Really hurting him, for being bright and ... and a worker.'

'But was Freddy part of the bullying, Mrs Gibbon?'

'Was he part of it? Peter didn't know, but Freddy was the leader, like always. To hurt Peter – the very one who'd helped him with his schoolwork. Did you ever hear of anything so shameful, and ... and sadistic?' She looked from Parry to Lloyd as she went on. 'Then he told me that long before the summer holidays he'd known Peter was likely to kill himself. And to think he'd got me to ask Peter's parents to keep him out of the enquiry into the boy's suicide. Now I learn it was Freddy who'd first put the terrible idea into Peter's mind. To see if he'd do it. Do what Freddy told him to do. To prove his power over people.' She paused, then looked hard at Parry. 'And I was as good as told by the police lady who looked after me yesterday that a girl at the college, the one from Brecon–'

'Josephine Oswald, ma'am?' Lloyd volunteered.

'That's right. She tried to kill herself too, didn't she? And she was one of Freddy's ... disciples as well.' The speaker swallowed, with difficulty because her throat was obviously dry. 'And all so Freddy could prove his power over people,' she repeated, huskily.

When it was clear that Mrs Gibbon wasn't going to continue without prompting, Parry asked: 'And it was here on Sunday night that you decided to ... to end his life?'

She breathed deeply, in and out, before replying. 'Yes. To atone for what I'd done in caring for him, nurturing him for all those years, only so he could grow into the monster he'd become. That's what finally pushed me over the top. The blatant evil in what he'd said to me. And the way he gloried in it.'

'Where and exactly how did he die, Mrs Gibbon? You mentioned your husband's handcuffs.'

She stroked her throat. 'I'd gone to the kitchen for something, and when I came back he'd fallen into a deep sleep. Sprawled on that sofa, he was, his body facing inwards, and all limp, with the lower hand pushed out at the back. That's when I thought of handcuffing his hands behind him, which I did ever so gently, not to disturb him, and ... and before I tied the bag over his head.' She blinked several times. 'Once he came properly awake, he ... he

406

tried to pull the bag off with his teeth, but he couldn't. Then, with his struggling, he fell off the sofa. It was soon after that all movement stopped. I was glad when it did.' She sighed and looked up. 'So that's how it happened. How I killed my adopted son.' Sonic seconds later, her shoulders began to heave involuntarily with silent weeping.

'It was pretty ingenious, considering it was on the spur of the moment, boss,' Lloyd reflected, as he and Parry were driving back to Cardiff. It was early evening. Mrs Gibbon had been charged, and was being held in custody at Hereford Police Station, pending her appearance before the local magistrates in the morning.

Since, on Mrs Gibbon's admission, the crime had been committed in Hereford city, the two South Wales officers were effectively off the case, though the handover to the other constabulary had taken some time.

'Ordinary handcuffs would have left more noticeable marks, of course,' said Parry. 'That rubberized magician's pair hardly left marks at all.'

'They were made for escaping from, though, boss.'

'Yes. But not in the short time he had left

to do it in. Before he lost consciousness. He hadn't used his hands to get rid of the bag, and, as she said in the formal interview, she'd sat on his legs long enough to stop him working the cuffs around and under his feet, even if he'd been switched on enough to think of it. And she didn't leave restraining marks doing that either.'

'And he certainly wasn't switched on, boss. Drunk and drugged, she said. Imagine waking up in that state, with no way of knowing what was happening to you?' Lloyd shuddered.

'That's right. And doing physical contortions blindfolded in that room would have been impossible. A nightmare in itself, with bits of solid furniture obstructing in every direction.'

'Frankly, I don't know how she managed to stay and watch, boss. Do you? And afterwards, carrying him through to the garage, putting him in the car boot, offloading him when she got to the college, and heaving him over that basement wall,' Lloyd listed, while opening a new tube of peppermints. 'That's quite a programme, isn't it? And the last part of it without being seen. It could have been accepted as suicide though. Like you said, nobody can *prove* asphyxiation, can they? It's got to be–'

'Arrived at by elimination, yes,' Parry completed. 'Leading to the conclusion that death couldn't have been caused in any other way. But it's still a hard one for a coroner to accept without a confession. And I believe Mrs Gibbon knew that.'

'But she confessed all the same, boss.'

'To avoid Mrs Hooson being brought in as an accomplice. Someone she hadn't intended to involve in any case.' The chief inspector paused while changing down a gear to overtake a long lorry. 'With the minus-zero conditions that night making it impossible to decide the time of death, it might have been excusable for the pathologist to decide Freddy really had been killed by the fall,' he contended. 'Yes, the weather was very much on Mrs Gibbon's side. She wasn't spotted in the college car park, because people had their curtains closed because of the cold. And nobody was hanging around outside either, for the same reason. She just had to wait for the right moment.'

'And Freddy's nakedness somehow made it more likely he'd chucked himself out of his own window,' said Lloyd, sucking hard on his mint.

'Well it certainly didn't suggest he'd just driven in from Hereford,' Parry responded glibly. 'As well as eliminating the chance of our picking up clues from his clothing. Dressing him after stripping the dressing gown off him would have been difficult, of course. No, she was much better off handling it the way she did, including, as she's just admitted, dumping his clothes in the local Oxfam bin Monday lunchtime.'

'After she'd put the wool rug in her washing machine. On cold wash.' Lloyd, shook his head over the lady's punctilious reporting of detail. 'And you think Beth Hooson was as ignorant about what really happened as they're both maintaining, boss?'

'Hmm. While it was happening, she probably was, yes. It was reasonable she believed Mrs Gibbon when she rang to say she'd driven Freddy to the school because he'd drunk too much. It was typical of the sort of things she'd always done to protect him. But when we told the media he'd been murdered, Beth Hooson must have twigged she'd been an accessory to something.'

'If without knowing it at the time,' said Lloyd firmly. 'She was honest enough in what she said to us in the shop too, about the phone call from Brynglas. I think it was just a matter of an innocent friend helping out in a simple emergency.'

'But she should still have reported to someone on Monday that Mrs Gibbon had driven Freddy to the college. That's if Mrs Gibbon herself wasn't going to.'

'Except, like Mrs Hooson told us, the only report she'd seen said the lad had committed suicide. Anyway, she was too loyal to report Mrs Gibbon for anything.'

'And Glenda Gibbon was too loyal to Mrs Hooson not to exonerate her before she got in too deep. Which she would have been if she'd had to lie to us,' Parry observed. 'There's no doubt Freddy drove Mrs Gibbon into doing what she did. He'd arranged one suicide, all right, and if we take the Oswald girl into account, Mrs Gibbon was justified in believing he'd intended arranging a great many more.'

'And Miss Strange saying he handled Josephine Oswald so tenderly, that was a load of old cobblers, boss.'

'Sure, which destroys the only decent thing we heard anyone say about him. He was just ... just "exercising his power over people", as his adoptive mother said. That was after she'd set up a suicide on her own account, of course. Freddy's.' Parry smiled grimly. 'There was a rough justice in what she did. And she might have got away with it, too.'

'Pity she didn't,' Lloyd muttered, but under his breath, because Parry didn't approve of coppers playing God.

The publishers hope that this book has given you enjoyable reading. Large Print Books are especially designed to be as easy to see and hold as possible. If you wish a complete list of our books please ask at your local library or write directly to:

Magna Large Print Books
Magna House, Long Preston,
Skipton, North Yorkshire.
BD23 4ND

This Large Print Book for the partially sighted, who cannot read normal print, is published under the auspices of

THE ULVERSCROFT FOUNDATION